A Sheep in Wolf's Clothing

AMY ALLEN

About the Author

Amy Allen is a trans woman from Virginia where she lives with her brother and two cats. She currently works in a used bookstore, surrounded by giants whose shoulders she longs to stand on.

A Sheep in Wolf's Clothing

AMY ALLEN

BELLA BOOKS
2024

Bella Books, Inc.
P.O. Box 10543
Tallahassee, FL 32302

First Edition - 2024

Editor: Heather Flournoy

ISBN: 978-1-64247-473-2

Acknowledgments

I owe a debt of gratitude to my beta readers, Evy and Emm. Their nitpicking made this story what it is. There, now you know who to blame.

Dedication

For my mother, my own Calliope, who dutifully told me about all those writing workshops. I didn't attend a single one, but it's the thought that counts.

CHAPTER ONE

Harper Zeale received the official request to track and kill a vampire the morning of her twenty-first birthday.

As soon as she had reached Chicago, she headed for the local guild headquarters. Since you couldn't just advertise *Hey, we track down supernatural threats!* to the general public, standard operating procedure was to create some kind of front. The Chicago Silversmiths, for example, styled themselves as an incredibly boring patent law office. There wasn't even any large signage, just a single tiny bronze plaque above the door that read "Shelley and Stoker." Presumably one of the branch's founders thought themselves very clever.

Stepping inside, she approached the modest L-shaped desk where a receptionist sat typing away at an ancient computer. She glanced up at Harper, who probably didn't look like either a future patent-holder or a traditional hunter. Her usual style included a leather jacket, a tank top, one of many flannels wrapped around her hips, and Chuck Taylors. Her undercut ginger hair was pulled back into a sloppy ponytail.

The receptionist, whose nameplate identified her as Sharon Myers, pursed her lips, studying Harper. Eventually she just shrugged and launched into the standard excuse for the uninitiated who walked in blindly. "Sorry, I'm afraid we're all booked up."

It took some fishing around inside her ratty brown messenger bag before Harper was able to pull out her laminated ID card. "I've got an appointment with Mr. Stoker," she said as she passed it off to her.

Sharon plucked the card from Harper's hand and looked it over with a small nod. "Ah, looks like congratulations are in order, Ms. Zeale. Finally getting turned loose?"

Once the ID was returned to her, Harper popped it back into her bag. "Yup. Big day. Are our guests from last night's raid still here?"

Sharon pressed a button somewhere behind the desk and another door at the other end of the small reception area buzzed, followed by the sound of a heavy metallic *ka-chunk*. "Stairwell at the end of the hall. That'll take you down to the basement level. The lounge is the first door on the left. One of the vampires was pretty close to feral, so he's sedated and under heavy guard. But the other two are fairly lucid. Good luck, Harper." That last bit was refreshingly sincere.

"Thanks," she said softly before heading for the door.

Harper found the stairwell and descended, occasionally taking the steps two at a time. Whether it was excitement or nerves—possibly both—she was feeling energized. She stepped through the double doors at the bottom of the stairs, which opened onto the basement hallway.

Farther down was another set of double doors with a brick shithouse of a man standing guard over them, most likely a guild Shield. He was wearing a black suit that strained against his form. She could only assume one of the rooms beyond held the sedated vamp. You couldn't get much from an unconscious witness, so she focused on finding the other two.

A door to her right was labeled as a unisex bathroom, and the one on her left had a worn-out plastic plaque identifying it as the lounge Sharon had mentioned. Harper paused just long enough to give the Shield a quick nod before stepping inside the room on the left. She immediately thought that "lounge" was a generous description. The floor was gray linoleum, the walls a faded robin-egg blue. What few windows the place had were draped with heavy blackout curtains, so the only lighting came from the lightly buzzing fluorescents overhead. Only the occasional support pillar broke up the otherwise monotonous space.

There was a modest seating area with a couch, some padded wooden chairs, a mini fridge, and a television attached to the wall that was currently off. A girl who couldn't have been more than eighteen was perched in one of the chairs, one leg tucked up under her, the other propped up with an arm around it, holding her phone as she idly scrolled. Her free hand held a medical blood bag, already half-drained, which she occasionally took a sip from like it was a juice pouch.

Draped across the couch was a man in his midforties who could have been mistaken for someone nursing a hangover. His head was propped up on a ratty throw pillow, left arm resting across his upper face. Newly turned vampires tended to go through a bout of sensory overload, so he was likely trying to block out the lighting, dim as it was. With his free hand, he reached out and fumblingly opened the mini fridge to pull out a fresh blood bag. The door had swung too wide, and he made a few feeble attempts at closing it again. The girl eventually took pity, freeing her propped leg just long enough to knock it closed before returning to her comforting posture.

Harper approached cautiously, fully aware that she was about to press her way into an extremely tenuous situation. Then again, that was a pretty accurate description of her entire job, so she knew she would have to get used to that. "Excuse me?"

The young girl looked over and gave her a weak smile. "They got you too, huh?"

It took a moment to process what she meant by that. "Got me? Oh! No, I uh…" She moved in closer, dragging one of the chairs with her to tighten the circle a bit, then settled into it with her legs crossed. She placed her messenger bag in her lap and fished out a spiral notebook and a pen. "I've been called in to deal with the vampire who hurt you."

That got the guy's attention, and he carefully pried his face free from the crook of his arm. "No shit?" He slowly sat up, opening the valve on the blood bag and taking a quick drink from it. "Don't get me wrong, I'm not going to turn down free vengeance. But what about us? Is *this* just it now?" He gestured with the blood bag.

"My friends are all wondering where the hell I went and I don't know what to tell them," the girl added with a hint of desperation.

Harper held her hands out to stop the wave of questions. "Let's back up a second. My name's Harper. I'm a Knife with the guild, kind of like an inspector or a detective." She gestured to the two vampires, encouraging them to do their own quick introductions.

"Demi," said the young girl. "Uh, shit, I don't know. I'm a high school senior?" Demi shrugged her shoulders uselessly. Harper just offered her a nod and a smile. She didn't need their life stories or anything.

The guy sighed, pausing to take another drink. "Ben. Cubicle wage-slave."

"Okay! Ben, Demi," she repeated. "First things first. If I can take down this guy, you should revert." She bit back the urge to say, "go back to normal." Yes, they would be cured of their conditions. But there was rarely any semblance of normal after experiences like this. That was why the guild included services like counseling. "To do that, I need your help. A description of the vampire, his favorite haunts, that kind of thing."

The carrot of a cure was enough to get both of them eager to offer what they could.

Demi sat up a little taller, planting both feet on the floor. "Oh! Hang on..." She started tapping and scrolling on her phone again. "I was at this house party, so I don't know if that super helps. But! I did snap a selfie with him. Want me to text it to you?"

Bashfully, Harper retrieved her own phone and held it up. It was an ancient flip phone, a relic from a bygone era, refurbished but ultimately too archaic for the task. "You can email it to me, anyway. Here…" She quickly jotted down her contact information on a scrap of paper and passed it off to her.

Demi opted instead to just trade the paper for her phone so Harper could get a good look at the picture and jot down some quick notes. Angular features with a chin that could puncture steel, black hair gelled into a dramatic sweep, dark and heavy eye makeup, tasteful five o'clock shadow. The dude must have used his centuries of living to craft the perfect douchebag look.

After returning the phone to its rightful owner, she looked over at Ben. "I know this is all still pretty fresh. Getting turned can be disorienting. But anything you can add will help."

He reached up and rubbed his hand back and forth over his shaved head. "Disorienting? I would say more head-fuck-y. A lot of it is a blur. Hell, I still can't remember what he looks like. But I was definitely out drinking."

"Bar?"

His brow furrowed in concentration. "Club. I wanted to dance. An awkward, aging queer looking for a distraction. There's this twink grinding up on me. He said so many nice things. Can't remember what, just the feeling. Looked into his eyes and everything felt all claustrophobic and warm—no, hot. I needed space and I needed him. We went to the bathroom." He wrenched his eyes shut tight. Desperately, he brought the blood bag to his mouth and took a long pull, and slowly his posture eased. "I remember…after he opened his own vein and made me drink, I thought it was all a bit ironic."

Harper wanted to make space for him to sort through all the scattered thoughts, but it seemed like Ben was onto something so she pressed a bit. "What was ironic?"

"Blood…" he said. "Red…The club. The lights? No. The name. The name was red."

Shit, I'm losing him. This is too soon. He should be resting.

But we need this. There's a million clubs in Chicago. Even if only a handful of them have red signs, it could take days to figure out which one he went to. Days we don't have. Push him anyway. Someone else can pick up the pieces.

Okay, pump the brakes, asshole. That's not how we do things.

Not my monkey, not my circus. We need to find the bloodsucker before this gets worse.

"Bloodsucker"? Are you serious? Fuck that, we're better than this.

Harper took a deep breath to calm herself down and silence the argument raging in her mind. The exhausting angel-devil double act could go back-and-forth endlessly if she let it. Each voice raised important points, but sooner or later she had to make a decision. This was her first official job, she was supposed to be a professional, and they were making it really difficult.

"Crimson!"

Harper nearly jumped as Demi cried out beside her. "Jesus, what?"

She looked between them, smiling broadly. "The club! It's called Crimson. When he was sweet-talking me at the party, he said if I wanted to find him again, I should go to Crimson. He was so smooth about it too. 'Oh, baby girl, you'd fit right in. It has the hottest people in town.'" She did her best to imitate how he sounded like, forcing her voice into this low, husky register.

Ben's face eased again as she filled in the gap for him. "Blood, Crimson, ironic. God, thank you."

Harper hastily scribbled that onto the page as well. She had the face, she had his favorite hunting ground. Now all she had to do was everything else. Easy as that. As an afterthought, she wrote down her contact information one more time before passing a second scrap of paper over to Ben. She was starting to think she should get some business cards made.

"Thank you both. If I do my job right, you should be feeling like your old selves again soon. Just be sure to take it easy. Reverting isn't any more enjoyable than the first part." She threw everything back into her messenger back and clambered off the chair. Harper hesitated for just a moment. She wanted to say something at least a little more comforting, a little less clinical. Her mom was great at that stuff, so she did her best to channel the woman. "It's going to be okay. I know this has kind of thrown your worlds upside down. Don't hesitate to reach out if you need anything."

It was hardly a rallying cry, but it got them both to smile. That had to be enough.

It did not elude Harper that she was entering a club on her twenty-first birthday with the express purpose of not partying. She was, in fact, painfully aware of it. As she made her way to the bar, she was forced to slip around clusters of people in various states of inebriation. Her eyes were constantly scanning the crowd for any sign of the vampire, but for the moment he was nowhere in sight. She'd passed the picture from Demi off to a guild Scroll who ran it through their database and got a handful of hits. She would have preferred going into this with more concrete information, but Harper knew there were still ways to narrow down her search. And there was no better place to start than with a hopefully observant bartender.

Finally, she managed to sidle her way up to her destination and leaned against the sturdy wooden bar. It took her a few moments to get noticed by the buff guy in the blood-red shirt with the word "Crimson" splashed across it. "What can I get you?"

She leaned in close to hear—and be heard—over the thumping bass. "Some pop and some information, if you've got a sec?"

"Just pop? Designated driver, I'm guessing." He scooped some ice from a well below the bar, dropped it into a glass, then filled it from the soda gun before setting the drink on a coaster in front of her. "That's one down. What kind of information were you looking for?"

Harper put a twenty on the bar to cover the drink and grease the wheels. "Looking for a guy, black hair, goth makeup, smooth as shit. Looks like a supermodel, flirts with anything that moves?"

He chuckled as he picked up the twenty. "I take it back. Guess you're looking for a different kind of high. Yeah, that sounds like Zack. He's here most nights. Guess you could be his type, but the waiting list is pretty long. Still, you're shooting your shot, and I respect that. Might be a few hours."

Bingo. There was only one Zack in the list of names she'd been given—Zachary Garfield. Harper knew it was stupid to assume that there was only one vampire in the entire city with that name, but the odds were looking good. Only time would tell, and if what the bartender had told her was true, she'd be waiting a while to find out for sure. She wasn't looking forward to that, eager for some proper action, but it wasn't like Harper had anything better to do. "You're the man. Don't let me keep you." She pushed away from the bar and took her drink to look for a vantage point—not to mention a dead zone where the music didn't punch her in the chest and crush her eardrums. After some dedicated scouring, she found the red underlit staircase that led to the upper balcony where things weren't so oppressive. A series of semicircular booths were set into the wall, and on a whim she picked one with a decent view of the dance floor as well as the upper VIP section. If this Zack guy was that notorious, she had an inkling he might have his own throne back there.

Her attention and confidence lasted roughly half an hour. What had begun as a careful scan was now idle people-watching. She'd drained the liquid from her glass, chewed through all the ice, and now it served as little more than a fidget toy. Harper checked the time on her phone and realized how little of it had passed, groaning desperately. This was the worst part. The goddamn waiting.

Around the hour mark, she contemplated going for another drink, but another glass meant an increased chance of needing to use the bathroom. Obvious dysphoria-based anxieties aside, time in the bathroom meant a chance for her to completely miss her window. So she sat, and she watched, and she waited.

She sat.

She watched.

She waited.

And then Harper started to worry. The bartender had said that her quarry came in "most nights." And Demi had mentioned meeting him at a house party, so there was every chance in the world she was planted here on her ass for nothing. And all the while he was out there, capturing someone else, draining them, or turning them.

Fuck.

That delightful spiral carried on for another thirty minutes or so, when finally she saw his stupid smug face. Part of her wanted to get this over with—bull-rush him and finish it. But that was an awful decision for several reasons. First and foremost, she'd look like a crazed murderer. And then everyone in the club would see that he wasn't human, creating a mass panic. Plus, she'd get chewed out by her parents and the guild.

And since she couldn't act until he made a move, she had to wait again. She had to just sit there and watch while he got a drink from the bar. She had to stew in her frustration as he ambled about, taking time to chat with every single fucking person he ran across. And even when all that was done, he sauntered right into the VIP section as she'd predicted—which meant the bastard was out of sight. Scrambling, she got up from her booth and found a better position where she could pretend to look out on the dance floor while still keeping an eye on what parts of the roped-off section she could see.

Zack was sitting on a couch next to a girl maybe a year or two older than Harper, whispering sweet nothings in her ear. There was every possibility he might drink from her right then and there. The only thing that kept her from panicking was the reports of the bodies he'd left behind. They were always littered in random places across the city with no discernible pattern. He probably liked this club too much to leave a mess.

So she watched and waited some goddamn more.

It was well past midnight when he finally took the girl's arm and pulled her up from the couch, walking her out of the VIP section and toward the stairs. He was taking her to a secondary location—this was it! As smoothly as her nerves allowed, Harper trailed after them while the pair moved down the stairwell and through the main door. She stopped off just long enough to deposit her empty glass on the bar before slipping out after them. To her immense relief, she caught sight of some blond locks moving out of sight down the nearby alley and continued her tail.

Just as suddenly, she had to pull up short. Zack had apparently decided to make this the scene of tonight's entertainment. Harper swiftly pressed herself up against the rough bricks of the dark alleyway, then ducked behind a nearby dumpster, desperately willing her breathing to slow. This was her big moment. *Happy twenty-first birthday! Go stop a vampire from siring half of Chicago.* Not that she was complaining exactly. As far as birthdays went, it didn't get much more exciting than this. But it was stressful now that she didn't have her parents acting as a safety net.

Even in this dingy alley, the atmosphere from the nearby club was still palpable—fragments of neon lighting, dulled thumping bass, chatter from people waiting in line to get inside. This dark, cramped space was only occupied by three bodies. There was Harper, hunkered down on one knee behind an exceptionally pungent dumpster. There was the cute, young blonde in the too-short, silver, glittering dress. And there was Zack.

While waiting for the perfect moment to strike, Harper ran the dossier back through her head. Zachary Garfield, formerly Zechariah Gairbekov of some European city that didn't exist anymore. Still a relative newcomer to the greater Chicago area, he made a habit of city-hopping to avoid too much attention. It made Harper wonder what was wrong with the slacker hunters in New York City or Los Angeles that they hadn't dealt with this clown yet. In the span of a month or so he'd managed to kill a handful of people, which was bad enough. Far more dangerous, though, was his propensity for turning innocent people against their wishes. Worse, he left them to figure out their new vampiric state alone and afraid—like poor Ben and Demi.

And now here she was, half focusing on Zack while the rest of her mental energy was used up, ignoring the rotting garbage in the dumpster that provided such meager cover. She watched as his head dipped down toward the girl's neck, a fang glistening in the red neon washing from the club.

It was now or never.

Harper pushed to stand and step closer, then cleared her throat, trying to sound intimidating. Unfortunately, she was already used to counteracting the effects of testosterone on her voice, so course-correcting along with that caused a situation akin to driving a car with a blown-out tire. Her voice shook, coming out at a pitch that was just a touch too low, before quickly ratcheting up a few steps, only to overshoot and go too high. "Ah, excuse me, miss. I—Ahem, I don't want to ruin the mood, but is this whole thing…consensual?"

There were several seconds without anything happening as Zachary held eye contact with his victim, who finally turned to look at Harper. Her pupils were dilated to an almost uncomfortable degree, and she gave a forced, robotic smile. "Oh yes. I'm very happy."

Harper clicked her tongue softly, perhaps trying a little too hard to be cool. "Y'know, I might've almost been convinced if you'd made her give me, like, a small nod or something. But that was so obvious. Shame." It wasn't great, not as far as snappy banter went. Nothing like the heroine in her favorite show. Harper never could get the hang of that clever dialogue. In the moment, she couldn't just think up witty stuff on the fly. She kept trying, even if she kept failing. But there was also a time to admit when you needed to stop screwing around, so she brought all of her attention around on the vampire.

Zack looked away from his prey, leaving her dazed and hypnotized and leaning up against the wall for support. He turned to fully face Harper and sighed. "Walk away. Or this is going to get very bad for you." His fangs were on full display now. A picture on a phone and watching him from a distance hadn't really prepared Harper for just how tall and broad Zack was. She wasn't short, but he still dwarfed her easily. With a growl, he lunged at her, teeth bared, ready to bite.

This part, at least, didn't make her nervous. This part was easy. In one fluid motion, Harper flicked open the clasp on a sheath at her hip and drew her knife, driving it straight into his chest, where the shriveled remains of his heart should be.

Zack drew up short and looked down where the knife was lodged in his flesh. He seemed shocked, for sure, but otherwise unimpressed. "Stupid. Incredibly stupid. If you know what I am, then you know that was pointless."

His smoking wound told a very different story, and Harper couldn't help but grin. That was no ordinary knife. Rather than traditional, reliable steel, the blade was made of pure iron and inlaid with veins of silver, available only by special requisition from the guild. The combination of those two notorious metals was more than enough to do serious damage to any number of countless mythics. Iron for various flavors of Fair Folk, silver for all the midnight dangers. Sure, wooden stakes were a classic for dealing with a vampire, but they were a pain in the ass to make and lug around. Her knife was always with her, like an old friend.

He muttered something she couldn't quite make out, his voice coming out raspy as more and more of him started to smoke and the skin on his face and arms started to crack and fade away. But she definitely made out one word. "Hunter…"

"Bingo," she said, finally sliding the knife back out of his chest. Slowly, Zack stumbled back the short distance to the brick wall, leaning against it next to the blonde. His flesh crackled as it caught up to his actual age. Harper wiped off the small bits of viscera and ichor from the blade on her pants before sliding it back into its sheath, clipping the cover in place. He looked as though he was probably attempting to cry out in pain, but by now his throat and lungs were turning to ash so it just came out as a whisper. Sad and grim, his body finally began to lose the last vestiges of composure, and he deteriorated into nothing more than a pile of dust on the dirty pavement.

"Well. That's that," she said softly, mostly to herself. Harper had done it. She'd killed the vampire. Hopefully, Demi and Ben would turn back to normal. Nobody else had to die, or suffer the indignity of being transformed against their will.

She'd killed the vampire. It was so easy.

It was *too* easy.

Harper decided that she really, really didn't want to follow that particular train of thought any further. Instead, she focused her attention on Zack's intended victim.

At the moment, she was curled in on herself, staring despondently at the pile of dust that had once been her attacker. Her feet gave out from under her and she slowly slid down until her butt was on the asphalt.

"Shit." Harper much preferred the ones who ran because it made her job far simpler. She didn't have to explain anything, or comfort them. But she also wasn't enough of a garbage person to leave her alone, so she awkwardly crouched down and joined her in sitting on the disgusting ground. "Um, sorry about…all that."

She worried away at her lower lip with her teeth for a few moments before finally attempting to speak. "Was… Was he—?" Blessedly, she cut herself off before asking the super-obvious question. Still, this was the moment. The veil had officially been pierced for this girl, and she was allowed to see the rest of the world, the real world. Everyone reacted differently. If they were fortunate, the sheer power of denial would sew that veil right back up and they would go about their lives as if the trauma was more mundane. If they were less fortunate, they would have a full-on breakdown and question everything they had ever known. This girl impressed Harper by landing somewhere in the middle, which was rare. "Well, I mean of course he was. The teeth and…that weird thing he did with his eyes, and he turned into dust when you stabbed him. Normal people don't do that. Are, uh…are you—?"

"Am I what? A creature of the night? Nope. Boring human."

The trembling blonde chanced a more fearful look at the world outside the alleyway. Harper could see a few telltale tears in the corners of her eyes. She was trying hard to maintain her composure, but the weight of it all was setting in. "Are there others? Like, other stuff out there?"

Harper wasn't particularly enthused about having to further shatter this girl's world. But lying to her now would probably be the worse option in the grand scheme of things. "There are. But hey, they're a lot like us. Some of them suck, some of them are pretty nice, and almost everyone is just trying to get by. You saw the worst of it tonight."

"Kinda saw the best of it too," she said, sniffling softly. After a beat, she carefully pushed herself up to stand again—an impressive feat considering the heels.

Harper stood up with her, no doubt looking like a newborn fawn by comparison. Harper was riding a wave of very complicated emotions. She'd managed to hunt a vampire all on her lonesome. But her hunt had also ended with Harper killing him. It wasn't just that she had driven her knife into him and ended his existence that was fucking with her, though. What really disturbed her was just how simple it had been. The reflexes were deeply rooted, and stabbing her blade into Zack's heart came so easily. Worst of all was the feeling of satisfaction she got from a job well done.

In an effort to keep distracting herself, Harper did something incredibly stupid and allowed herself a chance to examine the temporary damsel in distress. She was pretty in a very conventional way—not a bad thing, to be clear. Wavy blond hair, wide blue eyes, and that tight silver clubbing dress. "Mind if I ask you your name? Otherwise I'm going to have to keep referring to you as 'Cute Blonde' in my head."

The look she got in return told her that had been a bad idea. There was some warmth in those features for a moment, but her brow quickly furrowed and she closed herself off with her arms crossed. "Sammy. You?"

"Harper. I, uh—" She fumbled the ball so hard she considered calling the whole game. "I know this was a lot. I can put you in touch with some people that can talk you through all this. Get your head around it." She once again went through the awkward process of putting information on a scrap of paper before passing it off to her. The two of them stood there awkwardly for a moment, shuffling their feet. "Fuck, look, I'm sorry. That was so uncool of me. Just the epitome of inconsiderate."

"Yeah, kinda," Sammy said, not even bothering to soften that particular blow. "It's whatever. I'm gonna go home, take a long shower, get hammered, and have an emotional breakdown if I can find the time. Maybe I'll call your people tomorrow. I don't know. It's whatever," Sammy repeated, voice cracking slightly.

The urge bubbled up within Harper to offer an escort home. She had to viciously bite down on her lip to keep that from happening. Instead, she just offered an awkward half-wave and watched as Sammy left the cramped alleyway and hailed a cab. Glancing over, Harper contemplated hurling herself into the dumpster where she belonged. "Yeah. It's whatever..."

Normal was never on the books. Once she was certain Sammy had managed to get safely inside a taxi, she made the hike toward the nearby parking garage where her car was waiting. It was time to go home and nurse her emotional wounds while trying to be grateful she hadn't sustained any physical ones.

CHAPTER TWO

Harper started to turn her car toward the exit for the interstate, then at the last moment, flipped the turn signal lever back down and kept the vehicle in her current lane. The fastest way to get home was to take Interstate 57 south, and right now, she wasn't in the mood for fast. She redirected, aimed for highways, and sulked her way home instead.

Her car was a clunker, a Chevy Cavalier that was even older than Harper. It had been kept alive by sheer force of will and a helping hand from Morgan back home on the commune. The guy was a master at keeping ancient car parts alive. The seats had a couple holes in them and the fabric headliner above was drooping in more than a few places, but the car moved and it held her stuff. That was generally good enough. This was her trusty steed, and she would always hold a special place in Harper's heart. Her name was Lilith.

Harper reached for the volume knob on the dashboard and cranked it up. Club music was stupid and annoying and too loud. And yet, when it was riot grrrl punk and angsty nineties alternative chick rock churning out of her battered MP3 player through an auxiliary cassette adapter, ruptured eardrums were almost soothing. She cracked open the tall energy drink can in the cup holder and took a long sip as she piloted Lilith through the middle of a dying town.

Bikini Kill faded out, replaced by Tracy Bonham.

Harper was definitely okay. So what if she'd made a pass at a girl who nearly died? So what if that was super gross and lecherous? After all, that wasn't a huge deal in the grand scheme of things. The important part was that Harper had managed to slay the bad guy. She was a slayer. A killer.

Harper had killed a man. Yes, he was an awful man who had done terrible things. It should have been a comfort that she killed him. The world was safer now. But she had to kill someone to ensure that safety. She'd done it before. No doubt, she would have to do it again.

Mother, mother, everything was fine.

Harper was yanked from her moping by the rattling of her phone in the spare cup holder. She picked it up, using her index finger to carefully rotate the car's volume knob back down before flipping the phone open and holding it to her ear. "What?" She was in a foul mood and the world would just have to deal with it.

"Is this a bad time?"

Shit, that was Demi. Nice one, idiot, Harper berated herself internally. "No, sorry, it's cool. What's up? Everything okay?"

"Yeah! Um, me and Ben are both feeling pretty good. Well, I'm feeling good, anyway. He went to take another sip of blood and nearly threw up. They're running a few tests on us just to make sure, but…I think whatever you did worked. So. Just, y'know, I wanted to call and thank you. And let you know. I've got no clue how I could ever make it up to you."

Harper sighed with relief. "Get back to your life, stay safe, and don't tell anyone the truth."

"Okay. Wow. You're pretty cool, Harper. Thanks again! I'm gonna stop now before I ramble and make a fool of myself. So, uh…bye!"

"Take care, Demi. You're gonna be all right." She flipped the phone closed and tossed it back into the cup holder. Then Harper reached for the volume knob, pumping the music back up to its original volume. It was sweet of Demi to say that stuff. And it felt good to make a difference, to be a hero. But that was a small comfort in the face of what she had done. The price of being a hunter was steep.

Growing up on a commune colored expectations and behavior, arguably by design. So it really shouldn't have come as a surprise that Harper was the way she was.

Harper's family was a part of the Silversmiths, an ancient order of warriors, mages, and scholars who stood on the edge of the mundane world to blah blah blah…They were monster-hunters. The Silversmiths were a North American offshoot of a European guild, The Knights of Iron. Ever since humanity first discovered there were supernatural beings in the world, there had been those who banded together to study them, fight them, and kill them.

At least, that was how the guilds used to operate. "Monster" had become something of a slur, replaced with the word "mythic," and "hunting" had long since turned into a catchall term. Guilds like the Silversmiths didn't just take down the bad supernatural threats; they also helped the ones who were feeling scared or alone, and rehabilitated those who just wanted to be a part of modern society.

Being a hunter was essentially a community service and rarely included a paycheck, outside of per diems while on the job. The Silversmiths did have a few employees, but they were rare. Guild members either had to moonlight to put food on the table and a roof over their heads, or else find ways to rely on others.

Which was how Harper and her family had ended up in a sort of symbiotic relationship with their commune. It wasn't guild-affiliated in any way, but it was a good place for the Zeales to rest their heads, with food and comfort and all those things it was hard to not have in the twenty-first century.

Her home wasn't quite as off-grid as other, similar communities. They tried to be self-sufficient within reason, but some residents still worked day jobs. There was electricity, phone, and Internet—though the utilities were spotty at best—

but the lifestyle was still pretty radical by modern standards. The facilities spanned roughly one hundred acres and ranged from cabins first put together in the sixties, to the big dormitory building and a dining hall with all the amenities. Some of the members had workshops, while others maintained offices for remote work. It wasn't much, but it was home, and it meant the world to Harper.

Her parents had tried in vain to keep what they did a secret from the community, but that proved to be a monumental task. In the end, they came clean. While some commune members were concerned about the ethics of it—particularly those who came looking for a crunchy, free-love kind of vibe—most everyone respected the grind. In time, her family came to be seen as the holy knights of their little community.

Was there something noble about being a part of the Silversmiths? Certainly. Did she sometimes enjoy the pure joy of being a big hero? Absolutely. But most of all, this was her home. And sometimes it was a little too big and a little too close, and you didn't get to have a lot of secrets. But she loved it with her whole being. This was her family.

She brought Lilith to a stop in the big dirt parking lot. It was nearly two in the morning, and this far out from society, everything was still and quiet. Most of the outer lights were off, but the harvest moon overhead ensured decent visibility. A cool autumn wind blew across the commune as she stepped out from her car and pulled her jacket a little tighter around herself. It was difficult to be respectfully silent when everything in your vehicle creaked and clicked so audibly, but she did her best to retrieve her duffel from the trunk without waking up half the residents.

After fiddling with her keys for a moment, Harper managed to open the front door of the dormitory building. Years of stealth training paid off, and she only banged her shin on one couch as she slipped through the main living room and up to the second floor.

Harper had her own private dorm room upstairs—humble though it was—with a bed and dresser, a homemade bookshelf, a busted tube TV, and thrift store DVD player. She also had a brick of a laptop that she didn't use often. She flicked on the light of her bedside lamp, bathing the room in a gentle glow that wouldn't blind her. After dropping her duffel to the floor, she hung her jacket up on the hook affixed to the wall with a touch of reverence. The rest of her clothes didn't get the same treatment, unceremoniously shed and tossed in the general direction of her laundry basket. Once she'd managed to locate a pair of ratty gym shorts and climb into them, she flopped onto the mattress face down, passing out from various forms of exhaustion.

* * *

A knock at her bedroom door roused Harper before her alarm clock got the chance. It was difficult to tell if she was drowsy because the hour was ungodly, or because she still felt a bit like garbage. For the time being she went with the safe bet and assumed it was both. She continued to lie there with her face buried in the pillow, praying that if she pretended to still be asleep, the disturbance might leave her alone for a while.

When the next knock came louder and more insistent, she knew two things. First, she was not going to be left alone, and second, the disturbance was almost certainly her father. The day was not off to a fantastic start.

"Mm…Yes?"

"She lives," came the usual dry wit from the other side of the door. "Up and at 'em, Harper. There's work to be done."

Not wishing to have this conversation muffled as it currently was, she untangled herself from her blanket and clambered to her feet. With fumbling hands, Harper somehow managed to get a tank top on right-side out in a single attempt. She crossed the short distance and opened the door.

Sebastian Zeale was an intimidating man. Lean muscles, head buzzed, cheeks sharp, jaw protruding, always so serious. The only reason it didn't affect Harper too much these days was that she'd grown used to it. He was a terror when it came to the world of the supernatural, but he could be kind of a big puppy about hearth and home. He was already dressed for the day in standard-issue dad apparel—crisp khakis, navy polo, and loafers. You might never guess looking at him that he was a nightmare with a blade.

"I just finished a job last night. Don't I get a break?" She yawned as loud and obnoxiously as she could to drive home her current state, rubbing at her eyes.

He was unmoved. "You're a full guild hunter now, Harper. No such thing as a break, not until you're dead."

God, Harper thought but managed to stop herself from saying out loud. What a drama queen.

He continued, unaware of her internal jab. "A girl was eviscerated at a small college campus down south. The guild needs a Knife to go investigate."

Harper held his gaze for a moment, his piercing eyes versus her bleary ones. This was a common battle between them. Her father was a master of the heavy silence and the meaningful look, and she just hadn't managed to figure it out. Sebastian won the staring contest and she gave a helpless shrug with a heavy sigh. "Aye aye, *Jefe*. Would you be so kind as to grant me fifteen minutes for a shower?"

Finally, his face softened a bit with an almost imperceptible smile. "The boys in the city say you handled yourself well last night. Take an hour, get some breakfast too." Just like that, he was back to business, nodding thoughtfully. "But no more than that. The sooner you get down there, the sooner you can get this sorted. I'll be in my office."

"Copy that." Once he'd turned to leave, she shut her door and turned to look herself over in the standing mirror leaning against the nearby wall. She looked like hell. "A whole hour. Happy birthday to me."

One hour later and Harper almost felt like a human being again. A hot shower, some pancakes, and clean clothes—that were a carbon copy of her last outfit—were enough to give the semblance of an actual person. As she slipped her leather jacket around her arms, some psychological conditioning kicked in that made her feel like a knight getting armored up.

She stepped out of the dormitory building and into the crisp fall morning. A sudden presence came up out of her right periphery and a familiar weight latched onto her arm. "Hail, brave warrior."

She turned to look down at her childhood friend and smiled, whipping around to pull her into a hug. "Katie!" Pulling back just a bit, she made sure Katie got a full view of her tired smile. "You're never going to get tired of calling me that, are you?"

Katie completely ignored the question, choosing instead to poke her in the arm and demand intel. "Come on, I want details! How was it?" She tilted her head to the side slightly, her honey-blond hair cascading over her shoulder. Her blue eyes sparkled just a little bit in the bright fall sun. Harper thought she was done admiring the girl she'd known for so many years, but no dice. Even after all the time that had passed since their ill-advised kiss, there was still a part of Harper that remained foolishly attracted to Katie.

This enthusiastic digging had become a regular occurrence whenever Harper returned from a hunt with her parents. And no doubt, it was extra exciting now that she was an independent hunter.

"Well, I don't want to brag," she said before proceeding to brag. "I stabbed a vampire in a dark, dank little alleyway next to his favorite club before he had a chance to hurt his next victim. Turned to dust and everything." For just a moment, Harper's chest felt tight. Why the hell was she boasting? What she did wasn't glamorous or cool. Zack might have been unrepentantly evil, but she still took his life.

"Were they okay?" Katie asked with her eyes glimmering a little. "The victim, I mean."

"Yeah, she was...I mean, she was kind of traumatized, but I think she'll be okay." Harper rubbed her neck slowly, dropping her voice as she added, "Though I'm not sure I made things any better by flirting with her."

Without warning, Katie reeled back and delivered a not entirely playful slap to her arm. "You *flirted* with a traumatized girl? What is *wrong* with you?"

Harper flailed, trying to get away before Katie could land a second hit on her. "Would you keep your voice down? Jesus!" She sighed and leaned up against the wall of the dormitory. "I have no idea what's wrong with me. I was feeling confident and stupid. Now I just feel stupid." And really, wasn't that the crux of the entire issue? Take everything else away and Harper was just a big, romantic idiot. And all she had to show for it was one failed relationship, one misguided kiss, and one poor girl in Chicago who probably never wanted to see Harper again. She harbored all these idealistic, starry-eyed dreams, but at the end of the day, she was just this lonely weirdo. And Harper knew that if she didn't sort out her shit, she was doomed to a life of heartbreak.

Katie joined her in leaning on the wall, gently bumping shoulders by way of a silent apology. "Well. Don't let it get you down. You've done stupid stuff before and survived." The implications went unspoken, and for that she was grateful.

"Yeah, that's fair enough." Sighing softly, Harper glanced toward the commune office building. "Anyway, I should get going. Already got another assignment in the barrel."

"That was fast."

Harper scoffed. "You should have heard Dad this morning. 'No such thing as a break, not until you're dead.' But hey, we all have our parts to play." As she stood up, she opened her arms and Katie instantly went in for a tight hug.

"Yeah. You gotta go be a knight in shining armor." Katie let the hug linger a second longer, then finished with an emphatic squeeze before letting Harper free. Just as suddenly, she whipped Harper around and gave her a shove. "Go on. Better not keep the old man waiting."

"Fine, I know when I'm not wanted!" They were both giggling as she resumed her walk across the main courtyard of the commune.

Harper's parents were both lifelong hunters themselves, so it only made sense that she would be brought up to eventually join the "family business," so to speak. Her father, Sebastian, was especially old school. He was a taskmaster, a good soldier, and something of a traditionalist. He had trained Harper in combat and research from a young age. Her mother, Calliope, was the touchy-feely type, much more in tune with the modern mission statement of the guild. She was good at meeting both mundane and supernatural individuals where they were, providing therapy or counseling. She could also be a terror with plant magic, when the need arose.

Harper much preferred studying and learning about mythics. Her father had been under the impression that this meant she was developing an intellectual streak when it came to her hunts, but that wasn't quite right. Certainly she was familiar with ways of fighting them, should violence become unavoidable. But it was not fighting or defeating that truly interested her. It was the mythics themselves, the way they operated and moved throughout the world. Where possible, she tried to learn about their cultures, but that information was difficult to find—at least through Silversmith resources. Until the last century or two, hunters didn't care about cultural anthropology, they just cared about the hunt.

Sometimes Harper found herself wondering what it might take to bring their worlds together. Not just hunters, but all of humanity. Would it be possible to find unity, to pierce the veil that separated the mundane and the fantastical?

It was commonly accepted that the division was necessary. If everyday humans discovered just how much was truly out there, they would undoubtedly go mad. Worse, they might become violent. Surely humanity would panic and revive the old ways, killing mythics out of misplaced fear. But sometimes Harper could be overly optimistic. She needed to believe that people were capable of being civil. She wanted to hope that expanding everyone's understanding of the universe might lead to a better world, new developments, stranger magic, and—most importantly—an increased sense of hope and wonder.

She thought about this stuff a lot.

Sebastian kept his office obnoxiously neat and tidy. Even the forest-green color on the walls was perfect, not a speck of stray paint. One side of the room was occupied by two massive bookshelves that flanked a collection of framed documents and commendations from the guild. The opposite wall featured an intimidating collection of mounted weapons, centered on his beloved longsword. Much like Harper's knife, it was a specially designed tool. One edge was pure iron, the other silver, and a series of runes was etched along the central groove.

The far end of the room was taken up almost entirely by a massive window with heavy, white, spotless curtains. Sebastian sat at his equally large oak desk. The thing must have been a logistical bitch to get into the building. He was typing away at his own fossil of a computer, pausing when she entered.

Harper shut the door behind her and quickly slid into one of the seats opposite her father. "So, eviscerated girl?"

He reached for a manila folder already opened on his desk, rotating it around and pushing it across to her. "Malcolm-Baptiste College. Student by the name of Autumn Temple. She was found at a local outdoor party spot. Her chest was opened up, ribs pulled apart, heart removed—looked like it was torn out. Officially it was a wild animal attack, but—"

"A werewolf then." She picked up the folder and began looking through the few scattered documents the guild had managed to pass along. "My first ever mission alone and I get a vampire. Now it's a werewolf? I don't suppose they have anything juicier on the docket? Rakshasa? Rogue angel? Haunted mirror?"

"Oh, I'm sorry," he said, sounding not particularly sorry. "Is the important work of stopping supernatural threats not exciting enough for you?" The two of them shared yet another silent staring contest.

Harper inevitably lost, but she wasn't done being a brat yet. "I'm just saying, it's not exactly complicated. Silver-tipped bolt through the neck or heart, bing-bang-boom."

"Good. Then you'll be back with time to spare in case something…'juicy' should come along. Understood?"

This time, Harper was the one to initiate the contest of wills. Some part of her saw it as a rite of passage. The day she could make her father relent with nothing but eyes and pursed lips, she would finally ascend.

Alas, today was not that day. It felt as though she'd held out longer than ever before, but Sebastian still hadn't broken a sweat. She inevitably gave in first and stared down at the dossier instead with a small huff. "Yeah. I'll let you know when it's done." She flipped the folder closed and plucked it from the desk. By the time she rose from her chair, he was already back to work on his computer.

In one final childish act of rebellion, she slammed the office door shut with a resounding boom.

Maintaining her frankly immature demeanor, Harper stomped off across the commune grounds and found her feet carrying her toward the gardens of their own volition. They were taking her where they always seemed to take her when she was nursing her wounds—to her mother.

Calliope Zeale was, in many ways, the antithesis of her husband. She was warm and welcoming and full of life. She was a plush woman who had never been afraid of being a full head taller than her husband, nor of being solid and round. Her vibrant red hair was going more and more gray over time, and she seemed to wear even this proudly.

At the moment, she resembled one of those paintings where a humble woman gathers up the harvest, with her head scarf and long flowing dress. She used her apron to hold all the assorted produce before dumping it into a nearby basket. As Harper drew closer, she pushed up to stand, brushing the back of her hand across her forehead before raising it high and waving to her energetically. "Sweetie!"

"Hey, Mom."

Instantly, she gave a sympathetic pout and finished closing the distance between them before drawing Harper into a warm embrace. "Just finished meeting with your dad?"

"What tipped you off?"

Calliope chuckled as she finally let go after one last solid squeeze. "He does have a way of coming down on you too hard. Always leaves you looking a little deflated."

She clutched the manila folder against her chest and sighed sadly. "There was a moment this morning where he was almost nice. I swear, I thought—" She cut herself off, not wanting to put such obvious words to what it was she really wanted. It damn sure wasn't an extra forty-five minutes to get ready. But saying it out loud would have been so demoralizing. "Anyway. It's also this assignment. It's not exactly glamorous. Just a liberal arts college with a werewolf problem."

"There's nothing wrong with a simple job. Still…" Her mother got a mysterious smile of infinite amusement for just a moment before reaching out to pat her on top of the head. "Did anyone see this werewolf? Eyewitness reports, or even just rumors?"

"Doesn't seem like it. Just the one death." With a shrug, Harper popped the file back open to flip through the small amount of information again.

"Sometimes things aren't so simple. Could be a werewolf, sure. Could be a shapeshifter, or a particularly nasty demon. You know, the mission where I met your father—"

Harper's eyes rolled reflexively. "Ann Arbor, your first assignment together. You were chasing what you thought was a collection of dream goblins, turned out it was a bogeyman. Love at first sight. Storybook."

Calliope's smile was big enough to highlight the plentiful laugh lines in her face. "So. That version of the story is only half true."

Harper's eyebrows lifted and she leaned in, curious to hear the real version.

"I was partnered with a Shield at the time, Connor, and we ran headlong into this absolute prick of a Sword, some hotshot named Sebastian. Turned out the guild had double-booked. I hated him instantly. So self-important, with this whole 'I work alone' attitude. Could never get a smile or a laugh out of him. I was distracted, which meant it was far easier for me to get jumped by that bogeyman. Connor was badly wounded fighting it off, and I thought we were done for. That was when I saw the Sword in action. He was so strong and fearless, and his muscles…" A visible shiver of delight—or, God forbid, arousal—passed over

Calliope, and Harper tried not to let her mild disgust show. "Sorry, I'm getting off-topic. Yes, there is every chance this job will be unexciting. There will be a lot of those. But sometimes you'll get a pleasant surprise. You're free to complain if it sucks, but you should always be open to the possibility that nothing is what it seems."

Harper felt much better, which was sort of unfortunate, because some part of her was thoroughly enjoying being a brat about this. But her mother was right. You couldn't take the world of the uncanny for granted. Not everything was fully categorized and understood, and they were changing in equal measure with the human world. Hell, she felt almost hopeful now. Maybe. A little bit.

"Who knows? Maybe you'll even find a little love, just like I did." Calliope laughed brightly at that, but Harper didn't get the impression it was teasing. Her mother was simply a joyful person, and she wasn't too shy to show it.

For her part, Harper wasn't so sure, nor was she so enthusiastic. If prior experience was anything to go by, she'd probably have to settle for a lot of awkward letdowns. Love didn't seem in the cards, at least not any time soon. Maybe it was time to put love on the back burner and focus on being a decent hunter. "Eh, I dunno about that." She gently rubbed the back of her neck, refusing to meet her mother's kind eyes.

"All right, I'll stop. You've got a hunt, and I've got a harvest. No rest for the weary, eh?"

God, if she had a nickel for every time Calliope had said that… Harper smiled weakly and opted to steal one last hug before jogging away toward the dorms again. She needed to finish prepping and get on the road.

After repacking her duffel and checking all her supplies, Harper was feeling almost sort of okay. It was easier to push aside frustrations when you were working on something, be it chores or the hunt.

Harper stepped out of her small room to find Natasha leaning against the opposite wall, trying very hard to look casual and uninterested. The dark pixie cut and pale skin were all that remained of Nat's old goth phase. That phase had been left by the wayside the same day their rocky relationship ended. Though even without the aesthetic, Nat continued to maintain an air of unflappable coolness—right up until the point you saw past the mask at some of that hurt she hid so well. "Hey." There was a heavy weight to that single word.

"Hey."

"How, um—Are you…doing okay?"

"Huh?" She allowed the bag to drop from her shoulder, since it seemed like this might be A Thing That Required Her Attention. "Yeah, I'm fine. Frustrated with my dad, but that's nothing new."

"No, not that. Just—" Nat was really stumbling over her words, and it made Harper worry that something was legitimately wrong. When she made her next attempt at a coherent sentence, her voice was much lower in both pitch and volume. "Yesterday. You were all alone. What if something had happened? And we just—" She shut her eyes firmly. "I was worried that everything would get left how it was a few days ago. Which is to say, really fucking shitty, Harper. And for the past twenty-four hours, all I could think about was Sebastian breaking the news that you'd been hurt, or worse."

For a moment she just nodded along, letting all of that really sink in. She'd been so busy wallowing in self-pity she'd completely forgotten to call literally anybody and let them know she was okay. Poor little Harper, rejected by a girl because she had nearly just died. At the very least, she could have texted her father to pass the word along. She folded in on herself a bit, sighing. "Dammit, Nat, I'm sorry. I got a little caught up in my own head."

She smirked. "Yeah, Katie told me you did something pretty stupid. I'm guessing you got shot down?"

"Getting shot down implies I asked her out. I didn't make it past 'awkward flirting.' It went poorly, and then I just felt like an asshole. I can't shake that voice that says this is just going to keep happening." Speaking of being a stupid asshole, this was absolutely not a conversation she ought to be having with Natasha of all people. But it was far too late for that now. "Tell me it's not always going to be like this?"

After a moment of hesitation, Nat finally pushed herself away from the wall, glancing down at the military duffel bag on the floor. She let one more meaningful beat pass before looking up at Harper with an attempt at a smile. "Promise me you'll text this time, and I'll nurse your ego when you come back alive. Deal?"

She laughed. It felt good to be laughing with Nat again, even if it was awkward and strained and hesitant. "Deal. I'll keep you updated. With any luck, I'll actually have some free time when I'm done. And you and Katie and I can split a case of shitty beer and have a normal night."

"I'd like that."

Harper lifted the duffel back up onto her shoulder and somehow managed a cocky smile. "Besides, it's just a werewolf. How hard could it be?"

CHAPTER THREE

A large wooden sign on the island divider greeted Harper as she drove into the small town. "Welcome to Kitezh, Illinois—The Center of the Universe!"

Literally every town Harper had ever visited had some version of this sign waiting to greet visitors. Epigraphs were plastered up in the hopes of showing that this time, this place would be different. They were utterly ridiculous. Everywhere was the same; it was the unchanging law of America.

Not to say that these places were bad by any means. They were often...nice. Charming. Picturesque. Just oh-so-goddamn *quaint*. Which was fine if that was your thing, but it definitely wasn't hers. She drove along flat highways, past identical fields, desperately missing the energy of Chicago. Kitezh was one of those places that used to be strictly rural before a college came in and injected just enough life to make it something resembling a tiny suburb, but spread out across twice the land.

All the driving she had to do had left poor Lilith with an empty tank, so she pulled into a rinky-dink gas station to refuel her car and her body.

She sat on Lilith's trunk, chewing through a cheap hot dog, bobbing her head along to the steady clunk-clunk-clunk rhythm of the gas pump. It was the only entertainment available, aside from watching the huge swaths of wheat across the highway dance and sway in the gentle breeze.

A chunky click told her the tank was full, so she swiftly finished her meager meal, chasing it with the last of her energy drink. Harper dismounted the trunk with an unnecessary flourish, returned the nozzle to its resting place, and closed up the gas cap.

"Okay, lunch break over. Let's do this, old girl." Harper climbed back behind the wheel and pulled away from the gas station to drive the last few miles to the college.

Malcom-Baptiste College had apparently been some kind of religious school when it first opened. A lot of these places were. They served as training grounds for missionaries or pastors or whatever. But there wasn't exactly money in that, and schools had to stay afloat somehow, so they opened up to more and more diverse students. Before long, they were doling out degrees in everything from political theory to music theory.

The place was small enough that she was able to drive down the main thoroughfare and back in just a few minutes. Despite the size, it took an obnoxiously long time to find a parking spot. Harper inevitably had to settle for a space near the edge of the campus. Still, it was hard to be too sore about that when she felt like she could get anywhere within fifteen minutes, even walking at a leisurely pace.

She retrieved her manila folder from the passenger seat, turning through the pages to refresh her understanding of the situation. Autumn Temple, junior theatre major and wannabe actress. She'd been employed part-time with the school's administrative office. There was a small picture attached to the first page. If Harper had to guess, it was probably a professional headshot, just judging by the quality of the image. Autumn's smile was easy and warm, and her emerald-green eyes glinted with mischief. Her blond hair perfectly framed her face— touched with expert makeup—in curls and waves.

Harper quickly moved on from studying her image. Putting a face to the name humanized the victim, which only served to make her mad. So long as the girl was just a file and a story, Harper could keep some distance and not think too hard about the life that had been cut short, so she kept reading through the file.

Autumn was found dead early that morning, at a local party spot in the woods north of the college. Cause of death was assumed to be a wild animal, but a friend of the guild with access to the coroner's report thought there was something suspicious about the dimensions of her wounds. There were no records of a party in the clearing. Perhaps the most important detail for a hunter, of course, was the harvest moon glowing in the sky that night.

Caution—and her mother—told Harper that she could only ever make assumptions at this point. But come on, it was so obviously a werewolf. The problem wasn't figuring out what had done this, it was stopping them in time. Otherwise, she was stuck walking around this place poking everyone with a silver needle until someone sizzled. Time was running out.

But at least she wasn't completely lost. She knew that the beast had preferred stalking grounds. The moon would still be full for another two nights. There was the momentary thought that perhaps her quarry had a companion that would lock them away in the steam tunnels so they didn't kill again. But in situations like these, her father's advice had always been to follow your leads and trust your instincts.

"Shit, when is sunset?" Harper checked the time on the faded dashboard clock. "Early fall...so, that's...four hours from now. Just gotta find a vantage point." She slipped her messenger bag around her torso before climbing out of Lilith to go investigate. Her focus narrowed until the people and buildings were all just shapes. A major issue quickly struck her.

Vantage points were, no pun intended, thin on the ground. With a huff, she went back into the car and whipped out the map of Malcolm-Baptiste. After studying it for a moment, she found the lot she was standing in, noting the red circle her father had made to indicate the wooded clearing up north where the girl had been found. "Come on. Give me something." Her finger traced in a slow spiral out from the mark. The next closest spot was the campus football field, which wasn't ideal. How was she supposed to do her thing when everything was so goddamn flat?

"Whatever. I'll figure it out on the fly like I always do."

Even if the campus was small, she didn't want to make a bunch of trips back and forth, so she decided to load up everything that she would need. Fishing around in the trunk, she retrieved her trusty hand crossbow and a fistful of silver-tipped bolts. She silently gave thanks to the guild artisan who had designed this particular weapon as she folded it up and shoved it into her bag. The last thing she needed was to look like a crazy person toting a weapon around a school full of worried students. She also stashed a few granola bars and a bottle of water before securing the bag and slamming the trunk closed.

While crossing campus, Harper continued to look around for other places where she could get even the smallest amount of height. She passed a two-story building with a large wooden sign planted into the lawn labeling it "Randolph Dormitory." The height had potential, but she noted it as a last resort. There was a heavy electronic lock on the door, and she was willing to bet roof access was even more tightly controlled. She had the same concerns about the Wesley Science Building and the MacKenzie Gymnasium. As she drew closer to the football field, Harper was growing nervous that she might not be able to find an ideal location.

But then she saw it, rising up from the far end of the field. Sure, if you were looking at it objectively, it was just a rickety tower. It stood roughly fifty feet high on four thick legs with plenty of crisscrossing braces. The stairs spiraled up at regular ninety-degree turns, terminating at a small booth. It was nothing impressive, but in that moment, it might as well have been the most wondrous thing Harper had ever seen. "Oh, thank you, sweet baby Jesus."

As she approached the base, a few minor issues presented themselves. First, there was the chain-link fence that kept students from entering the tower. Second, given that it was the tallest thing around, her ascent was bound to be noticed by anyone giving the tower even a momentary glance. She wasn't looking to deal with campus security or, God forbid, the authorities.

"Ugh, I guess we're doing this." Harper reached into her bag and hunted around, careful to avoid stabbing herself on a crossbow bolt. Finally, her hand emerged unscathed holding a black felt-tip marker.

With practiced strokes, she drew a tight circle on the inside of her left wrist just below her Silversmith crest tattoo—a sword plunged vertically into an anvil. Within the circle, she added a series of intricate geometric patterns. Harper forced her hand to remain steady. Each line had to be perfect or she would end up with a shattered radius. She closed up the last line and completed the glyph, then looked around cautiously to be sure there was no one around.

Harper hadn't inherited her mother's gift for traditional magic, so she had to rely on other methods for calling up sorceries. Glyphs were a fairly common way, though they were also dangerous, and not just because of the aforementioned bone-shattering. Mages could draw power from the latent mana present in the air and ground, then weave it into fantastical spells. But activating a glyph could only be done by pulling from your own life energy. A single spell like this was fairly trivial as long as you weren't doing anything stressful. But it would drain you over time.

Sure, you were *technically* doing magic. It didn't make you a *mage*. Glyph manipulation was basically seen as the more socially acceptable version of blood magic—sacrificing a part of yourself instead of "working in harmony with the universe" or whatever. It was hardly what you could call a foolproof method, but she'd found that temporary spellcasting had gotten her out of more than a few scrapes. So she was fine with a little social stigma.

Harper flexed her arm a few times, then focused on the glyph. It was hard to give an exact breakdown of how this process worked. It felt a bit like plucking a piece of your own spirit and funneling it along the lines of the glyph, as if she had irrigated a portion of her body. Slowly, her entire form became encased with a warping of light and space that made her effectively invisible to all but the most careful scrutiny.

"Upsy-daisy," she said to no one in particular, realizing too late that talking to herself was counterproductive to a stealth operation. With as little scrambling as she could manage, Harper hauled herself up over the fencing, grateful that it was topped with a sturdy horizontal pipe and not bare chain-link—never mind straight-up barbed wire.

She started her way up the stairs, leaving the fence to rattle behind her for a few seconds. Halfway up the tower, she paused to look around just to ensure that no one had seen or heard anything. But the few students she could see in the distance were all busy chatting or hoofing it to their next destination. She released a small sigh of relief and finished her ascent. Taking that many stairs should have been easy, but keeping her cloak activated at the same time left her winded. Harper paused at the top to lean against the railing and catch her breath.

Turning behind her, she looked over the door for the small booth. In a fit of optimism, she tried the handle, but it refused to turn. "Oh, for fuck's—" Dropping down to one knee, she once again dipped into her treasured bag. With a bit more careful rooting, she was able to retrieve her small set of lock picks.

Closing one eye, she looked into the keyhole and grinned. "Have they changed this door since the fifties? A baby could do this." Harper pulled up a pair of tools and set to work disengaging the lock. The pins set with such ease that she was almost disappointed. In a few more seconds, she had rotated the lock and popped the door open. She scrambled inside, shut the door again, and finally stopped pumping energy into the glyph. "Hoo, okay. Let's just…take a second…"

Harper allowed herself a small break to get some water and demolish one of her granola bars. By the time she'd recovered, her phone told her that roughly an hour had passed since she'd parked. With some dismay, Harper realized what this meant.

It was time to wait and watch.

As the daylight faded, activity around the college faded with it. From her hidden perch, Harper was able to watch as students slowly filtered out of the assorted academic buildings and made their way back to their dorms, apartments, fraternities, and sororities. It was quiet, and based on her minuscule knowledge of college life, that was probably not the norm. She had to assume there was some kind of curfew in effect.

With sunset getting progressively closer, she doubled her efforts to study every visible inch of the campus. As good as this spot was, it didn't give her a perfect view of everything. That made her nervous. No matter how hard she tried to convince herself she was doing her best to follow the most logical leads, she couldn't shake those negative thoughts.

The moon is technically out. The wolf could already be out there wreaking havoc. I'm probably missing it while sitting up here like a fucking idiot.

Oh, what, you have a better idea? I'm all ears, genius. Come on.

Okay, fine, maybe this is the best we're going to get. Which is just going to make it that much more embarrassing when I screw it all up. Someone else is going to die and I'm going to lose my status with the guild. Jesus, and I was so cocky earlier. It's so easy to hunt a werewolf, I said. I can do it in no time.

Amateur hour, Harper, that's what this is. I can't believe you wanted something "juicier." You don't deserve juicy. You have to earn juicy. If you can't do this, what makes you think you can handle something more difficult?

All right already, stop laying into me. Us. Whatever.

You needed a wake-up call, dumbass. For example, you're currently missing something super obvious.

Oh, am I? Care to enlighten me? Us?

The girl. She's right there. Look at her, sneaking around. She's trying to be stealthy while walking through a football field. Like we wouldn't see her.

Harper finally cut off her internal dialogue and actually processed what she was seeing. Sure enough, out to the west, a lone figure was making its way across the open field toward the tree line of the woods. That would have been suspicious enough on its own. What really drew Harper's attention was the girl's destination. She didn't follow the well-trod path that led straight toward the clearing to the north. Instead, she looked to be heading for a random spot almost a quarter mile south of it.

Do it. Go after her. Even if she's not the werewolf, that's suspicious as hell. She's getting away, go!

Scrambling, Harper gathered up her things and shoved them back into her bag. As she flew through the door, she diverted some energy back into her glyph and felt the blanket of energy wrap around her once again. She descended multiple stairs at a time, knowing that if she stopped to think too hard about it she would inevitably take a nasty fall. As she hit the final landing before the ground, she opted to completely bypass the fence below. She lighted onto the railing and then hurled herself out, leaping over the fence entirely. As her feet connected with the soft grass, she tucked in on herself and went into a roll. When instincts took over, she didn't feel like nearly such a fuck-up.

As smoothly as she was able, she came up out of the roll and into a jog to chase after her target.

This burst of activity turned out to be somewhat unnecessary. While the girl ahead of her was certainly trying to move as inconspicuously as possible, her gait was fairly easy. Harper slowed her own pace once she had closed the gap between them to a comfortable fifty feet. From this distance, she was able to get a much better look at her.

The girl was most likely a student at the college, just judging by her age. She had dark skin and a halo of tight curls in a well-maintained Afro. Relatively short—not more than five foot two—and just a touch on the rounder side. She was dressed surprisingly nice for a potential monster who was going into the woods to find more murder. Like church-nice. The blouse-sweater-skirt combo was cute but not ostentatious. In her hand she carried a vintage leather suitcase that had clearly seen a lot of wear and tear in its life.

Harper's target crossed the tree line into the woods and continued for another hundred feet or so before coming to a sudden stop. Harper prayed she didn't make too much noise pulling up short as well.

She watched with growing fascination as the girl set the suitcase down onto the ground. She flipped the latches and pulled it open. It was only when she started pulling off her sweater that Harper understood what was happening.

She didn't undress in a hurry, nor did she do it sloppily. She performed each action almost like it was a holy ritual. She took the time to carefully fold her sweater before putting it away. Next went the sensible blouse, each button undone with great intentionality. The bra beneath was equally plain—flesh-toned and functional with zero frills. Then went the sneakers and socks. She undid the skirt—a length appropriate for a God-fearing woman. Which made sense, because Harper suddenly noticed a prominent golden cross hanging about the girl's neck. Was the good girl a secret murderer? That would hardly be a plot twist. But still, something was off here.

Harper's face felt hot, and she knew she should be looking away. Mythics were innocent until proven guilty, and right now she was treating this girl like she didn't have a right to privacy. But Harper couldn't shake the fear that she'd lose track of her if she looked away for more than a second, so she kept it as clinical as she possibly could. While the maybe-werewolf removed her hoop earrings and cross necklace and added them to the pile, Harper focused on studying her face. She took in the roundness of her face, the shape of her eyes, the fullness of her lips— Whoops, nope, that was no good. And as the bra and underwear were removed, she forced herself to only note the shape of her body and to look for any details that might stick out.

The only detail Harper could manage to focus on was "pretty." Which was very unhelpful.

"Ope!" the girl suddenly said through a light gasp, gritting her teeth. "There it is…"

Harper wondered what "it" was, until the girl stepped under a break in the branches overhead, bathed in soft moonlight.

Watching her strip had obviously been intimate. There was no way it couldn't have been. But that was nothing compared to the intimacy of what came next. Harper had seen a few werewolf transformations in her relatively short life. But not a single one had ever been like this.

With a chilling, inhuman growl, the girl dropped down onto her hands and knees. Bones still cracked and reshaped, forcing limbs into positions humans weren't meant to experience. The face still contorted, teeth still popped out and replaced themselves with sharper ones. Fur still sprouted from the skin like watching grass grow in high speed. But there were no cries of pain beyond the initial growl, no howls of agony, no fear, no cursing. One minute, she was one thing, and the next, she was another. She subjected herself to the process the way other people went to the dentist.

It was incredible. And, it was terrifying.

In the span of maybe sixty seconds, she had become an enormous wolf. Her dense black fur had the slightest curl to it. Her ears stood at attention, nose occasionally twitching, reminding Harper that she needed to take way more care from here on out. From snout to tail, she must have been nearly seven feet long. The top of her head could likely stand level with Harper's chest. Technically, that was small for a werewolf, but Harper's dumb ape brain didn't know that.

At some point during this entire process, Harper's hands had unconsciously reached into her messenger bag and retrieved the crossbow, unfolding it silently. She carefully placed a bolt into its designated place. This was the moment, of course. Harper had found the werewolf, and now it was time to bring her to justice. All she had to do was just pull the trigger. Release the silver-tipped bolt. Kill the girl. Very simple.

But something was still eating at her, not least of all the idea of killing a girl just for being a werewolf. That was the attitude of a hunter from a prior age. The implications there were far too disgusting to live with.

So Harper kept right on waiting.

Something caught the wolf's attention, and she started to wander away. She didn't seem to be hunting, exactly, though she was searching quite intently. Sniffing again and again, she was soon following after some errant scent.

Once there was a comfortable distance between herself and the wolf, Harper scrambled her way upward into the trees above. Up here, she felt more comfortable letting her spell drop again. She took in a long, slow breath, then released it nice and easy. It was time for some acrobatics.

While the werewolf made her rounds below, Harper followed from her place above, moving from sturdy branch to sturdy branch. It required an extra second of concentration to find her next perch, but it was far safer than the energy she would have to expend to keep her weave of invisibility active—especially since she had no idea how long this might take.

However, that percentage of concentration spent branch-hopping took away from dog-watching. Harper was a few seconds behind when she realized that she'd followed the werewolf to the party clearing. There were no more trees ahead to leap to, and all the momentum she'd built up now had to be stopped short. Her hands scrabbled at her current limb, breaking a few pieces of bark off in the process, causing them to fall down to the ground.

Harper bit down hard on her lower lip, holding her breath. *Fuck.*

As the bark hit the dirt of the clearing, the wolf paused midstride and began glancing around. Once again, her ears and nose began twitching attentively.

Oh fuck oh fuck oh fuck.

Just like that, she buried her nose down into the dirt and began sniffing around on some unseen hunt. The tree bark had been a momentary distraction only, and now she was back on the trail.

Harper's teeth released their hold on her lip and she allowed herself to breathe again.

That was too close. Take it easy. She's not going anywhere in a hurry yet.

Speaking of, what are we doing here? Back to the scene of the crime?

She wasn't comfortable taking her eyes off her target for too long, but Harper did at least take a brief glance at the surroundings, just to see what all the fuss was about.

There was a plot of scorched earth where bonfires were lit in the center, and various rotted stumps and logs they used for seating. Leave it to college idiots to actively ignore any semblance of safety. The place was a million tiny accidents waiting to happen, and yet somehow it was a supernatural force that actually brought the authorities in to clear it out. Off to one side was a patch of dirt that was far darker than the earth around it. She could still see a few strips of warning tape littered around it. That was where it had happened, then. For a split second, Harper thought she had some important revelation about the nature of the crime scene. But it was quickly silenced as the werewolf trailed back into her line of sight, approaching the bloody ground.

One of her massive paws began to lightly dig at the dirt. She certainly didn't seem proud of her accomplishments. In fact, the longer this went on and the more she sniffed at the ground, the more it turned into soft whining. Sure, it could be guilt, but... Hell, it could be hunger. The smell of blood without meat.

Harper was becoming concerned, because she knew less and less with each passing moment.

This sad whining and pawing continued. It turned downright pathetic as the werewolf crouched down onto her belly, pressing her whole body down low, ears drooping. Her noises finally died out, like she was resigning herself to keeping some kind of silent vigil.

This memorial—or whatever it was—lasted several agonizing minutes.

Reaching some sort of conclusion, the wolf stood with one last whimper. Her movements were much slower now, aimless. This made it far easier to trail after her, which Harper was grateful for. Her movements were surprisingly quiet for a beast so big, and it forced Harper to keep a consistent visual at all times, or she was in danger of losing track of her quarry.

Up ahead, Harper spotted a small break in the trees where a family of deer were resting together. The wolf was heading straight for them. She swallowed the lump forming in her throat. Something truly gnarly was about to happen here, and she wasn't sure if she had the stomach to watch it. But…she had to, right? That was the job. So Harper leapt for the next branch and settled herself onto it, waiting for the carnage to unfold. The poor bastards didn't stand a chance.

She could not have predicted what came next.

More like a puppy than a massive hound, the wolf trotted right up to them, announcing her arrival with a gentle yip. Not only did the other animals not freak out, they seemed downright delighted to have her. She drew closer and nuzzled each of them in turn, even the little baby doe. Once the greetings were finished, she made a series of circles before flopping down onto the grass in a partial arc around the family. Her posture was almost possessive, or at the very least defensive.

What in the ever-loving shit is going on? I expected a nature documentary, not a children's cartoon!

No, think this through, idiot. Maybe they're a local family of odothropes that she knows. Hell, it actually might be a rakshasa! Don't they shapeshift sometimes?

But the eyes…Not a hint of sapience there. Pretty sure these are just some regular-ass white-tailed deer. Which means…what exactly? They run away at the first sight of anything even vaguely dangerous. But this hulking wolf doesn't bother them one bit. Do they know her? Or can they just sense that she's safe?

I don't have nearly enough information here. Guess it's time to get comfy.

Yay.

With this entire night officially making no sense whatsoever, Harper settled down as well. She braced her back against the tree trunk and placed her bag in her lap, having long since stowed her crossbow again.

As adorable as the scene below was, it swiftly lost its novelty. But while the werewolf and deer were able to sleep to their hearts' content, Harper didn't have that luxury. She was forced to just sit and keep watch over them. All she wanted was to climb down and go find a crappy motel and catch some sleep. But she didn't want to wake up in the morning and find out there was another attack while she'd let her guard down.

So she sat on an uncomfortable tree branch and watched a big dog snooze with some forest critters. Cute, sure, but terribly dull. Every time she felt herself slipping, she would bite down hard on her tongue or cheek, or dig her nails into her side.

To help ease the boredom, Harper followed up on her earlier promise to Nat. She fished out her phone and dutifully set it to full silent mode, then opened her texts.

> *guess whos spending her night*
> *in a goddamn tree.*

lol seriously?

> *good news is im not dying to a*
> *werewolf*
> *shes a big puppy*

that sucks. what now?

> *an excellent question. no idea.*

wow, baddies beware.
harper zeale is on the case.

> *thanks jackass*
> *appreciate the vote of confidence.*

All she got in response to that was a winky face. Harper huffed. At least she was back to doing snarky banter with her friend. That had to count for something.

A few minutes later, her phone lit up with another message. She looked down at the screen and smirked.

um.
but in all seriousness,
thanks for checking in.

good to know youre not dead
ill let you know if anything
interesting happens.
which seems doubtful.

lol

That brief conversation didn't kill nearly as much time as she'd hoped. Harper was forced to resume injuring herself in the name of consciousness.

Harper's tongue was numb, her cheek was chewed up, and she'd drawn a bit of blood from her hip by the time the sky started to change colors. Sweet relief wasn't too far away. She just needed to make sure the girl was a girl again and then she'd officially done her due diligence. Which meant she could get some food and maybe some rest with minimal guilt. Not *zero* guilt, mind, but minimal was good enough after a failed night like this.

A slight rustling from below pulled her attention back to the werewolf. As quietly as she could, she rose up from where she'd been sleeping with her woodland friends and padded away.

Harper pushed herself up, intending to get into a crouching position to once again make her way across a few more tree branches. There was a sudden pop from her right knee paired with painful muscle tightness. Harper tried desperately to right herself, course-correct, put the weight on the other leg instead, balance herself with her hands. Something. Anything. But the damage was done. She was working with no sleep, off-balance, atop a branch a good ten feet in the air.

The world tilted, and she was powerless to stop it. The ground rose to meet her. For whatever reason, her first instinct was not self-preservation. All she could think about was all the precious items she had in her bag. She wrapped herself around it and rotated, hitting the ground hip first. Her world exploded in pain, and Harper wrenched her eyes shut for a moment to block out the stars bursting in her vision. "Augh! Son of a—"

Harper was cut off by a low growl that was way too loud for comfort. She pushed open her eyelids and found herself face-to-face with the werewolf. "—bitch."

CHAPTER FOUR

Farewell, cruel world. Let my headstone say, "Here lies Harper Zeale. Daughter. Hunter. Idiot."

Instinct kicked in, or at the very least it tried to. Harper sat partway up and reached for the knife at her hip. But the moment she attempted to twist her body to do so, a new wave of pain shot through her and she lost all interest in drawing her blade. It wasn't worth it. She'd be dead soon anyway.

The wolf pushed in, its growl either getting louder or simply *sounding* louder with how close it was.

No, not it. She. This was still that girl. No matter how terrifying she might be, Harper couldn't let herself forget. Even as she was getting eaten alive, she wouldn't go down thinking of this mythic as anything less than a sapient being worthy of respect.

The werewolf huffed, and her breath was visible in the cool autumn morning light.

Morning light! Harper only needed to stay alive a little longer and the werewolf would transform back. Even if she still tried to attack in her human form, Harper could deal with that.

Slowly, she raised up her hands in a defensive position. This time she fought through the pain in her side and shuffled back a few inches. "O-Okay, ow, obviously this is bad. I realize that. But there's no need to kill me. We can play this nice and easy, y'know?"

She got another huff in return. It was probably just projection, but she could have sworn this one was more dismissive than the last. But the wolf wasn't moving any closer, at least. She growled, low and guttural. "Hrng…Woh…Won't kill…" Her entire form trembled and she sank down onto her belly.

The process from the night before slowly started back up in reverse. All of the fur shed from her skin, drifting to the forest floor below. Harper was closer now than she had been for the first round, and the sound of bones cracking and snapping was almost deafening from this distance. Her arms and legs warped back into their human dimensions, torso collapsing, face reshaping as fangs popped out and dropped on top of the tufts of fur.

And just like that, the werewolf was a young college student again. She sat up with a protective arm around her chest, flushed and glaring at Harper. "Did you want to get one last ogle in? Or am I allowed to go get changed now?"

Harper winced as she lowered herself back down to the grass and dirt below, letting her eyes drift shut. "I'm not some perverted old man over here. Jesus…" A moment after she took the Lord's name in vain, she remembered seeing that cross necklace and winced at her lack of consideration. "Shit, sorry. Don't mind me, I'm just gonna catch my breath." Her forehead slumped down to connect with the ground. There were painkillers back in her car. If she could make it out there, everything would be okay. She could recover from this. Well, physically anyway. Her pride was another matter.

After a few minutes of lying in a heap, she was already feeling a little less terrible. The sound of approaching footsteps drew her attention back to the world around her. Harper lifted her head and saw the girl, now fully dressed, bending down and offering her a hand.

Harper hesitated for only a moment before she took it and was helped to her feet with surprising ease for someone so much shorter than her. A smaller, more subdued flash of pain burst along her right side and she grunted weakly. No broken bones, but she was bound to have some ugly bruising along her ribs and hip. Her eyes were having some serious trouble focusing. The blurry figure of the girl started talking to her again. "All right, here's the deal, hunter. I'm starving, and I'd say you owe me breakfast for tailing me all night. There's a diner in town where you can make it up to me."

Harper blinked a few times. Once her vision cleared a bit, she took a better look at the girl's face. Her assessment of "pretty" from the night before was quickly being updated to "freaking gorgeous." It was the eyes that really did it—umber with flecks of copper, wide and curious, and wholly unafraid. There was also none of the anger she expected to see, just an amused, almost puckish smile. She didn't know how to process that. "Mm. Harper."

Silently, the girl looked Harper over, practically scrutinized her with those dazzling eyes. It felt like she was able to completely pick Harper apart, easily drawing out all of her intentions—and insecurities. But finally, she concluded her appraisal with a nod, as though some bare minimum of acceptability had been met, and her lips spread into a warmer smile. The look was genuine and kind, and Harper was starting to understand how this girl could become friends with a family of woodland critters. She radiated an aura that was hard to classify, but it was welcoming, enchanting even, and it had one hell of a strong draw. "Esther."

A name. That was a good start. "Okay, then. Esther. You trust me enough to let me give you a ride, Esther? Or will I be forced to limp all the way there?"

"It'd be kind of stupid of you to go to all this effort only to kidnap me instead."

"First thing you should know about me—I'm pretty stupid."

That got a surprisingly bright laugh from Esther. It had a delightful tone to it. She didn't bother making it girlish or pretty. It was real and honest and it came from her belly. "I bet that's only kind of true."

"Guess you'll just have to find out." *Hey. No flirting while on the hunt. Bad. That's what got you in trouble last time. Stop it. We literally just decided yesterday that we're not doing this anymore, and you're already backsliding. Get it together.*

But she'd already said it, and it couldn't be taken back now. So, as they left the woods together—Esther walking with suitcase in hand, Harper limping—she took a brief glance over to see just how pissed Esther was.

Either her flirtation had actually landed, or her temporary companion didn't seem to care. She just smiled sweetly. "Guess I will."

Their conversation trailed off after that. The sun was barely peeking over the eastern horizon. Even if anyone was awake, they weren't outside. Everything was still and quiet as they made their way across the open field and between two academic buildings toward the parking lot. Harper noted Esther's accommodating pace, keeping her steps slow enough that she didn't end up ahead or behind.

Her keys were already out by the time they reached the car. She was desperately in need of relief and didn't have the energy to pretend otherwise. With a simple motion the trunk was unlocked and popped open, and she carefully set her messenger bag inside.

Harper fished around in her duffel for a few moments, eventually met with the delicious sound of a plastic gallon bag filled with various rattling pill bottles. She bypassed all the transparent orange containers and grabbed up the generic brand, extra-strength ibuprofen. She knew it was just psychosomatic, but just plopping the pill on her tongue and chasing it with some water already made her feel better.

While she busied herself with that, Esther was looking Lilith over, humming nervously. "Are you sure we're going to survive the trip in this thing?"

The learning curve here was steep. Her initial impression of Esther hadn't prepared her for someone with this assertive, biting sense of humor. She was already off her game, and this was only pushing her farther out of balance. And the last time she'd lost her balance, she busted her hip. "Be nice. Lilith has made it this long. I think she can handle it."

Esther smiled and reached out, giving the Chevy a gentle pat on the roof. "Sorry, sweetie. Didn't mean it. Just a bit of teasing. I believe in you."

Harper couldn't tell if that was sincere or if Esther was just humoring her. She decided to just assume it was both. She gestured to the suitcase in Esther's hand, then to the open trunk. "You can toss that back here, if you want."

There was a moment of hesitation, but Esther eventually took her up on the offer and carefully placed the weathered antique inside next to the massive duffel bag.

Harper shut the trunk and moved around to the driver side, climbing in behind the wheel. Esther joined in the passenger seat, and they headed off into town.

Diners were liminal spaces. One was very much like the other.

There was a theory that Harper had been cooking up for some time. If someone wished to move from one point in the country to another quickly, they did not need to use some kind of high-speed rail, nor break any land-speed records in their car. All they had to do was enter the bathroom of a hole-in-the-wall diner, and with enough faith or dumb luck, they would emerge from the bathroom of a totally different diner. Surely the fabric of reality was at its most malleable in places like this. Hell, maybe you could even crawl through the mirror into the world of Faerie, if the audience clapped along.

Did Faerie have diners? The Fair Folk needed to eat too, after all. Maybe some cozy little place that served dream pies and joy omelets and home fries—the regular kind, for variety's sake.

Wait, why are they called "Fae" or the "Fair Folk" and not the "Faer Folk"? Why is it "fairy" and not "faery"?

Who is making all these decisions?

Oh, right, humans. No wonder it's so inconsistent.

These were the things she usually contemplated on her own. She was not used to being with unfamiliar company, and it left her feeling awkward. Because if she didn't contemplate the magical nature of mundane places, other thoughts would inevitably start to break through.

I saw her naked.

I saw her transform.

She's like some kind of fairytale princess.

She's freaking gorgeous.

Anyone who wears a cross like that of their own volition is never going to be interested in someone like you, idiot.

My instincts are screaming at me that she's not the killer, so what the hell are we doing here when we should be out there continuing the hunt?

Well, the answer to that is obvious. A pretty girl asked you to breakfast. Maybe you could lie and tell yourself it's because she might have some clues or whatever. But the truth is so much more obvious.

Harper, you predictable bitch.

"So…" she started uselessly, with absolutely no clue what she was going to say next. She was saved from having to continue that thought by their waitress.

A woman in a slightly wrinkled dress and apron came sauntering over, managing to glow despite the hour of the morning or the bags under her eyes. Seeing the other girl sitting there, she actually started to beam a little bit brighter. "Esther! Delightful as always to see you, hon. Not often you come round with a guest. Full Moon Special?" She added a small wink to her question, and it made Harper wonder if perhaps this humble waitress was in on the joke. People in the service industry could be so observant, and no one ever realized how much they saw and heard.

"You know me well, Carol. Please and thank you!"

The spotlight of attention swung Harper's way next, and Carol looked at her expectantly. "And you, darlin'?"

"Uh…" She realized too late that she'd spent so long stuck in her own head she hadn't even looked at the stupid menu. She scanned it quickly and latched on to whatever popped out at her first. "Strongest coffee you've got. And this egg and sausage hash. Er, please and thank you." Esther and Carol both gave an approving nod as she tacked on the bit of politeness.

"Back in a flash, ladies!"

"So," Harper started again. "You didn't have anything to do with Autumn Temple's death then?" At this point, there was no reason to try and dance around things.

Esther's smile turned small and sad. "Disappointed? Trust me, I almost wish I could say that it *was* my fault. You could have this whole thing wrapped up neat and tidy and be on your way." She tilted her head curiously and gave Harper a steady look. "How did you hear about this anyway? Did someone flash the hunter signal up in the sky?" Esther chuckled softly at her joke, and it was just infectious enough that Harper cracked a smile herself.

"Nah, we have people that keep an eye out for suspicious deaths. If something pings their radar, they pass it along to one of us."

"Oh? Who is 'we'?"

The Silversmith ID was fresh enough that Harper still felt that itch to show it to people when she had the excuse. She retrieved it from her wallet and passed it off to Esther. "I'm part of a guild network. Makes it a little easier to do the job when you're not alone."

Esther gave it a look, and for a moment her brow furrowed. "Silversmiths," she mumbled.

Oh God, why had Harper not thought ahead for even two seconds? What was a werewolf going to think about her proudly proclaiming herself a *Silversmith*. They might as well have gone around still calling themselves "We Kill You, Inc." Harper decided she would add that to her mental list of hunter traditions that needed to be phased out.

Her distress was quickly supplanted by an obnoxious grin. "Harper *Zeale*? What are you, a detective in a pulp magazine?"

Uselessly flustered, Harper snatched her ID back and returned it to its proper place. "Shut up, it's cool."

"I didn't say it wasn't."

"Look, as long as you've got me trapped here paying for whatever a Full Moon Special is, can I at least ask you a couple questions?"

"Only if you put on a fedora and a trench coat, and jot down what I say in a little three-by-five notebook, gumshoe."

Harper groaned, and she could practically feel Esther drinking in her misery from all this needling. "Just—Listen, is there anyone else around here like you? Other werewolves?"

The girl's eyes flicked away suddenly. "No other werewolves." The phrasing was very particular and very suspicious. Frustratingly so. Perhaps in an attempt to deflect from that suspicious phrasing, she fired off another question of her own. "You didn't shoot me, but I'm sure you had plenty of clean shots. And I could smell the silver on you. Why didn't you?"

"Didn't seem right. You weren't doing anything wrong. You transformed, you went for a walk, you cuddled with some woodland critters. I've seen what a dangerous mythic looks like, and you didn't fit the bill. I needed more information." She played the evening back in her head, recalling Esther's incredible, seamless transformation and perfect behavior. "How'd you control yourself like that, anyway? I've only heard of a few werewolves who are that skilled, and you were like an old pro."

"It's a family curse. Like, an actual literal curse by a witch. Our ancestor was a witch-hunter reverend in New England. As it turned out, he'd managed to find one of the real ones, and she was none too happy about being burned at the stake when she'd done nothing wrong. Hexed his entire line to suffer at the hands of their 'true, bestial nature' or whatever."

A little light went off in Harper's mind. Despite the naming conventions, hunters and witch-hunters were not inherently the same. The Silversmiths weren't associated with any particular faith or belief system. They worked alongside priests, rabbis, and imams when the necessity arose. But witch-hunters were quite explicitly Christian, fueled by irrational fears and religious fanaticism. More often than not, they were simply vehicles to punish outsiders and deviants. The fact that they'd manage to kill an actual witch was kind of impressive, considering how otherwise inept they were.

The two were interrupted momentarily by Carol returning with their food in what must have been a world-record turnaround time. As it turned out, the "Full Moon Special" consisted of enough steak and eggs for an entire family, and a full jug of ice water. The second the plate touched the table, Esther was digging in without any shame. Since she didn't seem to be in any hurry to bolt for the door, Harper opted to put the interrogation on hold until they'd both gotten some food in their bellies.

There was something so reliable about diner food. You could never really say that it was high quality, or expertly made, or healthy. If you were being realistic, you couldn't even really call it "made with love." But it *was* made with good old-fashioned grease, and cheap as hell. It filled you up, and it tasted better than it had any right to.

Only when their paces relaxed a bit and Harper was on her third cup of coffee did Esther get back to it. "The Talbot clan doesn't really track with traditional magic, even now. So we've never actually gotten our condition properly healed. We just train from an early age to control it, usually getting a grip on things right around early adolescence." She paused to chow down on another hunk of steak, followed by a big glug of water.

Her family didn't like magic. Probably didn't like hunters either. They almost definitely would not be fans of a girl like Harper. Seemed safer to just nip this foolish idea in the bud now before her imagination ran away with ideas about romancing a werewolf, no matter how attractive or special she might be. No, her previous declaration had to stand, and those stupid romantic instincts needed to be shoved down deep.

"Well, if it's not you, then that means the trouble is still out there. Ugh, not even a werewolf, which means it could be damn near anything."

"Like I said, I *wish* it was me." Esther's face suddenly twisted up with a heavy pang of guilt. "Oh God…I must have been nearby when she was attacked. I could have done something."

Oof. Esther was going to end up with a bad case of survivor's guilt if someone didn't point out the obvious flaw in her logic. Harper shook her head and gave the girl an intense look. "Hey. Whoever or whatever did this was clearly not messing around. If you *had* been there, you might have gotten hurt, or worse. There could have been two corpses that night. Seriously, beating yourself up doesn't do any good."

She sighed and picked at the remains of her food for a moment. "Autumn was always so nice to me. Said it was cool I didn't judge her for who she was, and I felt the same way about her. Mutual respect." Her face fell. "She should be avenged, whatever that might look like. She deserves peace."

"Didn't judge her for what?"

Esther fidgeted with her hands for a few moments, looking away bashfully. "Er—Look, I know your whole deal is to dig into everything. But I'm not sure if it's my place to say. Just—" She stopped fiddling with her hands and instead began to idly toy with the cross around her neck. "Let's say people like me have historically been pretty cruel to people like her. And she appreciated that I wasn't, and never held my faith against me in return. Is that good enough?"

Harper added *that* to her mental list of good news. "Yeah, I got ya." Harper fished a wad of bills from her wallet and tossed them onto the table—more than enough to cover both of their meals along with a sizable tip. "C'mon, lemme give you a ride back to your fancy school so I can get back to work."

Esther got up and nodded with a somewhat dramatic sigh. "Yeah, you've got a job to do, I guess." The two of them exited the diner and made it about as far as Harper's beat-up car before Esther whirled around and looked at her with a disarming amount of intensity. "Listen, Autumn was a friend of mine. And if someone or something did this to her to make it *look* like a wolf did it, then maybe…maybe they were trying to frame me! There's no way I can just go about my life and pretend like nothing is going on. Let me help you."

Harper wanted to say yes to that. Even putting aside any stupid notions born from being teased by a pretty girl, it would be good to have backup. Esther was a student here, so she must know at least a handful of people. But getting a civilian involved—mythic or otherwise—was a bad move. You could ask them for information and small favors. But having this mostly normal girl tag along was an easy way to get her hurt.

"I really appreciate it, but no way. There's—" Harper stopped herself and lowered her voice as a guy in a trucker hat walked past them and into the diner. "There's still a killer on the loose."

"I can turn into a giant wolf," Esther said. It was a salient enough argument on its face, but Harper knew there was only one more full moon left, and then the excuse was moot.

Harper shook her head firmly. Denying Esther was harder than she was willing to admit, but it was for the best. "I can't. I'm sorry. This stuff can get...dark, and dangerous. And I'm not strong enough to keep myself and someone else alive while dealing with it." What she didn't say but almost did, was that she also wasn't strong enough to have that kind of shit on her conscience when things inevitably went bad.

Esther's face remained resolute, right up until that final sentence. And then she did the only thing that was worse than trying to force her way into this investigation. She looked at Harper with something like pity. "Harper—" She reached out, but her attempt at consolation was easily sidestepped. Her face fell and her hand dropped again. "Fine. Fine, I'll just go hide in my dorm until this is over, I guess."

"I know it feels kind of crappy, but that really is the best option. Let me at least give you a ride back," Harper said, making her own attempt at keeping the bridge from burning to a crisp.

She got a silent nod in return.

The drive to campus was an uncomfortable one. The two of them sat in silence the whole way. With each passing minute, Harper thought again about buckling. It would have been so easy.

I'm really sorry. I've been training for years to deal with mythics as a hunter, and I'm pretty good at that. I'm pretty bad at all the other stuff. The social stuff. The...people stuff. I have some issues I haven't fully worked through, and I would rather not add survivor's guilt to the list.

Y'know what? Fuck it. Come with me. There's absolutely no way it could possibly end in disaster. It'll be like a buddy-cop movie. Car chases and explosions and sexual tension. Four out of five stars.

Obviously, she didn't say any of that. She just brought her car to a stop down the main street of Malcolm-Baptiste and threw it into park.

Esther was the first one to speak. She cleared her throat softly. "You were right. It would be a terrible idea for me to tag along. I'd slow you down, or get hurt, or worse. I just thought... Well, it doesn't matter. Good luck, Harper. I really hope you find who did this. A lot of people loved Autumn." She placed her hand on the door handle, then paused. She was giving Harper one final chance to change her mind.

Wait! Yes, come with me. This isn't a buddy-cop movie. This is a coming-of-age romance set against a backdrop of supernatural intrigue. Sexual tension? No, emotional catharsis. We'll find the killer together and kiss while the guild cleans up in the background. Heartbroken hunter comes into her own and learns to love again. Five stars. Two thumbs up. What do you say?

The lump in her throat was massive, but somehow she managed to swallow it. "I can do this, Esther. Everything's going to be okay. So, thank you."

Esther smiled wearily and finally pulled the handle, releasing some of the built-up pressure inside the car. "I'll hold you to that." Harper yanked the latch beneath the wheel to pop the trunk, allowing Esther to grab her suitcase. Once she had it in hand, she stepped back onto the sidewalk and offered a final, half-hearted wave.

Harper put the car back into drive and pulled away, resisting the urge to stop and spew out one of the sappy monologues she'd been writing in her head. There was no time for sentimental notions about the power of friendship. She couldn't let a civilian get involved.

Only after she had driven past the sign for the college did Harper release a world-weary sigh. "I need a fucking shower."

Motels were a lot like diners. You could find them practically anywhere, and they all bled together over the years. She'd crashed in dozens of them with her parents while hunting. She knew even before she opened the door what she would find. Two beds, scratchy blankets, at least one busted light, a mini fridge that didn't work, and a shower that would just barely do the trick. That last one was the only thing she cared about right now. If she ever got the chance to actually sleep here, maybe she would find time to let the rest of it bother her.

This particular motel was still old enough that they used locks with traditional keys. She awkwardly shoved the key in and had to fight with it for a moment before she managed to actually get the door open. There was a kind of smug satisfaction in being so right about what she found inside. Once the door was shut and latched, she chucked her duffel and messenger bag onto the closest bed, then shrugged out of her leather jacket and stumbled toward the bathroom.

If she could just get in a shower, everything would be okay. It didn't matter if this place had freezing cold water and crappy toiletries. Hell, at that moment a cold shower probably would have been more effective. Harper decided she would play it by ear. She locked herself securely in the bathroom and let herself pretend for a while that the outside world didn't exist. There was no murdered girl, no vicious killer, no werewolf girl. Just Harper, and the dirty tiles, and the mass-produced tub, and the rusty showerhead. This was her entire world. She was queen of the bathroom.

Harper unbuttoned her flannel and tossed it to the floor, quickly followed by her tank top. Looking back into the mirror, she could see some telltale redness in the skin above her belt, but the rest was hidden beneath her clothing. Knowing the answer but needing to see it anyway, she climbed out of her jeans and took another look, sighing sadly. The center of the softball-sized spot on her hip was already starting to turn from red to blue. Before long it would be a beautiful rainbow of green and purple and yellow.

For a moment, she flashed back a few hours to when she had taken that tumble. Every time Harper thought she was getting good at her job, she had to do something to screw it all up. The mighty hunter couldn't even keep herself steady on a tree branch.

Oh no…

Far too late, she realized she'd been looking in the mirror a while now. She knew the kind of dysphoric depression that would follow if she kept that up. Harper turned her back on the giant mirror and swiftly discarded the last of her clothing, got the shower running, took a moment to marvel at how hot it was, and finally hopped in.

Washing the grime of the woods off herself was a decent start to not feeling like a total mess. It wasn't a solution, but it was a temporary boost. She practically shoved her face up near the showerhead, letting the hot spray of water give her a nice jolt. Spitting some of the water back out, she brushed her hair away from her face. She turned to grab up the crappy little bar of soap and the water struck her injured hip, causing Harper to briefly cry out and grimace. "Fuck! Fuck fuck fuckity fuck." Rather than pull away, she forced herself to let the onslaught continue. She needed to get used to the pain. She needed the reminder of her mistake. If a bruised hip was enough to shut her down, then she was never going to make it on her own.

As she submitted herself to a bit of self-flagellation and pretended it was for her own good, she found her thoughts turning to Esther once again, because of course they did. A girl like that deserved to go to school without living in fear of some murderous psychopath stalking her campus. Harper only had one choice—get her shit together, solve this problem, and let everyone carry on with their lives.

CHAPTER FIVE

Harper guided Lilith back into the campus parking lot, eventually finding a spot to leave her. She threw the gear shift into park and turned the key. And then she simply sat there for a moment, letting the silence wash over her.

Okay…The werewolf didn't do it. That's all right. It's fine. A girl was opened up, heart gone. What else can do that? No other werewolves, according to Esther. Could maybe be a shapeshifter that mimics a wild animal. There are mythics that eat hearts, but for whatever reason they usually prefer fetuses, not co-eds. Hmm, a witch could maybe use a heart for a nasty ritual. Oh God, did I screw myself over by wishing for a rakshasa?

There was one other thing she thought was worth trying, though it wasn't something she had a lot of faith in. But when options ran low, you had to examine every possible avenue. Harper grabbed the map from Autumn's file and got out of the car, moving around to the trunk. It took a bit of rooting around in her duffel, but she managed to find what she was looking for. After she closed the trunk, she laid out the small map printout on top of the lid, then dangled a short chain from her hand. The end was capped with a simple copper pendulum in the shape of an inverted teardrop. She waited for it to stop swaying before looking down at the map with a weary sigh. "Can't believe I'm doing this. All right, little guy. Nothing complicated. Filter out the…werewolf energies? Just help me find any other mythics around here. I'm desperate."

Her mother had taught her that she had to be patient with things like this. You had to concentrate and wait while the mysteries of the universe did their thing.

God, she was tired of waiting.

The pendulum continued to hang there, suspended by her hand above the middle of the map, not moving an inch. Of course it didn't. This was stupid.

A full minute passed, and she was seriously considering packing this in. Which was exactly when the pendant gave a little jump. Harper gasped, clamping her left hand around her right wrist to keep herself steady. "Wait! Do that again." It jumped once more after a few seconds, this time in a different direction, slightly more animated. There was one last jolt before it went straight back down below her hand. Harper deflated a bit, until she suddenly noticed that it wasn't actually still. The movements were almost imperceptible. It was as if there was a magnet just below the map forcing the pendant into its position. She moved the chain experimentally, but the pendulum remained locked in place above the dead center of the page.

Concentrating for a moment longer, Harper noticed the thing was almost vibrating. It wasn't locked between gravity and a magnet. It was the center point between multiple nodes, each one exerting equal force, until the pendulum could no longer choose a location and was left pinned between all of them.

"Great. It's broken. I can't even use the most basic magical item without ruining it. So much for that. Now we have to do this the old-fashioned way…"

With a bit of rearranging, the map and pendulum were back in their rightful places and she had her bag around her shoulder again—sans crossbow this time. Harper retrieved the next tool from within the duffel bag.

Obviously you couldn't just go around telling people that you were part of a secret society involved in a supernatural investigation. But you still needed to exert at least a little authority to get what you needed. Licensing for private investigators in the state of Illinois was hardly complicated, but applicants had to be twenty-one years of age. Iowa, however, was another matter. Their requirements were almost embarrassingly simple. By the time she was nineteen, Harper had cleared all the necessary hurdles and was authorized to act as a private investigator in the neighboring state. She may not have had any jurisdiction in Illinois, but the legal mechanics hardly mattered. All she really cared about was the authority a legitimate license offered her during the hunt.

Bless you Hawkeye State, she thought as she tucked the leather holder into her jacket pocket and turned to stalk the school grounds.

Now that Harper wasn't examining the campus through a filter looking for verticality, she was able to take in far more details. Unfortunately, she had no frame of reference for what a college was like. It was just a bunch of big buildings. Some of them were single story and wide, others were taller with a series of identical windows peppered with decorations. There was a central building labeled as the "student union." As she walked past, Harper heard the sound of an impressive bell ringing out across the campus, singular and long. One o'clock.

She could only waste so much time wandering aimlessly. The clock was ticking—literally, it would seem—and she needed to make some kind of progress. Harper slipped her hand into her jacket pocket and wrapped her fingers around the license inside. As if it were some kind of totem or talisman, she let herself draw some confidence out of it. Harper Zeale, Guild Hunter, was an awkward mess. But Harper Zeale, Private Investigator, knew how to talk to people and get what she needed.

Choosing a cluster of students at random, she walked up and briefly displayed her credentials. "Excuse me. Private eye. Rebecca Temple hired me to look into her daughter's disappearance. She thinks there's something the sheriff's department is missing, or maybe even lying about."

She watched quietly as the students looked at each other. Some unspoken *thing* passed between them. Eventually, a towering girl with platinum hair in a long, tight braid took over as spokeswoman. "Sorry, we don't really know anything. Autumn was cool. Literally nobody would wanna do…y'know…*that*."

Harper dug her hands casually into her jacket pockets again and looked them over. No pings on her bullshit detector. Granted, the damned thing could be a little faulty at times. But they were all looking various degrees of miserable. The only thing she could sense was a kind of social barricade. Harper was an interloper here, not a student. She wasn't getting the silent treatment, but this itty-bitty scrap looked to be the only thing they would let her have.

"Right, well, I'll be around. If you should happen to think of anything, let me know." Harper was starting to think she might need to invest in two sets of business cards.

The students nodded, a couple of them giving her polite waves as she stepped away in search of her next interview.

As it turned out, Harper's first attempt was pretty exemplary of what the next hour would look like.

"Private eye. Rebecca Temple hired me to look into her daughter's disappearance. She thinks there's something the sheriff's department is missing, or maybe even lying about."

"Whoa, damn. Yeah, fuck those pigs. But honestly, I got nothing."

"Private eye. Rebecca Temple hired me to look into her daughter's disappearance. She—"

"You're like a year older than me. What are you gonna do that they haven't already?"

"Private eye. Rebecca Temple hired me to look into her daughter's—"

"Sorry, I've got a—I have a thing. I need to go."

This was exhausting. The only achievement Harper had managed so far was making a name for herself as that weirdo who was going around questioning every person she ran into. Going on zero sleep, an aggravating pain in her side, and a mild case of hopelessness, she wandered toward the center of campus again. There was a large lawn set between the student union and one of the dormitories, with intersecting paved pathways that centered on a charming circular fountain. She allowed herself a quick break, popping a squat on a heavy stone bench.

Something was seriously wrong here. She got an honest vibe from everyone that she'd spoken to so far. Nobody was outright lying to her. They were just kids who were sad or angry about losing someone so popular. The issue was all that…other stuff. The look that passed between the first group she questioned. The way Esther had said "no other werewolves." And whatever the hell she'd done to break her useless pendulum. There was some big inside joke here, and Harper was still on the outside.

Her attention was diverted before she had a chance to put the pieces together. On the other side of the fountain and past the other benches, a pair of students sat in the shade of an oak tree. There was a taller one with wiry hair dyed a vibrant purple. She was in the process of bawling her eyes out.

The other was a tiny little thing with a fringe of brown hipster bangs and thick-rimmed glasses, holding her and offering some minor comfort—though it was obvious she'd been crying pretty hard herself.

Harper couldn't make out the full conversation over the noise from the fountain, but she caught a snippet that lit up the inquisitive center of her brain.

"I know, it's awful, it's just…awful!"

"She was such an angel, and now she's gone."

"Yeah, she was perfect."

"If I ever find who did it, I'm going to tear them apart."

That didn't sound like the idle chatter of two girls who merely knew Autumn. Those two cared about her. A lot. Everyone else had been merely bummed or upset. But they were in mourning, the way Esther had been. They were sad and angry and—

They're vulnerable. They might talk to you.

Holy shit, are you kidding me? That's easily the worst thing I've thought in a while.

I'm right, though.

That's not the point! Yes, we're still going to talk to them. Because they seem to have a connection to her. Because they're likely to want closure. Because that's the job. But we're not going to be an asshole about it. No pushing. Give them space. Seriously, what is wrong with you?

She let her internal dialogue continue as she got up from her seat and made her way over to where the girls were sitting. Harper cleared her throat softly. "Excuse me."

Dye-Job just gave her a steady glare through running makeup and pathetic sniffles, terrifying despite her sadness.

Tiny was a bit more gentle but still clearly closed off. "Can we help you?"

"Actually, I think you can. I'm investigating the death of Autumn Temple."

Dye-Job finally spoke, voice dripping with bitterness. "You're definitely not a fucking pig."

Harper flashed her license once again, the motion feeling as natural as breathing. "Private eye. Rebecca Temple hired me. She thinks there's something the sheriff's department is missing, or maybe even lying about."

"Bullshit she did." Tiny wasn't able to hold the other girl back, and Dye-Job was instantly up on her feet, eyes full of fury. "If Rebecca hired a dick to look into this, she'd have told her daughter's *girlfriends* about it. And she damn sure wouldn't have brought in a normie to do the job. So, you wanna try that again, Red? Or maybe I should just go ahead and paint the quad with your fucking blood, because I am not in the mood for whatever the hell this is."

It was stupid of Harper to not prepare for that anger to be turned back onto her for intruding on this moment with questions. Though a part of her was also distracted by that word, *normie*. "Okay, listen—"

"Izzy!" A familiar figure had suddenly placed herself in the middle of their argument. "Hang on!"

"Esther?" Harper and Dye-Job both said at the same time. They continued, almost comically, in unison, "Wait, you know her?"

She looked back and forth between them, holding out her hands as if she were trying to calm down a pair of wild animals about to tear each other apart. "It's a long story," she finally offered placatingly to Dye-Job, "but I can vouch for her." She then turned to Harper, her expression too complicated to properly parse. "Izzy and Zooey are friends of mine. So can we please take a breath and calm down, here? Please?"

Izzy seemed like a girl who only felt things strongly. And yet the moment Esther said "please," she was instantly back down on the grass. "Fine. Whatever. If this story is so long, then you'd better start telling it now." She nestled herself against a tree, desperately reaching for her girlfriend's hand. Zooey held it without missing a beat.

Esther sighed with visible relief on her face and lowered herself to the grass.

This seemed like yet another insular thing, so Harper turned to leave. She was definitely not welcome here. But she felt a hand clasp her wrist, stopping her from running away. She looked back and saw Esther holding her in place, shaking her head firmly. "You're not going anywhere. Sit."

Flushing, Harper dropped to sit cross-legged on the grass and looked around bashfully.

With tensions eased, Esther cleared her throat before glancing back toward Izzy and Zooey. "Okay, just—Promise you won't freak out."

They did, in fact, freak out.

Tiny/Zooey was fretting and fussing away over Esther's brush with danger. "Are you kidding me? I can't believe you let her see you transform. God, she could have shot you. And then you go and have breakfast together? What were you thinking?" It wasn't like Harper could blame her. Last night, she very much did have a crossbow trained on the girl in question. If she were a different sort of hunter, there could have easily been another death on campus to deal with.

Esther just waved her away, huffing softly with just a hint of a low growl. "The nose knows, okay? It's not something I can explain. A million little details, all filtered through my brain at lightning speed. She didn't…smell bad."

"I will literally never understand what you mean when you say shit like that," muttered Dye-Job/Izzy.

"I'm not asking you to understand it, I'm asking you to trust me."

This little argument was going nowhere fast, so Harper cut in. "So, wait, you all know about Esther being a—well, y'know. How'd that happen?"

All three of them shared a look that was incredibly significant. That outsider feeling was rearing its ugly head again. This silent argument continued for several seconds. Esther raised her eyebrows and cleared her throat, Zooey responded with a kind of low uncertain noise, Izzy just scowled and shook her head. Finally, Esther threw up her hands in the classic "we're talking in circles" frustration.

Izzy grumbled. "All right, fine, tell her. But if shit goes sideways, it officially becomes your fault, Talbot."

Harper was getting a bit annoyed with everyone talking around her and about her, instead of actually including her in any of this. "Look, whatever it is, I've seen crazier, I promise you. Werewolves are tame in my line of work. And I've already proved I'm trustworthy—or at least not trigger-happy."

With a shaking sigh, Esther gestured grandly to the school around them. "Nothing about Malcolm-Baptiste is normal. Most of the student body and faculty are mythics, and the few humans that go here have their own quirks."

"Holy shit." That was a lot to process, which would have taken up precious time and energy. So, she chose to not process it at the moment. The hunt was on.

However, somewhere deep inside her, Harper was flailing and dancing excitedly. This was enormous. This was huge. And she'd stumbled right into the middle of it. "What do you mean by 'quirks'?"

"Magical aptitude, hexed, cursed, or otherwise unable to participate in human society." It sounded a little bit like Esther was repeating something from a school brochure. "We've got an alchemist and a technomancer in our year. Someone in the graduating class lost their name and all their memories before age ten to the Fair Folk. That kind of thing."

That all made a shocking amount of sense. Hunters had guilds and communities, surely mythics must have had their own organizations. "Okay, so is this…some kind of secret training ground?"

Izzy scoffed at that. "God, I wish. We just have to do regular boring college shit like—Crap, I have an essay on *The Old Man and the Sea* due next week. But some of us, y'know, we can't exactly go to a regular school and make it through okay. Can you imagine having to deal with a normie roommate, trying to hide our monster shit?" It was weird to hear someone from the supernatural world use that word. You weren't really supposed to say *monster*, as the connotations were too tangled. Was this a generational thing? A cultural thing? Regardless, Harper wasn't about to go stepping in it now.

All of this prompted the next obvious question, though Harper knew asking about something so intimate could be a massive social faux pas in certain circles. "And you two are…?"

For a moment, there was a silence of the same caliber that her father was capable of inflicting. Esther's friends seemed to be weighing things in their heads, balancing out some invisible equation. "Isabelle Vaughn, banshee," Izzy finally said. She then gestured to the other girl. "Zooey Halloway, my literal Manic Pixie Dream Girl. Autumn is—" She cut herself off almost violently, a few tears instantly pricking the corners of her eyes. She looked pained. "Shit. Autumn *was* a shapeshifter."

It was obvious why Esther generally looked human. But looking around, it seemed as though every single student was a human too. "How do they keep this kind of thing under wraps?"

Zooey motioned toward the student union building. Up at the very top was a small, peaked section. It looked like it might have been the source of the ringing bell she'd heard earlier. "Mass variable glamour. Keeps everyone looking human, regardless of their condition. That single piece of magic is half the reason this place costs as much as it does. But it's worth it. I know my wings won't suddenly pop out when I go into town."

The comparison may not have exactly been one-to-one or anything, but Harper could respect someone wanting a place where they knew they could be safe. "Thought about getting a glamour one time. Just to get away from the awkward conversations and all. But it seemed like...I dunno, cheating."

"I don't understand. Why in the world would you need a glamour?" Esther looked earnestly confused, which was just precious.

Like it wasn't super obvious. The jawline, with the vaguest hint of stubble, the clear Adam's apple, the try-hard girl voice. Still, this entire trip was taking such a strange turn that Harper wasn't sure she had the energy to be snarky or rude at the moment, nor to simply evade the topic. "I'm trans. It'd just be nice. To have that. To look..." The word *normal* hung on her lips and she quickly put it away. That wasn't quite right. But she didn't know what to use in its place, so she opted to just let the sentence go unresolved.

Izzy clicked her tongue softly, and for the first time since they'd met, she had a genuine smile on her face, though it was clearly not directed to Harper. "Autumn never cheated it," Izzy said. There it was. The thing Esther didn't judge her for. "She said she refused to use her shapeshifting to lie about who she was. Which seemed stupid and noble."

"It was," Zooey agreed, soft and sad. "Harper." She looked over with a sudden, steady seriousness. "You really think there's something suspicious about her death?"

"Yeah. Now more than ever. Unfortunately, this also puts me back at square one. The list of possible suspects went from one to zero, and now it's shot up to...however many people go here."

She got a smirk from Izzy, which was maybe the friendliest expression she'd managed to elicit from her thus far. That felt like a kind of progress. "You know we're not just gonna sit on the sidelines while you solve our girlfriend's murder, right?"

"My offer still stands too," Esther reminded her.

Hell.

Harper already had to deal with this once. When it had just been Esther, she'd been able to summon the necessary fortitude to turn her down. She wasn't sure she could do it a second time, especially with two more people making demands. But that was no excuse. She was the hunter here, she was the one who knew how to actually do this stuff. It didn't matter if they were mythics, they still weren't fit for this. "No, no way. Why is everyone so eager to put themselves in harm's way?"

"It's what Autumn deserves," Esther said, repeating her sentiments from that morning.

"It's what Autumn would have done, if it had been either of us," Zooey continued.

"I want to make this fucker bleed," Izzy concluded.

I'm so tired. And after almost twenty-four hours, all I've managed to do is waste time following a false lead and question a bunch of random students for precisely zero information. Nobody else will even talk to me.

I just have to add "keep these three alive" to my job description. Nothing difficult about that.

Harper scrubbed at her face for a moment. "All right. Fine. But I'm serious, this person is a vicious killer. When things go bad, you all had better be nowhere in sight."

"Well, yeah. Someone's gotta watch Esther's back. This girl wouldn't hurt a fly." Izzy reached out and poked Esther playfully in the center of her forehead.

She grunted and swatted the hand away. "Okay, just because I'm not a violent person doesn't mean I'm helpless. I'm not just some damsel. Now, Harper, can you please just explain what comes next?"

Oof. She glanced around her, first at the other girls, then at the campus around them. What *did* come next? The way Autumn died could have been random, but it seemed incredibly personal. Someone close to her was the most likely candidate for an attack that violent. "Without much to go on, I need information and leads. Autumn was in the theatre department, yeah?"

"All three of us..." Zooey seemed to get hung up on verb tense and eventually removed the issue altogether. "All three of us. Her, me, and Izzy."

"Okay. That's good. Those were the people she spent the most time with. I need to talk to them, as many as will let me."

"Yeah," Izzy said. "She practically lived over there. I suppose we could try to wrangle them all up in one place. Can't make any promises, but it's worth trying."

Esther got a nervous look on her face. "What about me? I'm the outlier over in religious studies. I know plenty of people, but the overlap between my social circle and Autumn's was pretty slim." She gestured to Izzy and Zooey, implying that the two of them might have been the majority of that overlap.

"You're coming with me. This case got a lot more complicated, and I can't keep wandering around this place in a haze, not knowing what half these buildings even are. I need a guide." She had an idea for something else that Esther might be able to help with, but she didn't want to overwhelm her right out the gate.

Esther's face lit up a bit at that, seeming genuinely pleased to be of use. She popped up to her feet gracefully and once more offered a hand to Harper. She took it and let herself be hauled up to stand. "Right, then. No time like the present."

"And you can just go there? Literally any time?" Harper could hardly believe some of the stuff she was learning about this place. But for some reason, it was the twenty-four-hour gym that currently had her attention.

A lot of her training with Sebastian had been pretty homebrewed. If you wanted to take a run, the commune had more than enough acreage. If you wanted an arm workout, there was always wood that needed chopping. Squats? Go work in the garden and your legs would be screaming before long. The idea of a free, full-time gym where you could explicitly train whatever you needed sounded heavenly.

She motioned to the next building curiously. "Okay, this place. Walked by it earlier. Don't understand in the slightest. Why would students need a union? Are there dues?"

Esther gave another one of her earthy laughs. "What? No. Or, well, yeah kind of, that's—I mean it's covered by tuition. It's mostly just a central meeting building. That's where the student council meets, there's a lounge, a bunch of club rooms, the bookstore. I think that's where the school paper operates out of. It's a multipurpose building for all the stuff that doesn't fit anywhere else."

It felt good to finally have a sense of the place, and Harper was infinitely grateful to Esther for not judging any of her questions. Well, not too much. She couldn't quite be sure if it was because her questions weren't actually that stupid, or because Esther was just that nice. But she decided not to worry about it too much. "So everything is contained here. You can leave and do stuff if you want. But it's all pretty much here. Y'know, it kinda reminds me of my commune—"

Shit. Don't talk about that, dumbass.

People don't know what that is.

Or they don't care.

Or both.

She was interrupted from any further deprecation by a gentle, excited cooing from Esther. Harper looked over at her and saw a slight glint in her eyes. "Wow, really? You live on a commune?"

Anyone else asking that question would have made Harper nervous that she was being fucked with. But Esther's earnestness and enthusiasm were blinding. "Um, yeah. I mean, it's not that big a deal. It is what it is."

"No, I think that's great!" There was a bounce in her step now. "There are religious groups across the world who live in communes and intentional communities. After all, it's the same principle as a classical monastery or convent." Just as quickly, the energy faded and she hung her head slightly. "And I'm realizing…you probably don't care about that stuff."

In truth, Harper was of two minds about that. Her experiences with religious people were so incredibly hit-and-miss. There had been really competent priests who could run a flawless exorcism or deliver holy water in bulk. And there were members of faithful flocks who had looked at Harper like she was a freak. But no denying, there was something quite beautiful about watching someone gush about their passions. Waffling on where she fell, she eventually opted for the middle road approach. "Maybe you can gush a bit when the hunt is over. You could even come and visit!" Okay, that might be a step too far, she told herself quickly, so dial it back, Zeale.

To her surprise, her companion actually began to glow just a little bit and hurried to gesture to the next building they were approaching. "Er, here's the library. I imagine that one's pretty self-explanatory. Books. Computers. All that. Which I think covers just about—Oh! Doctor White!" Esther cried out suddenly, her hand waving up in the air back and forth in a wide arc.

Harper turned her gaze down the sidewalk, where a woman was walking toward them. Her dirty-blond hair was up in a loose bun, a pair of fashionable glasses propped up on her nose. She had on a classic blazer and pencil skirt combo with reasonable heels. She was upsettingly gorgeous.

Feeling a bit overheated—for absolutely no reason in particular, of course—Harper removed her jacket and wrapped it around her waist, then sloppily rolled up the sleeves of her flannel. It definitely didn't have anything to do with the sudden appearance of this beautiful woman.

Dr. White smiled warmly as she drew closer. "Esther, you know damn well you can just call me Imogen. I want to stay approachable."

Esther's face lit up with a mischievous grin. "Why do you think I do it every time?" She turned back to Harper and gestured. "This is Dr. Imogen White, president of our humble little school."

Imogen gave a fond laugh. It sounded like exactly the kind of thing a person did after a lot of practice. She was clearly the sort of woman who wanted everyone to find her easy to get along with. She wanted to be liked. There were worse things to want. "So, who's this?"

"Harper. She's a potential transfer student," Esther said easily, and Harper was at once impressed and disturbed by how convincingly she lied. "I'm giving her a truncated version of the school tour."

"Nice to meet you," Harper said, extending a hand. "I grew up homeschooled and then did some online learning, but it just wasn't landing right with me. Decided I wanted a proper college experience, if only for a year or two."

Dr. White took her hand and shook it firmly. "Well, you could certainly do worse than MBC. I think we're currently up to about twenty percent of our upperclassmen being transfer students and commuters. We try to encourage all kinds to study here."

Esther started clicking her tongue and shaking her head. "I'm already giving her the sales pitch, you don't need to double down on it, or she might get annoyed instead of interested."

The president threw her hands up with an overly dramatic sigh. "All right, all right, forgive me. You never really shut it off. It lives with you, burrows into your brain, day after day. You start dreaming in speeches and pithy statements. Trust me, kids, never go into academic administration. It's not worth it." Imogen chuckled softly to herself and gave the both of them a subtle nod of the head. Her eyes flicked down and she seemed to be scanning Harper a moment longer, though it wasn't clear what the specific target was, not until the woman spoke again. "That's a fascinating tattoo you have there."

Following her line of sight down, Harper saw the Silversmiths crest tattooed big and bold on her flesh.

Shit.

CHAPTER SIX

Great job, idiot. You plastered the crest of your guild in permanent ink on your flesh. There are bound to be plenty of mythics out there who know that symbol. The fact that you haven't been attacked on sight yet is fucking impressive. And now the president of a college full of mythics has seen it, and knows exactly what you are, and she's going to make you leave before you can solve this murder. And that's if we're lucky. Maybe we'll end up like poor Autumn. A corpse left out for someone to find. It's been a good run.

Flustered and caught off guard, Harper could really only mumble her way through an explanation. "Yeah, uh, it's part of an old family crest. I dunno, it just seemed cool…" God, she was bad at this. She couldn't even pull off a single lie about an ill-advised tattoo.

"Oh!" Imogen perked up, adjusting her glasses slightly before locking Harper's gaze with her own. "I actually have a bit of an amateur fascination with the symbolism and history behind family crests. Maybe you'd like to stop by the administrative building tomorrow afternoon while I have open office hours. We can talk about it a little more."

"Uh. Yeah. Sure, we can…We can do that. Tomorrow, then."

"Lovely." Imogen was beaming as she gave the two of them a curt nod before continuing on her way.

Once she was a few dozen feet away, Harper allowed herself to release the breath she'd been holding, shaking a little bit.

Esther looked at her sympathetically. "It's okay, Harper. She has that effect on a lot of people."

"Huh?"

"Well, she's beautiful and friendly. But she's also a woman in power. That's a dangerous combination. But I promise, she's super easy to talk to. You'll be fine."

Well, the good news was that Esther just assumed she was flustered because Imogen was hot.

The bad news was that Esther assumed she was flustered because Imogen was hot.

"Yep. It's just a little nerve-racking, I'll be fine." Harper rubbed her neck and cleared her throat several times. "Um. So you said that's the last of the tour, right?"

She nodded and smiled. "Well, short of me dragging you in and out of literally every building we can find. Kind of a waste. Why, did you have an idea for what to do next?"

"Wouldn't be very good at my job if I didn't." Harper puffed out her chest a bit, trying to recover from her momentary terror by being overly cocky instead. "How good is that nose when you're not a wolf, anyway?"

"Wait, what?"

The two were once again at the clearing in the woods. Now that Harper wasn't investigating the place from a distance, more details stuck out to her. There were a lot of lingering scents that even her stupid human nose could pick up on—booze, weed, and sweat, of course. Hiding underneath all of it was the coppery smell of old blood. It was a strange enough experience for her, but judging by the look on Esther's face, she was having a much tougher time.

They walked silently over to the spot where Autumn's body was discovered. Esther bent down and started gently brushing the dirt with her fingertips, pinching a small clump together and bringing it to her nose. Hovering over her shoulder, Harper watched, fascinated. It made her wonder if hunters ever paired up with mythics, or why it didn't happen more often. There were so many things they could do that she would never be able to.

"Would you mind...standing over there a little? Downwind? It's just...I need to isolate scents, and you're distracting." Esther's eyes went a bit wide, perhaps replaying what she'd just said in her head. "Not—I mean, not in a bad way! In a good way. No! In a neutral way."

Distracting. Well, with that little nugget of a confidence boost, Harper was only too happy to stroll a few feet back and give her some space to do what she needed.

While she waited, Harper turned her attention to the rest of the clearing once more. The strange thing was there wasn't a whole lot to go off of. Sure, there were tons of bottles and cans lying around that students hadn't bothered to clean up. There were footprints everywhere from law enforcement coming and going from the scene. But otherwise, the place was relatively undisturbed. Even the blood was localized to a pretty small area.

She could feel something forming in her mind. It was strange, right? After all—

"That's weird. That's...really weird." Thought process interrupted, Harper returned her attention to Esther. She was once again rubbing the dirt between her fingers, still slowly inhaling it through her nose.

"Did you find something?"

"It would be more accurate to say I found nothing," she mused, more to herself than to Harper.

That didn't sound great. "Nothing?"

Esther let go, the tiny particles of dirt falling back to the ground. "Literally nothing. Which is impossible. *Everything* has a smell. Even stuff you think wouldn't, like water or plastic. No matter how faint, there should always be at least some small scent to latch onto. What I'm getting here, once you get past all the obvious traces? It's a black hole where a scent should be."

"Okay, so what does that mean, exactly?"

"Not to be extremely unhelpful, but I have absolutely no idea. Luckily, I know someone who might be able to give us a hand with this." Esther pulled a handkerchief from her purse and looked like she was about to drop a fistful of dirt into it, presumably for safekeeping.

Harper could think of at least a few reasons not to do that and reached out to lay a hand on Esther's arm. "Hang on." From her trusty messenger bag, Harper fetched a tiny sampling kit. While most of the contents weren't going to do much good with grave dirt, she figured the small plastic jar would be far more useful than a bit of cloth for holding important evidence. Unscrewing the lid, she held out the container, and Esther bashfully dropped the dirt inside.

"Yeah, I guess that would probably work better."

With a few twists, Harper secured the contents inside the vessel before passing it off to Esther. "There you go. Less likely to spill out inside your purse, and probably a bit better for keeping that stuff fresh and maintaining the nonscent. Should we go bug this friend of yours?"

Once Esther had stowed the jar inside her purse, she took a look at her watch and sighed sadly. "Unfortunately, we're kinda out of time for today. It's getting late, and I need to eat and get ready for nightfall when—" She held her hands up on either side of her head, palms out, simulating tall wolf ears. "Well, y'know. Rawr."

There was a part of Harper that kind of wanted to stick around. She wanted to see that incredible transformation again. She wanted to spend time with a big cuddly wolf and maybe snuggle up to her and good *God* she had such a one-track mind, didn't she? "There's still a killer on the loose. Want someone to watch your back?"

The offer was legitimate, but she hadn't really expected Esther to actually give it any consideration. It was a shock to see the girl take a moment to think it over. "Seriously? You saw how boring it was last night. I mean…if you really want to, I guess the company would be—"

A sharp ringing from Harper's bag interrupted the answer, and she reflexively fished around inside until she found the offending phone. If it were anyone else, she would have silenced it on the spot. But when she saw the blocky letters spelling out "Zooey (Pixie?)" she figured it could be important. "Shit, sorry, just a second." She flipped the phone open, catching a suppressed giggle from Esther as she answered. "Hey, what's up?"

"Harper? Uh, me and Izzy did some poking around. If you want, we can pull together anyone who's available and wrangle them in the theatre. Maybe after that we can grab dinner and uhh...debrief? Is that the right word?"

She could just make out Izzy's voice in the background. "Probably don't need to be so formal about it, babe. Just tell her to get her scrawny butt over here."

"Please tell me you didn't hear that," Zooey muttered.

"Afraid I did." Looking at Esther, all Harper wanted in that moment was to tell them that she couldn't make it, that she was too busy chasing some other lead, especially when it seemed like her companion was willing to let her stick around. But ultimately, she knew there was only one option, and the hunt came first. Always. "And you can tell the pot that the black kettle is on her way." Flipping the phone closed again, Harper sighed apologetically. "Duty calls. Zooey and Izzy came through, so I need to get over to the theatre."

"Oh. Okay." It wasn't much, but the fact that Esther sounded just as disappointed as she felt was comforting.

"But maybe...text me tomorrow when you're no longer, y'know, rawr," Harper said while imitating Esther's wolf-ear hand gesture. "We can do breakfast again or something, and figure out our game plan?"

"Totally!" Esther said excitedly, practically bouncing. "I mean, it's just—It's exciting. Being all investigative and everything. I'm glad to help with whatever. Okay! See you tomorrow, then." With a hasty wave, Esther quickly whirled around and made her way down the path for her dorm.

Any more confidence boosts and Harper was going to start actually feeling legitimately good about herself. She decided yet again to not let herself get hung up on stupid fantasies and took one last look around the clearing for anything of note. But the light from the sun was starting to fade and the damned place wasn't offering up anything else useful. Whatever thought had been manifesting earlier was far away now. "Stop getting so distracted, jackass. You're better than that," she muttered before turning and making her way across campus to meet up with the others.

Harper wasn't entirely sure what she'd been expecting, and yet somehow this still managed to defy her nonexpectations. The school's "theatre" was pretty much just a big empty space with the walls painted black and chairs scattered around. There was the beginning of a set in the center—though it was just a bunch of wooden boards screwed together into a platform.

A decent collection of students and a pair of professors occupied the chairs. She had to admit, she was impressed. Harper had kind of assumed they'd maybe get a handful, that most people wouldn't bother coming out for this. A bit nervously, she turned back to look down at Zooey. "What did you tell all these people anyway?"

She shrugged with a small smile. "Well, I know Izzy saw through your cover earlier and went a little bit apeshit, but it's a pretty good excuse. 'Hunter' can be a four-letter word, depending on who you're talking to. But a private eye, hired to investigate what happened to her, that's more tolerable. It's all just labels anyway. You're trying to find who or what killed her, that's the important thing."

Harper looked back toward the assembled drama geeks and cleared her throat. "All right, folks, I wanna keep things moving along nice and smooth. I'm going to be in the—" Her mind blanked, somewhat ruining the air of authority she was going for, and she hurriedly looked back at Zooey.

"The green room."

"I'm going to be in the green room. Izzy will send you back one at a time, we'll go over the events of the last few days, and then you're good to go. Easy peasy. Make sure to get your stories straight before talking to me." She gave a playful wink, but her dumb joke mostly got her a few uncomfortable coughs. Harper sighed deeply and turned to walk away. "C'mon, Zooey."

A "green room," as it turned out, was basically just a small lounge. All of the furniture looked like it had been cobbled together from multiple trips to thrift stores. This much, at least, she knew from experience. The living room in the commune dormitory had a very similar vibe. A large corkboard on one wall was covered in papers of varying sizes. The largest one displayed what she assumed to be a miniature plan for the set, though she couldn't begin to make any guesses beyond that. Other pages featured sketches of costume designs and specific pieces of scenery.

Another wall supported two big frames featuring posters from previous productions. One corner of the green room was dwarfed by a noisy fridge and counters ladened with bags of chips and boxes of cookies.

Harper sat on a shockingly comfortable couch with her messenger bag tucked in next to her, notebook in her lap. Zooey sat next to her, mostly there to act as a friendly face for the other students and to fill in any other info she might need.

A flash of purple hair in the doorway paired with a firm knock on the doorjamb signaled that Izzy was ready to send in the first person. She gave a quick thumbs-up to the pair before disappearing from view.

The first to enter was an older woman, probably in her early sixties. She had "bohemian" written all over, down to the scarf around her shoulders that was clearly designed to be tattered. Her wide, circular glasses sat halfway down her nose. Her hair was a nest that had no clear beginning or end. "Ah, the detective! I'm so glad to have you here. Dear Autumn was taken from us far too soon. And if she has been struck down by someone within our very midst, then the truth must be brought into the light!" She'd started talking as soon as she entered the room and only finished her introduction by the time she had delicately graced the chair with her presence.

Zooey gestured to her with a weary smile. "Colette Bishop, head of the department."

Harper was fairly certain she could have figured out the second part based on context clues alone. "Right, uh, well let's start with what you remember from the last time you saw Autumn." She held her pen at the ready, hoping she would be able to capture the pertinent information buried underneath the monologue of flowery prose that was bound to be dropped on her lap.

"Naturally! We'd just finished rehearsal for our latest production, perhaps nine o'clock or so. I stayed behind with my stage manager to go over some notes and decide what needs to be refined. We're still early in the process, so needless to say we had plenty to talk about! Autumn left along with the other students, off into the night, and unfortunately, into the arms of danger. I'm afraid I was far too engrossed in my work to see if anything was amiss."

Yup. Flowery. Harper placed a few question marks next to the woman's name. The only thing Colette was guilty of murdering was normal speech. Still, Autumn's death was pretty damn dramatic. What if her killer was one of those chilling, artistic types who wanted the world to witness their grand vision? "Thanks. Uh, look, I'm sure it's not fun to think negatively about your students. But can you think of anyone that might have wanted her…removed?"

Colette held her hand dramatically to her forehead—Harper wondered if she did anything in a way that wasn't dramatic—and sighed wistfully. "I imagine if this were some tawdry murder mystery, I might cast aspersions on her understudy, Scarlett. Taking out the competition to assure her place in the show. However, here in the real world, such a thing would be ridiculous."

Regardless of the impossibility, she made a note on the page, writing the girl's name with a question mark next to it. "Right, thank you, Professor. I won't take any more of your time." She waited patiently until the woman had taken her leave before looking desperately at Zooey. "Please tell me this isn't going to be our entire evening."

"No, Colette is about as intense as they come. I figured we should go ahead and get her out of the way first."

"You have my infinite gratitude. What's your read on Scarlett? Think she might have been onto something there?" She idly tapped her pen against the page.

Zooey scrunched up her face in thought. "She doesn't strike me as the type."

Granted, Zooey wasn't a hunter, and she didn't have the instincts that Harper did. But she did know the girl, so it canceled out at that point. "Well, let's bring her in and find out."

Zooey looked toward the doorway where Izzy was leaning against the frame, arms crossed, apparently taking her job quite seriously. "Hey, can you grab Scarlett?"

"You got it," she said with a quick two-finger salute.

After a few moments, a tall, mousy girl made her way into the green room. Despite being nearly six feet tall, she tried hard to make herself shrink while scurrying her way up to sit in the interrogation chair. Scarlett was constantly fidgeting, picking at a loose thread in her chunky knit sweater. "Um, h-hi."

Hoo boy, maybe Zooey was right. This girl doesn't seem capable of violence.

Then again, she's an actress. Could be she's putting on a show to keep suspicion off her.

Yeah, I'm sure this college student is actually a murdering mastermind, seamlessly fooling everyone around her with this act. Sure, Harper.

How about you shut up? We need every angle we can get. Let's see what she has to say.

"Hi, Scarlett. So, what can you tell us about that night? Notice anything weird?"

Scarlett switched to fiddling with her sleeves, pulling them all the way down over her hands. "N-No! That's the thing." Scarlett was staring hard at the floor, then shook her head desperately. "Autumn was in a great mood. She was acting up a storm. I mean, watching her, I knew I didn't need to worry about having to go on stage for this show. I could hide out in the back and do some stagehand work instead. It was kind of a... relief." She looked up finally, a slight shimmer to her eyes.

Holy shit, she's crying. Can she do that on command?

I don't know whether to hug her or give her a standing ovation. Focus. Dig.

"You didn't want the part?"

Scarlett sniffled and shrugged. "It's always really fun to get a big role in theory. In practice, it's crazy stressful. Colette seems to think I can pull it off, but…I don't know, it's gonna be rough. Even more so because everyone's going to be watching and thinking 'Autumn could have done it better.' And they'll be right! I've got the part by default. It doesn't feel earned."

The notebook in Harper's lap stared up at her, waiting for the pen to make its decision. After a few silent seconds, she put a dark X next to the girl's name. The motivation just wasn't there. It hardly mattered whether she had the will to commit that kind of violence—and Harper seriously doubted she did. She saw the role as a burden on both her talent and her spirit. Sure, it could have been a standard "be careful what you wish for" scenario, but Scarlett just didn't fit the profile.

Harper looked up and gave her what she prayed was a comforting smile. "Then you just have to work extra hard to be sure it's a performance worthy of her memory."

Her kindness was met with a more emphatic sniffle, but at least the girl's shoulders weren't trying to envelop her ears anymore. "Tall order."

Zooey got up to give Scarlett the hug that Harper couldn't. "You're gonna do awesome, sweetie." Keeping a hand on her back, she guided her out of the room before sharing a hushed word with Izzy to bring in the next person.

After her companion settled back onto the couch, a mountain of a man strolled in casually. Unkempt gray hair and an equally unkempt gray beard, Hawaiian shirt, cargo pants, and sturdy boots gave an immediate impression of an easygoing, affable soul. He settled into the chair with a wide smile.

"This is our technical director, Marcus Hill."

He extended an enormous hand, and Harper took it, already knowing what was about to happen next. Marcus's handshake was strong, enough that her entire body was jostled slightly. Marcus was the kind of guy who could only give one sort of handshake.

A glamour could do a lot to cover a person's appearance, but it didn't change the body beneath the magical illusion. And as soon as she felt the craggy skin beneath, she realized she was dealing with a golem.

Strong enough to do serious damage to a victim. Could easily tear a girl's chest open.

Fine, he's strong. Lots of mythics are strong. Look at this guy. He's a softy. Nobody that laid-back is going to do that without a damn good reason. Golems are protectors, so unless one of the words inscribed on him is "murderous," he would be physically incapable of hurting someone.

"Good to meet you, Marcus," Harper said as she pulled her hand back and tried to subtly massage it. "Care to tell me what happened after rehearsal the night of Autumn's murder?"

His amiable exterior faded and he gave a solemn nod. "I'm not proud of it..." He cleared his throat. "I was back in my office working on some last-minute changes to the lighting plan that Colette had asked for. She wanted a gobo with a tree for act three, which meant moving a bunch of lights around and adjusting their position. I needed to make sure everything was laid out before shop hours the next day. I was...a little stressed out by the time I had finished. So I put on some Eagles and broke out my stash of whiskey for a drink. Or two." He released a weary sigh and gave his beard a few soothing strokes. "One of my students was killed, and I was here getting drunk. It's not that I could have done anything about it. It just sucks, you know? It doesn't feel good."

What was supposed to be an interrogation had quickly turned into a series of miniature therapy sessions for an entire academic department. Harper sympathized, but she couldn't go around giving everyone comforting words when she was supposed to be hunting down a killer. "Thanks for your honesty, Marcus. What-ifs suck."

"They sure fuckin' do. Anything else I can do for you?"

She shook her head and shrugged. "Not unless you saw anything suspicious."

"Sorry, kiddo. I was in my own little world that night. Not gonna let that happen again."

After he left, Harper took a second to focus back up. Something occurred to her that she felt almost stupid for not thinking to ask earlier. God, there was so much to keep track of. Too many spinning plates. In spite of her initial worries about involving others in her hunt, she was grateful to Esther, Izzy, and Zooey for everything they were already doing. "Hey, Izzy?"

She popped back into the room. "What's up?"

"Anybody *not* here that I should try and track down?"

Izzy frowned. "Hmm. Tripp and Mikaela had choir tonight. But they both said we could catch up once they were free. Although…" She glanced over at Zooey and they shared a quick nod. "Shit. Lakshmi said she probably couldn't make it but didn't have a great excuse. And she's tech crew with us, so she wouldn't have been at rehearsal that night."

After she wrote the name down, Harper looked over at Zooey. "Why 'shit'?"

"Well, we never really got any concrete details from Autumn about it. But there was…static between them. We assumed it was probably just stupid drama. What if it wasn't?"

"Only one way to find out," Harper said. "Still, we should at least finish up here."

The next few students to come through the room were a blur of more names and faces. Each of them was just as torn up as the rest. And every single one expressed the same concerns as Marcus. What if there was something they had missed? What if they had asked her to hang out with them instead of going off to do their own thing? It was just a string of regrets, which was touching, but not exactly useful.

"One more," Izzy said from the doorway. "Evan. He was pretty tight with Autumn. Football player. Solid dude."

"Yeah, send him in." Harper wiped the exhaustion from her eyes and looked down at her notebook. It was covered in words and names, circles, strikethroughs, underlines, question marks, and more. "God, I just need…*something*. Anything."

As promised, Evan exuded "solid dude" energy. He planted himself firmly in the chair and immediately went into an easy slouched posture with his knees spread about as wide as they would go. "Private eye, huh? That's dope."

"Yeah, super dope," she said half-heartedly. "So, you and Autumn were fairly close, yeah?"

He gave a nervous look toward Zooey, then back over his shoulder at Izzy. "Whoa, I don't know where you got that idea. Nah, I know Temple preferred the ladies."

"No, I...Not like that. Just...You got along well, right?"

"Oh! Yeah, for sure. Autumn was cool as hell." He brushed his fingers back through his well-maintained hair and gave an easy smile, apparently grateful he wasn't being accused of something like that.

She set the pen down. "I just need to know if there was anything weird the last time you saw her. Even if it seems super innocuous."

"Innoc...?"

Dear Lord, give me strength, Harper prayed silently. "Even if it seems dumb or unimportant."

"Right yeah. Well, look, this isn't normally the kinda thing I do, but...As we were leaving the theatre, she got this phone call."

Instantly, Zooey and Izzy shared a look with each other, both of them shaking their heads in unison. Izzy frowned. "Wasn't us. I was hanging with Zooey in her dorm, waiting for Autumn to get out of rehearsal." Her face fell slightly. "Got nervous when we didn't hear from her, but I figured she was probably working on an assignment or something."

"Dude, that's why it was weird. When she talks to you guys, it's real casual and she'll keep walking with us. But she was all like, 'I gotta take this,' and then walked off to the side to answer it. And I was all, 'That's weird,' so...Like I said, I don't usually do this kinda shit. But I got curious and hovered a little closer. She was all hush-hush, could barely make anything out. Sounded serious though. Something about 'You wanna meet right now?' and whatever. I thought I heard her mention the woods, but

I didn't wanna snoop any more than that. If she caught me, it would be over for me. Autumn could be savage, and she didn't hold back when you overstepped. Hell, wish I had now. If she was too busy busting my ass…"

Harper shook her head and did her best to give the guy a smile she hoped was comforting. "It's not your fault, Evan. And this is a huge lead. Seriously, thank you."

"Am I cool to go then? Homework and shit."

"Yeah, man, you're good." He got up and nodded to the room before taking his leave. Harper looked toward Zooey and shook her head. "God, no wonder I'm fading here. I haven't eaten since this morning. I believe I was promised dinner?"

Izzy chuckled. "At the finest establishment around."

"She's talking about the dining hall," Zooey helpfully translated.

"You two really know how to show a girl a good time."

CHAPTER SEVEN

This felt weird. The whole thing felt really weird. Harper was getting the smallest taste of the life she never had, and it was, in a word, weird. She had a crappy plastic tray with what could generously be described as a burrito and a glass of pop and it was *so* weird. She was sitting on a crappy plastic chair at a flimsy table with a couple of college students who were also a banshee and a pixie, and *that* was the part she could handle. "Okay. Not a super helpful exercise. But at least we got something."

Izzy sighed dramatically and shoved a forkful of spaghetti in her mouth, slurping some stray noodles and chewing through them before bothering to answer. "Barely. Is this what it's always like?"

Harper plucked a stray black bean from her plate and popped it in her mouth. "It can be. Sometimes a case can be really quick. I thought this one was going to be, until I actually saw Esther in action. Or, I guess, lack of action. Just a big, fuzzy sweetheart."

Shaking her head, Zooey picked at her salad but wasn't eating much at the moment. "I'm really sorry, Harper. I wish there was more we could do."

"Look, there's something else that's been gnawing at me." Izzy looked at Harper almost conspiratorially. "Autumn was a shapeshifter. She wasn't completely helpless. If there was a fight, or even if this really was some wild animal, she wouldn't have gone down like that. She'd have turned into a goddamn bear or whatever and mauled the shit outta them."

Harper pulled up her mental image of the woods earlier. She'd scoured the place for any signs that weren't ruined by heavy-booted flatfoots with no sense of maintaining a crime scene. Finally, it struck her. She had been missing an obvious detail because she was too busy distracted by some other shiny clue.

There was no major damage to the trees or foliage, no signs of a struggle. The blood in the dirt had been pretty tightly localized. There were no animal tracks except Esther's from when she padded around there last night. Whatever happened, it happened fast. Whoever Autumn met with, they were obviously someone she trusted, and they were strong enough to get to her quickly.

She sighed and took a giant bite from her burrito. Every time she thought she had something, it turned out to be useless. Or worse, it just opened the potential subject pool up all over again. Clearly Autumn knew a lot of people. Anyone might have been able to use that familiarity against her. Hell, Harper still didn't know if they were looking for one person or multiple assailants. "Yeah, I see what you mean. Mega-suspicious."

"Hey, I had another idea," Zooey said softly.

"I'm listening." Harper hated how little she had to work off of. At this point, she was willing to accept anything that people had. Whatever might give her a lead.

"We still have a spare key for Autumn's dorm. And I'm willing to bet the school hasn't changed the lock yet. The warning tape on her door was removed earlier this afternoon so it's no longer an active crime scene. Do you figure maybe your super sleuthing might find something?"

That sounded just the tiniest bit sketchy, and Harper smirked at the two girls. "I have to assume spare keys aren't generally a thing for dorm rooms."

Izzy grinned in return. "They're all marked to say reproduction is forbidden. But there's a guy at the local hardware store who has a soft spot for lovebirds. He also has exceptionally greasable palms."

"Hell, all right, let's do it." Anything to keep the hunt moving was good. She stood up and grabbed her empty tray, eager to get back to work.

Harper ran her hand across the wall while she stared at the mess of play programs taped to it. Next to them was a poster from the Broadway production of *Wicked*—a show big enough and gay enough that even Harper had heard of it. The dorm room was pretty good for getting a feel for what kind of girl Autumn was. But it had yet to really offer up anything she might call a proper clue. The bed was covered in fuzzy pink pillows, and there was a small collection of pill bottles on top of the dresser that Harper recognized in a heartbeat.

Beyond aesthetics and obvious information, the place had been pretty well picked clean by flatfoot vultures. She glanced back at Zooey with a small shrug. "Sorry, not sure if there's much here I can work with. The fuzz already cleaned out her trash, took her computer, all the usual stuff."

"It's okay, Harper, I know it was a long shot." Zooey just shrugged right back at her, doing her best to give a hopeful smile.

"Eh, I can't be perfect and amazing all the time. Sometimes things just don't pan out, ya know?" Harper perched herself on the solid frame of the girl's bed and idly tapped her foot against the wall. To her surprise, the painted cinder block she hit with her toe had just the smallest amount of give to it. "Then again, maybe I am incredible."

Hastily, she dropped down to her knees and felt around the large block. There was a break in the thick layer of white paint. She spent a few seconds trying to get a grip on it with her fingers, but it wasn't playing along. "Come on, I'm begging you, let me have this." If prying it loose by hand wasn't an option, then Autumn must have been using something else to dislodge it. She was sure of it. "Either of you have any way to move this damn thing?"

"Look who you're asking." Izzy practically shoved her aside and crouched down in front of the brick. With a practiced motion, she retrieved a multi-tool from a small pouch on her belt and got to work. "I gave Autumn one of these things for our anniversary. I'd bet anything that's how she did this."

That's a weird gift.

No, wait. Actually, that's rad as hell.

I need one of those the next chance I get.

Harper and Zooey watched quietly as Izzy searched through the various folding tools before selecting one that was sturdy enough to work the brick-free. It still took some time to dislodge. Harper hoped whatever was hidden inside was important enough to require this much trouble.

Finally, she jimmied it enough that she was able to get a better grip and wrenched it free. "Hell yeah. Multi-tool saves the day once again." Izzy stood back up and gestured grandly to the hole in the wall. "Care to do the honors?"

Reaching into the dark crevice, Harper pulled out several objects, inspecting each as she pulled it into the light. "Weed… Pipe…Fucking jackpot!" She held aloft a composition notebook. "Let's see here. 'Journal. Do Not Read. Yes, Izzy, That Includes You.' Hah, I'll be damned."

Izzy quickly plucked it from her hand, glaring at the cover. But just as quickly, the anger faded and she sniffled softly. "God, that's so her. Even though she knew full well that would never stop me. Still…" She hesitated for just a moment before passing it back to Harper. "Don't think I'm ready for whatever the hell that has to say. This, on the other hand…" She bent down next to her and grabbed up the baggy of weed and the pipe. "We'll spark up in her honor. That notebook's all yours, gumshoe."

Zooey giggled softly, following it up with a little sniffle of her own. "I think she'd be happy, knowing it's being put to good use."

Once Harper had put the brick back in place, she stood and slid the journal into her messenger bag. "Between that and the evidence Esther found, I just might manage to work this out after all."

There was a beat as the two girls exchanged a look before Izzy glanced at her more seriously. "That's the other thing we wanted to talk to you about. Esther's a good little Christian angel. I don't really know why she's volunteering to help you with this. Like, there's absolutely no good reason for a religious studies major to want to play detective. But she's got her mind set on it, and I don't have the heart to tell her she's an idiot. So let me be clear." She leaned in close, holding Harper's eyes with a burning, righteous fury that was honestly terrifying. "If she gets hurt? I will hunt you down, and I will wail and keen and howl until my throat is raw and there is blood leaking from every hole in your body. You will never know peace. Am I clear?"

Logically, Harper knew that she could handle fighting a banshee. She'd gone against worse and survived. Hell, the banshee were a part of the Fair Folk. Nine times out of ten, the only thing you needed to deal with them was iron. That was exactly the reason Harper's knife had been designed the way it was. And Izzy almost certainly wasn't trained in combat either, not as far as Harper could tell. Yeah, she could definitely take her.

But that declaration…It did not leave her thinking logically. It left her shaken, and she could only nod dumbly, shrugging her shoulders a few times. "Yeah. Crystal."

Just like that, Izzy was right back to her old self. "Good! Glad we're on the same page. That just leaves our last few suspects from the theatre department."

"Yup." The mild adrenaline spike hadn't quite left her system. Harper's body felt a little twitchy and she moved a little too quickly for the door. "Better get to it, then. Onward!"

At the southeastern corner of campus, where the school bled into the town of Kitezh, sat a humble little church building. Most of it was brick, though the front edifice was wood, painted bright white. The damn thing even had an old-school steeple. It couldn't have held a congregation of more than a hundred or so.

The sign out front read "Kitezh United Methodist Church—All Are Welcome!" Harper noted the little rainbow flag hanging off it and cocked her head. "I have several questions."

Zooey just shrugged. "Being a mythic doesn't preclude you from being religious. Just look at Esther."

"Speak of the angel—that little olive branch is her doing." Izzy motioned to the flag, beaming with pride. "I still wouldn't set foot in the place. But it's a nice gesture."

Well now, that raises a question. Did she do it out of the goodness of her heart?

Or did Esther make the push because she's gay?

Harper, you predictable bitch.

While Harper puzzled over the flag for a moment longer, clusters of students were leaving the church. Her assistants waved over two of them. Once they reached the sidewalk, she dropped that useless line of questioning for a far more important one. "Hey, I'm guessing you're Tripp and Mikaela?"

Tripp looked to be a frat bro through and through. Teal polo, salmon shorts, boat shoes, the whole deal. Mikaela had a flower-child vibe that instantly reminded her of home, right down to the peasant shirt and flowing skirt.

Tripp spoke up first and gave Harper a once-over. "*This* is the private eye?"

"Wow, way to make yourself sound super innocent, idiot." Mikaela playfully kicked him in the calf. "I can see it. Maybe more Veronica Mars than Dick Tracy, sure. But she has the steely eyes."

It was only getting later, and Harper was losing energy faster than she cared to admit. "I get it, I don't fit the profile. I just need to know if either of you saw anything out of place the night Autumn died. Nothing is too small." While they deliberated, Harper retrieved her notebook and pen.

"Not really. Pretty normal night," Mikaela said, almost sounding disappointed. This was becoming the norm with everyone she talked to. They all just wanted to help, and seemed legitimately upset that they had nothing to offer. It would have been sweet if it weren't so frustrating. Autumn was just a popular student who was in the wrong place at the wrong time. The only good news was that it made the list of people with legitimate grievances shorter. "I stuck behind with Colette to go over show notes and talk about what else needed to be done." Okay, this was the stage manager, then. She jotted a quick note next to her name. It would be pretty stupid of this girl to kill off the lead actress. It only made her job that much harder.

"Yeah, I had to get back to the frat ASAP, so I booked it out of there fast." Ah. Frat boy confirmed. She made another note. "We were getting ready for a 'fraternity event' on Saturday." Harper could practically hear the quotation marks.

"He means they were getting ready for a kegger," Mikaela translated.

She laughed and wrote it down just for posterity. "I had an inkling." So she had one person who stayed behind, and one who was too busy putting together a party. Those were easy alibis to confirm. And it made Harper that much more curious to meet this Lakshmi girl, the only person so far with even a hint of motive. "I appreciate you two taking a second to talk to me. I know this all sucks." It felt like an insufficient way to put it, but that didn't make it any less true. A friend had died. It sucked.

"I really enjoyed playing opposite her," Tripp added. It was the first time he'd said something that didn't make Harper dislike him. "She was really fucking good. Made me a better actor."

Mikaela nodded along. "She was so easy to work with. Any time you gave her a note, she took it seriously and seemed to appreciate the criticism. I just—" She stifled a small whimper. "Yeah. It sucks."

Everyone said their goodbyes, and Harper walked with Zooey and Izzy back across campus. They walked together in silence for a time, letting the quiet of the growing night wash over them.

Once they reached Randolph Dormitory, Izzy pressed her student ID to the electronic lock and popped the door open. She lingered in the hallway with Zooey and sighed. "Lakshmi's in room 203. She wasn't on great terms with Autumn, so us being there would probably just make shit even more awkward.

And that only makes your job harder. Plus, we've got shit to do."
She gently patted the pocket of her jeans where she'd stored the
pipe and weed with a grin. "Just promise me that, if you think
she did it, I get first blood."

It had been a long day, and Harper couldn't stop herself
from laughing a little. "You've got a deal. Seriously, thank you
both for sticking your noses into my hunt. I'd be so fucking lost
otherwise."

"It's been...I don't know. Therapeutic." Zooey smiled
weakly. "Good luck, Harper. Don't hesitate to call us if you need
anything else. This whole thing is a mess."

"Will do," Harper said, offering one last awkward wave
before striding down the hallway toward the stairwell.

Once she found the door she needed, she knocked firmly,
resisting the urge to properly pound the solid wood. The girl
was a suspect, but that was all. Without more to go on, she
couldn't get too aggressive. There was some telltale movement
from inside the dorm room, and after a few seconds, the door
finally opened.

Lakshmi was an Indian girl roughly Harper's height. The
first few strands of her otherwise black hair were dyed almost
pure white. Her purple hoodie must have been nearly two sizes
too large given the way she was nearly swimming in it. The
moment she saw Harper, she groaned and flinched. "Fuck. I
should have known. I told myself I should just go do the damn
thing. Son of a bitch."

The interrogation was off to a bad start. "Uh, yeah. Guess
you already know who I am then." Harper ran her fingers
through the long side of her hair and sighed. "Is now a bad time,
or...?"

"No. It's fine. We might as well do this." She stepped aside
and made room for Harper to walk in.

One look at the room was enough to tell Harper what she
was dealing with. Crystals on every available surface, a poster
of a large hand demonstrating proper palmistry, a full shelf of
tarot decks. Lakshmi was one of the school's human students. A
witch.

The massive gaming computer on her desk did throw Harper for a loop. But even witches needed hobbies outside of the supernatural. One of the two computer monitors showed a menu screen for some game Harper wasn't familiar with. Granted, Harper didn't know much about *any* video games except for the stack of battered cartridges that came with Nat's hand-me-down Sega Genesis. And this looked a good deal more complicated than *Gunstar Heroes*—a game that had already pushed Harper's skills to the limit, much to her friends' infinite amusement.

Lakshmi went right back to her computer and picked up where she left off while Harper was forced to sit awkwardly on the edge of her bed. "Go on, then. Hit me with it."

"Uh, right." Harper fumbled slightly as she pulled out her notebook, briefly dropping her pen to the floor. Everyone up to this point had been fairly agreeable, if light on information. This was the first time she'd come up against any resistance, and she'd allowed herself to get rusty. After a moment of further awkwardness, she had her pen back in hand. "Where were you the night of Autumn's death?"

She didn't even get a verbal answer. Lakshmi took one hand off her keyboard just long enough to gesture to her gaming setup before going right back to playing.

"Right, fair enough. Do you have anyone who can corroborate that?"

"That depends. Can you trace gamer handles and IP addresses? Unless you know who LiterallyFigurative or xX_PsychoKing_Xx are, no. Which is a shame, because I'm sure they'd be only too happy to tell anyone and everyone just how hard they were stomping my ass that night." She hammered the keys a bit harder. "Would you just fucking—Hey asshole! Stay on the objective, or go back to casual play."

"You obviously prefer getting to the point. You weren't the biggest fan of Autumn." Her pen hovered over the page, ready to jot down anything that might be of note here. She didn't even bother phrasing it as a question.

She clicked her mouse furiously. "No. Which apparently put me in the minority. Everyone thought the sun shone out her ass. Nobody's that perfect."

Harper quietly wrote "angry" next to Lakshmi's name. After a beat, she added "jealous?" Still, neither of those made her a killer. If anything, she raised a good point. Up until now, everyone had glowing reviews of Autumn. But she couldn't have been flawless all day, every day. What else was she, when the golden child persona dropped? "So what happened?"

"Yeah, because I'm gonna tell you that."

Her grip on the pen tightened momentarily, but she felt it starting to resist, threatening to break. She forced her hand to loosen back up before she snapped her poor writing utensil. "Look, I don't know Autumn. Right now she's just memories and public opinion. And I'm sure you know, pretty much everyone around here *does* think she was perfect. I doubt that's possible."

Lakshmi was silent for a while. The game on the screen had since gone to some kind of results page. Finally, she turned her chair around and looked at Harper with barely suppressed disgust. "Ugh, so...It happened at the wrap party last spring. Zooey and Izzy weren't able to make it. They'd just started dating Autumn, and I was—Look, I was into her. And she had two girlfriends, so I figured I was safe to shoot my shot. I managed to get as far as planting one on her lips before she gently pushed me away. She gave me the whole rundown. She appreciated it, but she wasn't interested, all that. She was being nice enough, but it just was such a slap in the face. Like she was willing to date those two, but I wasn't good enough? A burnout and a wallflower were more attractive to her than this hot piece?"

Jesus, even the girl who hated Autumn was just jaded because she got shot down at a party. "I'm sure you understand, this doesn't look great. She hurt you. Who's to say you didn't decide to hurt her right back?"

"And what are you going to do? You're not a cop, so you can't arrest me. You could put in an anonymous report, but this is all so fucking thin. You've got nothing. So how about you get the hell out of here?"

"We're not done yet."

Now that she had turned her attention away from the game, Lakshmi had a better chance to really scrutinize Harper. Her eyes seemed to be flitting everywhere and it was impossible to tell what pieces she was putting together. Not until she spoke again. "Holy shit, you're worse than a cop. Shouldn't you be out there hunting down monsters instead of harassing me?"

Yeesh. It had been awkward enough to hear Izzy use that word. But when someone in Lakshmi's position said it, the nuances felt even more tangled. And Harper did not feel at all prepared to try and unpack that. "My job right now isn't hunting mythics. I'm trying to find Autumn's killer. And I don't have a lot of reasons not to consider you a suspect."

"I'll give you more when you earn it, hunter. Come back when you've got actual proof."

"Oh, you can count on it." Harper stood from the bed and stormed out of the room, shutting the door a little harder than was probably necessary.

God, she needed to get back to her motel and go over everything. She needed answers, and she needed some fucking sleep.

Harper sat down on the uncomfortable motel bed and spread out everything she had so far. Of course there was her notebook, several pages filled to the brim with hastily scrawled text. Just for posterity, Esther had given her some brochures about Malcolm-Baptiste College. She had her list of suspects. Even though plenty of them seemed incapable of doing this, she needed to follow up on their alibis.

With Evan's tip-off about that mysterious phone call, Harper put in a request earlier that evening with a guild contact. Molly Chen was a blessing, capable of getting her hands on all sorts of official documents through her job as an administrator with the state police. She was good, efficient, and—most importantly—subtle.

She pulled up her name in her phone's address book and made the call.

"Harper, figured I might hear from you again."

"Sorry if this is too soon. I'm just anxious for anything useful at this point."

"Well, the good news is her phone records had already been combed through."

She groaned, already knowing exactly what the next part was going to be. "And the bad news is that the final number to contact her before the estimated time of death was a burner phone. How close am I?"

"Burner phone. Every goddamn time. I'm sorry, Harper, I know that's not what you wanted to hear."

"Well, it's not ideal. But it's not your fault, it's mine for wanting to get an interesting case."

There was a chuckle from the other end of the line. "That was your first mistake. There's a reason 'interesting times' are considered a curse. Anything else I can do to help? I hate coming up with nothing. Maybe there's another angle."

She tried to think if there was any other worthwhile lead she could have Molly follow up on. But Harper was dealing with a lot of loose threads and none of them seemed to fit her wheelhouse. "Not yet. But I'll be sure to pester you if something comes along. Thanks, Molly. You rock." Harper hung up and gently massaged her temples. That was that. No definite identity on the caller. Go figure.

The only other major lead she had at the moment was that... scent-hole? She'd never heard of any mythics being able to do something like that. But that didn't mean the answer didn't exist. She simply had to ask someone who was more versed in being a know-it-all. And she had the perfect know-it-all on speed dial.

The line rang twice before he picked up. "Harper. Is everything all right down there? Or have you already finished up?"

She looked down at her scattered documents and sighed. "No, Dad. There have been some major complications."

"Oh!" He chuckled softly and she braced herself for A Comment. "Sounds like you got that 'juicy' case you wanted after all."

"Ugh, yes, Dad, but I'd appreciate a cap on the sass for now. I need your help with something."

"I hope things haven't gone that bad that quickly. Do you need your mother and me to come down there and provide some backup?"

She rubbed the bridge of her nose aggressively. Her parents were great in a fight or helping with a wound. But this was still just an investigation. Her specialty. "No, I just need to know if there's anything out there that can disguise its scent. Like, fully and completely. Not with deodorant or chemicals. Something supernatural."

There was some shuffling on the other end of the line, and she could just imagine him pulling down some massive leather tome, flipping through it slowly. "That's actually a new one. Sounds like you've got a real chin-scratcher on your hands." More shuffling. "How'd you come upon this revelation? Human noses aren't exactly known for their sensitivity."

"I've…conscripted a local to help out."

"Nothing wrong with backup. Who'd you find?"

Her initial impulse was to leave him in the dark. Harper couldn't be sure her father would be nearly as accepting of an entire school of mythics. Hell, she wasn't even certain he'd approve of her working together with her initial target. That need for secrecy was canceled out by her need to show off. "Well, it turns out that there was a werewolf in town. But it's pretty clear she didn't do it."

There was another one of his famous pauses. "And what's the genesis of this iron-clad deduction?"

She ran down the basics with him, carefully avoiding any unnecessary information for the time being. Unless it became absolutely vital for him to know, she kept the truth behind Malcolm-Baptiste a secret.

"So, yeah. Scent-void. Very mysterious. Kind of at a loss here."

"Well done." The words hit her like a spear in the chest. As much as the two of them butted heads, sometimes you just wanted to hear that dear old Dad recognized something worthwhile in you. "You stayed your hand and analyzed the situation. You made the call, and it seems to be working out for you. That's good work, Harper." The praise was short-lived, and soon it was right back to business. "Unfortunately, I'm just as stumped as you are. I'll put in a few calls and let you know if I come up with anything useful. Beyond that, well, you know the grind. Boots on the ground, talk to people, take it all in. You can do this."

It was only when she spoke up and heard the hitch in her voice that she realized she was getting legitimately emotional. Stupid. "Yeah, thanks. Um, thanks. Yeah…"

"Good night, Harper."

"Mm-hmm, night, Dad." She flopped back against the pillows, groaning as she dug her palms into her eyes. No time to get hung up on that. She could worry about this surge of emotions later, when all this was done.

That left just one more piece of evidence. Harper picked up Autumn's journal and began slowly flipping through it. She did her best to only focus on names and events that really stuck out to her. A lot of it was the obvious stuff—fights she would get into with Izzy, makeup sex with Izzy, adorable things that Zooey had done.

Harper was doing her best to harden her heart to all of this. Autumn seemed like a good kid. The pain of losing her was palpable and painful. It was a tragedy. But the moment she let herself get stalled on that, she would lose all the necessary threads. Still, there was a definite splinter lodged in her chest while she turned back to the beginning and started perusing it fully.

The early entries didn't stick out to her much. Nothing much worthwhile.

It wasn't until May of that year when she finally saw something relating to her biggest suspect.

So. Lakshmi kissed me tonight??? It was kind of okay, obviously pretty sloppy and fumbling. We were both drunk, so I don't want that to be a comment on her skill level or anything. I don't know, she's cute, and she's really talented at all that complicated tech stuff behind the scenes! But...she can be pretty abrasive, even more than Izzy. I don't think it would be super healthy to date her. So I don't regret shooting her down. Mostly. She looked really hurt, but it's got to be for the best in the long run, right? How bad could it get?

Harper grimaced at that question. The answer was "pretty bad." She flipped past a few more entries until she saw her name again.

Okay, turns out things with Lakshmi can get pretty bad after all! We were never close, but we were usually pretty friendly. She doesn't talk to me anymore, and the few times I've tried to reach out to her she's been super bitchy. Jesus, that feels mean. But it's kind of true! I turned you down, big deal. Rejection is a part of life, girl. I know it sucks. Honestly, sometimes I get worried she's going to escalate beyond just being a jerk. If looks could kill...

Turns of phrase hardly seemed like a viable reason to accuse someone of murder, but Harper couldn't deny that Lakshmi was looking worse and worse the more she read. All she needed was another good piece of evidence and just maybe she would have an excuse to dig further.

Harper looked back toward the diary, but all the words began to dance and spin. Glancing at the clock, she saw that it was nearly midnight and sighed. She was going on thirty-six hours without sleep. There was work to be done, but she was no good to anyone exhausted like this.

Much to her dismay, Harper needed to sleep.

CHAPTER EIGHT

You couldn't quite say Harper was well-rested that next morning. A stiff mattress and thin pillows didn't exactly make for a comfortable night's sleep. But she'd slept in worse places, and this time she didn't have to worry about her father's horrendous snoring or her mother's sleep-talking.

She stepped out of the bathroom, toweling off from another mediocre but mercifully hot shower, fully intending to give Esther a call. But she'd been beaten to the punch. There was already a text on her phone waiting for her.

> *Hey! I dont know if you can*
> *even get texts on that fossil.*
> *Meet me at the diner in one*
> *hour?*
> *Breakfast/lunch/whatever*
> *on me.*

Ignoring the slight burn in her cheeks, she quickly texted her back.

yes jerkface :p
i do have unlimited messages
see you there

She rushed to dress in her usual apparel of jeans and a flannel, stepping into her ratty shoes and flinging on her leather jacket before rushing out the door.

Get a grip, idiot. It's not a date or anything. Just food for energy. To fuel the investigation. Get your head in the game. A girl died.

The previous day, exhaustion had gotten the better of Harper and she hadn't even really taken much note of the diner that Esther had brought her to. Now that she was a little more coherent, she took a brief moment to actually take it in. The building itself was long and blocky, fairly squat. The inside had one long bar that she imagined usually featured truckers and other loners. The rest of the space was taken up by booths and tables, and of course the requisite jukebox. The neon sign on the top explained in bright letters that this particular establishment was called The Landlocked Atlantis. Which she had to admit, as far as diners went, was a banger of a name.

When Harper entered, the bells hanging on the door jingled pleasantly. The booth she had shared with Esther the previous morning was empty, so she moved to claim it and slid into place.

Based on the text from Esther, there was probably still a good half hour before she would show up. Harper was glad for that, as she wanted a bit more time to go over Autumn's journal. Her reading the night before had been interrupted by her stupid flesh-prison's need for sleep.

Once she had a hot cup of coffee courtesy of Carol, she retrieved the journal and plunged right back in. There was a much more recent reference to her main suspect, and Harper dog-eared the page before giving it a proper reading.

At least Lakshmi knows how to be subtle about her growing hatred for me. She does her best to bottle it up whenever my girlfriends aren't around. But that just makes it worse when we run into each other alone. Sometimes I'll see her hand start to flex, and I find myself wondering if she's about to slap me in the face or put some kind of curse on me. I'm not sure which would be worse. I know I don't help things any. I don't know how to rebuild a bridge once it's been burned. If someone gets on my case, then I just have to return fire.

Why do people like me again?

So, anyway, every time she digs in, I get defensive. Today, I escalated without even thinking about it. I told Lakshmi she was psycho, that she had some kind of obsession with me. I didn't know what else to do. She had to see that she was being completely ridiculous! It was a drunken kiss and a fumbled confession at a party. We've all had those. But part of growing up is taking your knocks and moving on with life. You don't spend months acting like an asshole over something that small. And she didn't even say anything in return. She just seethed and stormed off. I don't know, I hope that's the end of it. I don't care if she keeps hating me. I just wish she'd stop making a thing out of it.

Harper paused and read the passage back over again, then put a big bracket around it with her pen. She flipped through the rest of the pages until the sudden cutoff point, but the girl's name never came up again. Maybe Lakshmi really had let things go after that. Or maybe she reached a breaking point and did something monumentally stupid.

Something else stuck out to her as she gave the final pages a closer reading. "Huh…"

Kind of a weird night. I was finishing up work over in admin, and I went to say bye to Imogen. And she's at her desk, wallowing and drinking wine. Like, a lot of wine! So obviously I ask her what's up. She tells me she's been thinking about Jackson, and how much she misses him. And I don't know if that's a brother or a husband or an ex or whatever. So I sit down and ask her about him. Guess he died in an accident or something, she was vague. At some point she fishes out an extra glass and pours me some of her wine, and I'm sure as hell not gonna turn down free booze.

I'm pretty good with people, I guess. Everyone seems to like me, though I don't always know why. Guess I know how to wear a lot of masks. The joys of being a shapeshifter. Anyway, I'm studying her pretty intensely. And I realize that she's not just sad—like, there's a part of her that's kinda angry. Which makes sense, grief is fucking complicated. After a second, she snaps out of it and gives me this sad little smile. She's all "Sorry, Autumn, you probably don't care about an old widow's moping."

The more she read, the more curious Harper got. She had promised to meet up with Dr. White that afternoon. That had mostly been a lie to get the administrator off her case. Now she wondered if there might be something there after all.

I tell her I don't mind, and that maybe we could talk about her husband again sometime. Sure, it was a little weird at first, chatting with my college's president about her dead husband. But it was pretty obvious that Imogen was in need of someone to be a listening ear. It must be lonely at the top...
Okay, yes, the free drinks didn't hurt either.

"Harper!"
Her head snapped up as Esther greeted her and sat down across from her with a bright smile. It was almost overwhelming how much that friendly face brightened up her morning. She casually closed up the journal and put it away. "Mornin', sunshine. Don't you look perky?"
Esther's glow seemed to increase for just a moment, and she shifted a bit in her seat. "Grabbed a shower before coming over. Didn't want us wasting any time."
"I like the energy, hold on to that. We're gonna need it."
Carol returned with a refill of her coffee and beamed at Esther. "Y'all need some time?" She glanced subtly between the two of them, though the implication wasn't fully lost on Harper and she felt her face grow warm yet again.
Since Esther was clearly the kind of customer to consistently get the same thing, she just glanced across the table with an eyebrow raised, implying the unasked, *Are you ready?*

"If it ain't broke, don't fix it. I'll do that hash thing again. Uh, please and thank you," Harper hurried to tag on. Like it was some kind of code phrase.

"And I'll just get the usual, please and thank you," Esther chirped.

Carol nodded and turned to bring their orders to the cook, slipping out a very quick, "Be back with that in two shakes, you girls have fun!" Harper chose once again to ignore any implications.

"So!" Esther bounced just a little in her seat, obviously excited by all this. "Got any new developments?"

"Kind of? I caught up with Zooey and Izzy after we looked at the clearing last night. We spent a while interviewing practically the whole theatre department. I think I might have found someone I can comfortably consider a suspect. But she's not willing to talk to me unless I can hit her with something concrete." She ran back over the evening, some of it still a sleep-deprived blur. "There was something else, though. I didn't really piece it together at the time, but that whole party spot was fairly undisturbed. It seems like whatever happened, Autumn might have gone out there to meet someone she knew, and…Well, it was probably pretty fast. Izzy seemed sure she could hold her own if there had been a fight."

Some of Esther's excitement drained a little. "Yeah. Two steps forward, one step back."

"Shit, we should be so lucky. Two steps forward, then three back. Still, it's not all bad. They also helped me check out Autumn's room. I managed to find a little hiding spot behind a loose cinder block. She was keeping a journal in there."

"Oh! Wow, mysterious. Was there anything useful inside?"

This felt like a bit of a gray area. It wasn't right to just go revealing Autumn's secrets to everyone. But the journal made it obvious Lakshmi was a serious thorn in her side. And it wasn't painting the college's president in the best light, either. Esther seemed fond of the woman, and she didn't want to go and ruin her impression of Imogen. She opted for omission instead. "Still going over it all. There was a lot, and it can take a while parsing out the useful information. Plus I kinda…passed out last night before I could finish." Technically that was true.

"Yeah, I can imagine you were pretty wiped out. Did Zooey or Izzy have anything else for you?" She idly propped her chin in her upturned hand.

Oh, ya know, Izzy just threatened to make me bleed out every pore in my body if anything bad happens to you. And something bad will probably happen to you because we're chasing down a killer capable of disguising their presence and opening up a girl's chest in no time flat. A creature that eats hearts? I'm at a loss, and if you get hurt, I'm not gonna live long enough to regret my failure.

She buried that whole internal monologue deep down and shrugged. "Nah, after that I just went back to the motel and followed up on a few leads. A contact from the guild was going over Autumn's phone records, only to find out she was called from a burner phone. I checked in with my dad too, but even he doesn't know of any mythics that can disguise their scent. Called it a 'chin-scratcher.'"

"Oh, right, I guess it's kind of a family business, huh? So he's a hunter too. Are you two close?" she asked curiously.

She rubbed her neck a bit, trying to decide how best to answer that. It was complicated. "Hmm, well. I guess? I mean, I love the guy. But he was also my tutor and my drill instructor. We spar a lot, literally and metaphorically. We drive each other crazy. I'm way closer to my mom."

Esther's head canted to the side slightly and she smiled fondly. "Been there. Like I said, Dad trained all of us to keep our other side in check. Sometimes he could be a little intense about it."

Carol eventually returned with their food. They spent a while in comfortable silence, tucking into their meals. But the lingering curiosity prompted Esther to resume asking questions. "What about your mom, is she with your guild too?"

"Yeah. She's a Stave."

"Sorry, she's a what?"

"Oh, right. Guess that was kind of inside baseball, huh? Basically, people tend to find niches, and there's big, important terms for each of them. A Stave is anyone who specializes in magic—my mom is a druid. Plants and animals and all that. Dad's a Sword, which means he does all the heavy grunt stuff, and he's especially skilled in fighting. I'm a Knife, more focused on stealth and investigation. Scrolls are your research nerds, Keys are spies and hackers. You get the idea."

Surprisingly, Esther started to giggle a little. "Sounds kinda hokey. But kinda cool, too." There was just a tinge of admiration in her voice that sent a little shiver along Harper's spine. "Maybe I'll join your guild too," she said, and it didn't seem as though she was completely kidding. "Ooh, what do you think they would call someone like me? Like a…a Fang, or a Claw! Maybe a Nose?"

As Esther said that, it hit Harper that the girl was talking about something that simply wasn't done. And that wasn't because the Silversmiths had something explicitly written in their rules prohibiting mythics from joining the organization. It was simply a byproduct of their very nature. Hunters were humans, and mythics were their own thing. Sure, the guild could help rehabilitate or aid mythics. But guild agents had always been humans. Cases like this, where Harper was receiving help from a werewolf, were simply rare instances of assistance. Which was a shame, because she'd been finding Esther to be a real boon. This kind of thing *should* have been far more common, and the fact that it wasn't, spoke to some baked-in prejudice that the guild hadn't yet taken the time to examine within itself.

Come to think of it, Harper still hadn't taken the time to examine those prejudices in herself, either. She was trying, really. But the more she learned, the more biases she realized she had to correct. And not for nothing, finding out the truth about Malcolm-Baptiste had brought it all into sharp relief. It was a constant struggle.

Harper wasn't in the mood to dash Esther's hopes, so she tempered her answer as best as she could. "Hey, after all this shakes out, who knows? Anything's possible, I guess. But, y'know, don't quit your day job. Literally, hunting doesn't pay for shit."

Esther just continued to laugh at that, rolling her eyes. "Sure, because there's so many options for high-paying jobs with my degree."

"Oh yeah. You're...religious studies, right?"

"Yep. Despite being literally cursed for our religious fervor, my family just kept right on worshipping. Dad's a pastor, and I think he hoped I'd do the same. Honestly, it's—" She stopped herself for a moment, gnawing on her lower lip in thought before continuing after some kind of internal conversation. "I don't always agree with everything he preaches. But I find a lot of religion itself fascinating. How it ties together culture and faith, and how it's so private and yet so public, and—" She stopped herself once again, quickly shaking her head. "Gah, I'm doing it again. I'll shut up."

Had you asked Harper a day or two before, she'd have most likely said that all that religious stuff just didn't do anything for her. But Esther's passion and enthusiasm were just contagious enough that she found herself suddenly caring quite a bit. And there was a bit of overlap between her own interests and what Esther was talking about. "I asked, didn't I? So, what kind of jobs do you get with that kind of degree?"

She gave a wry smile. "Well. A lot of religious leaders tend to study it. So I guess I'm kind of cruelly keeping my father's hopes alive. But there's also plenty of academic potential. I could get a masters, even a PhD. I could write a book, maybe become a professor myself."

Harper's head tilted a bit at that. "Wait. So...you go to school, and you major in something so that you can go to school *again*. And you keep schooling hard enough until you become the teacher for a bunch of new students. Isn't that, like, mega recursive?"

"Sometimes knowledge is its own reward. We've reached the point in sapience where we have the luxury to just sit around and think about things really hard."

Most of what Harper knew about academic, studious types came from guild Scrolls. And their research always had very practical, real-world applications. They passed along the information to other hunters, who then used that to improve their ability to meet with, or deal with, supernatural beings. But the concept of learning something for the sake of pure curiosity wasn't totally foreign either. Sometimes she did find herself rather enthralled with the nature of mythics, not because it would make her a better hunter, but simply because they were so fascinating to her. "You've got me there. Well, whatever floats your boat, Professor Talbot." Without really thinking, Harper started idly swinging her legs when she suddenly felt her foot brush against something, and it took her a moment to realize she had bumped Esther's foot.

Before she got a chance to apologize, Esther countered the movement and lightly rubbed their ankles together, maintaining steady eye contact. "Your support is appreciated," she said with a light chuckle, her umber eyes shimmering with more of that playfulness, daring Harper to do…something.

Well, fine then. You didn't become a hunter without being at least a little hard-headed and stubborn. If Esther was going to taunt her, then Harper was going to call her bluff. It was time to tackle the question she'd been pondering for nearly twelve hours now. "Can I ask something kinda personal? No pressure if you're not comfortable answering."

Esther eyed her curiously as she sliced another chunk from her steak and popped it in her mouth. "Ask away."

"Izzy mentioned that you're the one who convinced your church to put out that rainbow flag. I guess I just wanted to know—"

"Here's the check, ladies!" Without warning, Carol planted the bill on the table between the two of them, interrupting Harper's flow and disrupting her confidence.

Too embarrassed to start over, she opted to just reach for the slip of paper, but Esther beat her to the punch, dropping a few bills onto the table with a grin. "Ah-ah. My turn, remember?" she said, which Harper silently hoped meant they would continue taking turns, so to speak. A dumb thought, a predictable thought, but there it was. "Now, what were you saying?"

Whatever momentum Harper had been building up, it was long gone now. She decided to abort her stupid line of questioning and get back to work. "Uh, nothing, it's stupid. C'mon, I wanna get back to campus so we can talk to this friend of yours that can unlock the secret of our anti-scent mystery." She quickly shimmied her way out of the booth and looped her bag over her shoulder, rushing for the door a little faster than was probably necessary.

"So I'm presuming you know someone who does dirt magic?" Harper asked with a sly grin as Esther led her down the dormitory hallway.

"Alchemist, actually. And look, I know that you're the big scary hunter with way more experience in the world than me. But if you try to tell me there's dirt magic, I'm going to actually slap you."

"Oh, sure," Harper said, as casually deadpan as she could manage. "Dirtmancers are a rare offshoot of lithomages. They're niche, but they're extremely helpful under the right circumstances."

Esther stopped walking and stared at her for a few seconds before her face contorted into a forced frown that tried and failed to hide the amusement underneath. "Oh, come on, Harper!" She reached out, no doubt intending to deliver a playful mock-slap to Harper's cheek. But reflexes honed from years of training kicked in, and Harper expertly caught Esther's wrist instead. "Hey!" She gasped with a bit of suppressed laughter before making a second attempt with her other hand, which met the exact same fate.

It was only now, as Harper had Esther firmly immobilized, that she realized what she was doing and her face began to burn. "Shit, sorry. Old habits." Despite apologizing, she hadn't actually released her hold. "That was a dumb joke, and you gave me proper warning. Should've just let you slap me."

"No, it's okay, I don't mind." After a beat, Esther seemed to catch up to what she'd just said and stammered out a clarification. "I-I mean, no harm done, y'know?"

"Good. I don't want to hurt you."

"You've made that abundantly clear." Esther was finally able to pull her wrists free once Harper relaxed her grip—though she did so slowly, almost hesitantly. "Don't worry, I'm tougher than I look."

"You've made that abundantly clear," Harper said with a soft chuckle, then made a show of looking back up and down the hallway. "Anyway. Which dorm do we need?"

"Right. They live just over here." Esther led the rest of the way down the hall, pulling up short at one door in particular. "Oh, and, just some warning. Rowan can be a little abrasive, but they're a good person."

"I'm sensing a pattern with your friends," Harper mused.

She just shrugged and turned to knock on the door.

"Enter," came the voice from the other side.

Esther offered a knowing smirk and raised her eyebrows before opening the door and stepping inside with Harper in tow.

In a way, it was sort of impressive that this student had managed to turn their dorm into something that almost resembled the kind of lab an alchemist would have. Lots of little vials filled with bubbling liquids and wall hangings with alchemical symbols on them and shelves stuffed with Tupperware full of ingredients. Hunched over at a desk was Rowan. They were the very embodiment of the word *haggard*. Judging by the worn-out coffee maker and the empty energy drink cans nearby, this budding alchemist got most of their fuel from caffeine and other chemicals, which tracked for someone in their field of study. Their clothing was apparently only there for its functional purpose—plain shirt, worn-out jeans, Coke-bottle glasses.

It made sense to bring this to an alchemist. There was an easy pitfall when it came to the uncanny. You assumed that everything was mystical and ineffable, but that was just leftover spiritualism from the Dark Ages. Enlightenment had a fascinating dual effect on the world. For those stuck in the mundane world, it only further solidified how unnecessary superstitious beliefs were.

But for those familiar with the entwined worlds, it revealed the threads of sense hiding beneath the seemingly inexplicable.

Rowan had already taken the dirt that Esther had brought them, dividing it up between multiple smaller glass containers. To some, they added a strange liquid compound. To others, they added other sundry materials that Harper was utterly clueless about. On one container, they added nothing at all, only drawing a few glyphs on the glass in permanent marker. She could have sworn she recognized one or two of them, but without proper study, she would never have been able to say with any certainty what they meant.

"I've never seen this side of you before, Esther. It's fascinating," they muttered softly, picking up one of the vials and giving it a gentle shake, then holding it up to the light and inspecting it more closely.

"I suppose. This is definitely the first time I've ever brought anyone grave dirt in an effort to solve a murder." She shrugged humbly, glancing down at her feet. "Feels good to be useful. Instead of just giving 'thoughts and prayers,' ya know?"

Rowan gave a low chuckle as they repeated the shaking and lifting process with another vial. "Well, I'm glad to hear you've come to your senses, at least a little bit. How much longer before you've given up entirely on the Big Man Upstairs?"

"Wow, tell her how you really feel," Harper said, just a tad more defensive than she'd meant for it to sound.

Esther just giggled softly. "Oh, don't worry, this is nothing new. I think Rowan asks me every other week when I'm going to become an atheist. And I continue to remind them that I can turn into a wolf during the full moon. Believing in God is hardly the strangest thing about my life."

"And then I remind her that most 'supernatural' phenomena have observable and consistent rules. Besides, most mythics don't claim to be the creator of everything, with dominion over all creation."

Harper was happy to stand back and watch this playful banter for a moment. It was just kind of…nice, to see more of Esther and what her life looked like before some asshole hunter came around and nearly killed her. It was good to see that she had a full existence, and friends and beliefs and—

Oh no. Oh crap.

What had started as a "you're cute" crush was quickly turning into a "I want to know you better" crush. She'd caught a whiff of that whenever Esther started getting all enthusiastic about her studies. But now it was fully coming down on her what she'd blundered into. That was not good. Harper would much rather get shot down by a damsel in distress than actually fall for someone at this point. It was preferable to yet another bout of heartbreak.

Quick, change the subject.

Do something, anything!

"So. What's the verdict? Anything showing up?" The question had come out just a bit too desperate, and probably made her sound more amateur than anything.

"Okay, well, this is probably gonna take longer than five minutes. Either make yourself comfortable or go find something to entertain yourself with. This is not a process for the impatient."

Harper glanced at her phone and shrugged. It was officially afternoon, which meant it was time to go follow up with a college administrator. "I've got a date with Imogen White anyway, so I guess I'll be back after that."

For just a split second, a look crossed Esther's face, though Harper didn't know exactly how to read it. So she did her best to ignore that before she ended up utterly overthinking it.

Rowan just chuckled and actually looked up from their work for a moment with a shit-eating grin. "Ahh, you must feel like the belle of the ball right now. Some alone time with Dr. White. I hope she's gentle." They then did something with their eyebrows that was kind of impressive but mostly infuriating—raising one, lowering the other, then switching them back and forth to create a kind of wiggly effect.

Harper slapped them, hard, on the shoulder. "Jackass." She turned and looked more seriously at Esther for a moment. "I'll call you when I'm out."

"Yeah, of course," she muttered, sounding strangely bashful.

Not wanting to push her luck, especially after some of the strange moments they'd had already, she made her way out of Rowan's room. But Harper had barely made it halfway down the hall when she heard the door open and shut again, followed by Esther calling out after her. "Harper, wait!"

By the time she'd turned around, the other girl had already jogged up to her, looking slightly distressed. "Everything okay?"

"It's because I'm gay."

"Wait, what?"

"The—the flag. I came out to the congregation last year, and they got that new sign made and added the rainbow flag as a show of solidarity. I just…wanted you to know that. Since it sounded like you were curious. And…now you know."

"Oh." Jesus, what was she even supposed to say in this situation? Hooray? Yippee? Huzzah? Let's make out? "Wow, okay, cool. Thank you. For telling me. Um, I'm gonna go see Dr. White now, bye!" Whirling around, Harper awkwardly speed-walked toward the stairwell, looking to put as much distance between herself and that awkward moment as she possibly could.

Holy shit. She's gay. Holy shit.

Okay, let's calm down, that doesn't necessarily mean anything.

Why else is a cute girl going to explicitly tell you that she's gay, genius? Oh, and by the way, the correct response in that scenario is, "I'm gay too," but I guess it's a little late for that. Still, who knows, maybe once we have everything wrapped up here, we might actually find the courage to ask her out. Now there's a true test of our mettle.

Last I checked, we were explicitly not going there. Avoiding the pain and all that.

How about we consider it…exposure therapy.

Harper, you predictable bitch.

Stepping into the administrative building, Harper approached a desk being manned by a kid with pale skin and a mop of black hair. He glanced up from whatever project he was working on, looking like a deer caught in headlights. "Um, hello, w-w-welcome! How can I help you?"

In spite of the nerves and the stutter, he seemed to be doing his best. Harper wondered for a moment why they had put this poor student on the reception desk when she remembered Autumn's file. A girl that charming and popular, she almost definitely worked the front desk whenever she was on duty. With her gone, others had to take over. She felt bad for him and looked for any way to make this interaction as blissfully brief as possible, for his sake.

"Dr. White invited me to stop by. Is she available?"

He nodded a few times. "Yes, she's got open office hours right now. I d-don't think anyone is in at the moment." He gestured down the hallway to her right. "Third d-door on the left. You can't miss it."

Harper offered a grateful nod and kept moving, letting him get back to his work.

Something about the concept of freely entering the woman's workspace felt…unnatural. Sebastian never had "open office hours." If he was in his office, you didn't bug him without prior authorization. Everything about this was foreign.

The door was open, so she poked her head in, glancing around for a moment to try to take everything in. It was shockingly nice. The walls were painted that particular brand of off-white that somehow managed to feel extra warm and inviting. There were multiple plants on the floor, on shelves, and one hanging in the window. Framed degrees hung on the wall, along with some motivational posters and artwork.

Imogen White was idly clicking away at her keyboard, but eventually she took notice of her visitor. She glanced over toward the door with a professional smile. "Ah, there you are. Harper, right? Please, come on in, make yourself at home."

Harper pushed the door closed behind her, then planted herself in one of the plush chairs across the desk.

Once she was settled, Imogen's smile turned more casual—though there was a slight glimmer of something in her eyes. "So. You're a Silversmith?"

Fuck.

One-hit KO.

I'm screwed.

Her face must have displayed a reaction as visceral as she felt in her chest, because Imogen began to laugh softly. "It's all right. I was in the guild for a while, back in the day."

All the tension in Harper's body instantly retreated, swiftly replaced with a wave of confusion. "Wait, seriously?"

"I married into it. My husband, Jackson, was a Sword. He grew up with all that. Like you, I'm guessing."

Right, that name she got from Autumn's journal. The details were getting filled in now.

"It seems somehow rude to ask what happened to him."

"I imagine you can probably figure out the broad strokes." Imogen studied her for a moment, then nodded her head as she seemed to reach a conclusion. "You must be Calliope and Sebastian's kid. I can see the family resemblance."

She sat up a bit at that, surprised that Dr. White could pin her so easily. "You know them?"

Imogen leaned back in her chair, shrugging her shoulders. "Met them once, maybe twice. Jackson and I even visited that commune. Are they still living out there with all those hippies and tree-huggers?"

"Hey, be nice, I was born and raised on that commune." She was flushing, God help her. If anything was going to help Harper get past the realization that she was developing any genuine feelings for someone, it was focusing on something much baser. Like being teased by a hot, older woman, for example.

Throwing her hands up, Imogen gave a much more gentle laugh. "Easy there, kiddo. Not judging. Every hunter has to make the lifestyle work for them. Anyway, I didn't call you in here just to poke and prod about your parents. You're here investigating Autumn Temple's death, right? Such a shame, she was a good student, a good actress, and a good worker."

"Were you close to Autumn?" She watched the woman carefully after posing the question. She needed to see it, to know if there really was something fishy going on here.

A look of pure grief crossed her face, and Imogen swallowed hard. "Somewhat. We talked on occasion about life. She would tell me about her girlfriends, and I would tell her about Jackson.

I don't think it happened more than maybe a handful of times. But she never seemed to be suffering through the interactions. Though obviously she appreciated the fact that I let her drink in here." Her sadness gave way to a bit of fond laughter.

Imogen wasn't exactly helping her case at the moment. Sure, it sounded like she genuinely missed Autumn, and it seemed less likely that she had any hand in the girl's disappearance. But plying her student with alcohol so the girl would play the part of her therapist was...pretty skeevy. Still, that was none of her business, no matter how sketchy it was. There'd be time to unpack that later on. "Sorry, I'm sure you understand. Gotta follow all the trails I can."

"Only too well." Imogen gathered herself a bit, tapping her finger against her chin thoughtfully for a moment. "So, you assumed Esther was the culprit, right up until the moment you actually met her and realized she couldn't hurt a fly. Guess your mom and dad taught you to be cautious and not go murdering every single mythic you run into." Just for the briefest of seconds, Harper thought she detected something in Imogen's voice. Pride, probably, or hope for the future generation. "That puts you back at square one."

"My first lead didn't pan out, but I'm not dead in the water yet."

"Ahh, the eternal hope of the young. Hold on to that for as long as you can. Growing up, you start to get pretty jaded." Her sadness started to resurface a bit, and Harper could see the exhaustion there, even as Imogen tried to hide it.

"Not planning on it any time soon. Still, I bet you're not totally tapped. If you've got anything rattling around in there, I'm happy to hear it."

"Well, unfortunately we don't keep a record of what everyone here at Malcolm-Baptiste is, mythically speaking. We request that students self-report if their particular heritage or condition might create issues around the school. Nobody *has* *to* reveal if they're Fae or Fiend. So it's hard to give you a full profile of who the most likely suspects might be. But..."

"But?" Harper repeated, leaning forward, intrigued.

"You might want to ask your new friend Esther about the group she runs. I believe it's called the Repentance Club? It was registered as some kind of religious club, but I've heard rumors that it's more of a support group for students who are especially dangerous. Esther's heart is no doubt in the right place. I'm sure she wants a space where students can be honest about their impulses and the difficulties that come along with repressing them. But, well, supposing someone is having trouble keeping a lid on those desires, getting a thrill out of hearing all those secrets…You understand?"

That seemed like the kind of thing Esther probably should have mentioned. Yeah, anonymity was important, but also a girl had died. She was going to have to investigate this. "Thanks for everything, Imogen. It's kinda nice to know there's another Silversmith around. I'll try not to pester you too much with this stuff, you've got your own thing going on."

"Oh, don't worry about that, dear. I have to say, it's kind of a thrill to be in the game again, if only tangentially." She gave a wistful little sigh. "Yeah. Maybe it's not so bad for me to brush off the old instincts. I know how tough it is, working on your own."

Not wanting to give away just how much help her new friends were giving her, she kept mum about how much she was presently "on her own."

"Here." She grabbed a business card from her desk and scribbled something down on the back before passing it to Harper. A phone number. "Call me if you need anything."

"I appreciate it." With that, she stood up and gave a casual little wave to the president/former hunter. "Thanks again. I'll get out of your hair now." As Harper exited the building, she contemplated the conversation she'd need to have. If Imogen was right, this could be a huge lead. But it was also bound to be a really sensitive subject.

Crap.

CHAPTER NINE

Sitting on an uncomfortable metal bench outside the administrative building, Harper fiddled with her phone but found it difficult to push the button to actually call Esther. She needed to know more about this group, but that meant pressing her about it. There was no way in hell this was going to be a fun conversation. But finally, she found the strength to actually do it, and nervously brought the phone to her ear. "Hey."

"Hey! How'd it go?"

"Enlightening. Turns out there's more to your president than meets the eye. She kinda knows why I'm here now, and, uh…She told me to ask you about the Repentance Club?"

Things on the other end went quiet for a moment—not the imposing, aggressive silence of her father, but something altogether different. This was a girl forcing herself to choose her words carefully. "Dr. White told you to ask me that?"

"Yeah, she said—"

"And you think that's a good idea? 'Hey guys, I know things are tense around here right now and a lot of you have really complicated feelings about humans, so I brought a freaking hunter to meet you!' I bet that would go over great." She scoffed. Esther Talbot scoffed! "It's a safe space, Harper. But that safety is tenuous. And introducing someone who does what you do could be disastrous."

"Esther..." She started softly but was uncertain how she should continue. "I have no intention of going in there to accuse everyone I see of doing this. But other than some dirt we gave to Rowan, we're a little light on leads at the moment. But fine. It's your support group, so it's your call."

"You're right, it *is* my call. You're an outsider here, Harper, and sticking your nose in things has consequences."

Her chest hurt. Her *everything* hurt. Harper had been so delighted to find a place like this, to discover there was an entire community of mythics just going about their lives. She wanted to see more, know more. And Esther had just zeroed in on the one thing she absolutely did not want to hear in that moment. She was a visitor to this place, a fetishist, and a *threat*. When the hunt was over, she would leave and never see Malcolm-Baptiste or any of these people again. Of course it was stupid to think she might ever be able to fit in here. But every now and then, it was really nice to hold on to stupid hopes.

There was a long, drawn-out sigh and a few more seconds of silence before Esther spoke again. "Well...Ugh, I mean I only *started* the group, and I facilitate discussions. But a decision like this, it's too big for me to make alone. So...*God*, this is such a bad idea."

"All right, all right, forget I asked. I'm sure something else will crop up. I don't want to sow a bunch of discord in a group of students who are already having a hard time."

"I'll put it in the group chat and let them decide. Okay? Just don't expect any miracles."

She shook her head slowly, deciding to bite back the comment about Jesus-girl being so realistic toward miracles. "Wait, what's a group chat?"

"You are truly a mysterious creature. How do you live?" It was almost a disappointment to hear Esther return to some of her earlier biting sarcasm. The two of them had been developing a rapport together that created a warmer atmosphere. Sure, Esther would occasionally do a little playful teasing, but Harper had really stepped in it now, and things were no longer light and fun.

"I live on a commune," she reminded her quickly.

There was a soft jingling noise on the other end of the line. "Touché. Look, I just got a message from Rowan. Meet me at their dorm."

Harper massaged her temples and nodded. "Yeah. See you in a few." She flipped the phone closed a little harder than she meant to, groaning pathetically. "Smooth, Zeale."

"A mage did it."

Harper's eyebrows shot up. So did Esther's. "And the margin for error is…?"

Rowan smirked and held up one of the small vials of grave dirt. "I mean, of course there are things I could be missing, or factors I'm not accounting for. But you came to me for my opinion, and my opinion is 'mage.' This is important information, intentionally obscured through magical means. I found traces of mana being manipulated to cloud the senses."

Harper hummed thoughtfully as she took the vial from them, staring intently at it as if it would suddenly provide her with any direct insight. Obviously, it would not. "Sorry, not doubting you, but I have to make sure I exhaust everything. Magic comes in a lot of flavors. There are mythics that can manipulate mana too."

"Yeah, but the details spell it out a little clearer. Here." Rowan grabbed a nearby notebook and flipped to an empty page, then picked up a stray pen. With a steady hand, they drew a cluster of straight lines, all intersecting at roughly the same angle, as though Rowan was practicing a bit of hatching for a drawing. Next to this, they created a much more intricate pattern of swirling lines that broke off into more and more fractal branches. "Humans have to force mana into doing what they want. Even your crunchiest earth mage still has to do a lot of manual weaving to cast a spell. So the energy gets forced into these very neat patterns. Mythics use mana through much more natural means. You end up with complicated magical lines that fragment and split into chaotic subdivisions." Rowan gestured once again with the vial of dirt. "The magic residue in this was forced into position. Violently so. That's the work of a wizard, a witch, a druid, whatever. You're looking for a human."

"And thus, man is once again shown to be the true monster," Harper said softly, somewhere in that gray area between extreme irony and extreme sincerity. It made a kind of twisted sense that the person killing a supernatural being was a fellow human.

Esther's head snapped toward Harper and she furrowed her brow. "Really? Can you not, right now?"

Oof. Harper had really jammed her hand in a hornet's nest. So much for Imogen's Very Helpful Tip. All it had gotten her was awkward tension with her temporary partner. "Anyway. That narrows things down significantly. How many students here are magic-users?"

They cast their eyes up to the ceiling in thought for a moment or two. "Can't be more than a couple dozen."

Esther gnawed on her lower lip for a moment. "Wait, but… The way she was attacked. Is there magic that can do that?"

"Magic can do anything." Deadpan and unenthusiastic, Rowan held up their hands and wiggled their fingers in what could only technically be called jazz hands, despite the pure lack of jazziness. "You could create a small concentration of concussive force in the chest and then push out. Or do it more surgically, peel things back, open things up, all that. But, without a look at what happened to Autumn directly, I can't say for sure, ya know? Could be a magic-user was just the one covering the tracks of whoever actually did it. There might be multiple villains here. Still, I hope this helps."

Harper nodded and gave Rowan a pat on the head. "Ya did good, kid. Thanks."

They instantly swatted her hand away. "Hush. Oh, and hey, Harper?"

"Yeah?"

"If you find anything else weird?"

"Yeah?"

"Take it to someone else. I'm not your personal CSI lab. You want my help again, it's gonna cost you."

She couldn't help but grin a little bit at that. Rowan was an asshole, but that kinda made them likable in her book. "I'll stop by the bank and grab a stack of twenties."

"Now you're speaking my language."

Esther had remained eerily silent through this bit of light banter, and they left the room in an uncomfortable silence. This continued all the way down the stairs and into the foyer of the dormitory.

Harper needed to get away from here. She had something she needed to do anyway, and it would give Esther some time to cool off. It was for the best. Definitely. Lightly clearing her throat didn't quite manage to clear the nerves from her system, but she pressed on regardless. "I know at least one mage I need to go interrogate. Do...Um—"

"Go ahead." Christ, she still sounded so bitter. "Classes are going to be picking back up tomorrow. I have a few things I should take care of. Stuff I let slide since—" Esther sighed. "This whole thing was a really bad idea, huh?"

"No way. If you hadn't been there to save my ass, Izzy probably would have attacked me. Something really bad could have happened. I wouldn't have met Imogen, I wouldn't have been able to interview Autumn's entire department, I wouldn't have a suspect. You stuck your neck out for me even after I told you to leave it alone, and I'm better for it."

And now I'm asking you to stick your neck out for me a second time. I pushed my luck and now everything is weird. I'm sorry.

Just say it, jackass. Tell her you're sorry.

Two words. It's not that hard.

It actually was that hard, and the words died in Harper's throat. Like she was hoping Esther would suddenly turn out to be a mind reader.

Esther nodded. "I'll call you. Y'know, if...Well, when the club makes a decision. Good luck, Harper. I really hope you've got the right person."

"So do I." She knew how to read between the lines here. If she wrapped this up, she wouldn't have to barge her way into the Repentance Club. She could go back to the commune, and Esther would be free of the asshole hunter that had turned her life upside down. Yeah, that was definitely what she was thinking.

Without another word, Esther pushed her way through the front door, leaving Harper alone. That was for the best. Totally.

Feeling miserable and guilty, Harper started for the stairs. This next bit wasn't going to be much fun either. But at least it would make for a decent distraction. She climbed back up to the second floor and found room 203, knocking firmly. The door eventually swung open to reveal Lakshmi once again seated in front of her behemoth gaming rig. Judging by the gestures she was making in the air, she hadn't even bothered to get up, manipulating mana to operate the handle so she wouldn't have to pause.

"Figured you'd show sooner or later. Was just hoping it wouldn't be sooner."

"Hey, you're the one who said to come back when I had solid proof."

"Ah, so you've brought the recording of me killing her, and the letter in my handwriting confessing to the crime?"

She didn't wait for permission to move over and sit down on the edge of her bed again. Harper pulled the journal and one of the vials of dirt out of her bag and held them both up, though Lakshmi wasn't even bothering to look in her direction. So she just launched into it anyway. "You told me things were awkward between you and Autumn after your botched confession." Fuck, she was letting her own issues color things. "Botched confession" was so unfair. Too late now. "But it was a little more than that. Things got so bad, she was starting to worry you might have put some kind of hex on her."

Lakshmi just grunted and continued to play her game, almost as if Harper wasn't even there.

She pushed on regardless. "Someone at the scene the night she died used magic to disguise their presence. And right now, the only person who had an issue with Autumn is also a witch. So let's try this again. Anything you wanna tell me?"

"Bullshit..." was all she got in reply, muttered through clenched teeth.

Harper was getting tired of this. She was already in a foul mood, and Lakshmi's attitude was just making it worse. She stood and stepped closer, whirling the chair around. The girl tried to keep the chair rotating all the way around, but Harper stopped her with a firm hand on her shoulder, using her other hand to whip Lakshmi's massive headphones off and toss them aside. "You wouldn't even have to be there in person. A lock of hair and an effigy are all you would need to burst her open like that. Then you can go investigate at your leisure. Maybe take her heart for yourself since she wouldn't give it to you? Another easy spell and no one would ever know you were there."

"Holy shit, what has gotten into you?" She struggled, but a nerdy little witch had nothing on a girl with training like Harper.

"Been getting real tired of the runaround, Lakshmi. Admit to what you did and this all goes a lot smoother. But please, try me. My afternoon took an unfortunate turn, and I'm itching to let loose."

Damn, girl. You wanna maybe dial it back a few notches? This is not how we do things.

I'm still figuring out my style. Maybe I'm the bad cop. The loose cannon. How would you know?

We're not a cop at all, moron. We're a hunter. Meaning we actually respect the concept of "innocent until proven guilty." A girl's diary and a clump of dirt laced with mana do not equal guilt. So let the little gremlin go before she starts fighting back the only way she knows how, and you take a fireball to the face.

Growling, Harper released Lakshmi's shoulder and took a step back. Her nerves were all firing arrhythmically and her breathing was rapid. She was shocked to find that her other hand was resting on the grip of her knife at her hip, having already popped the clasp on the sheath. "Sorry. Shit. Sorry. That was... Sorry." She subtly secured it again and took her hand away.

Lakshmi looked her over, then did the worst thing she could have in that moment. She pitied her. "I thought I had problems. Do you need a minute or something?"

"It's you. It has to be you." She slumped back down on the edge of the bed and started fumbling to pick up the journal and vial again. "Because if it's not you, then it's back to the drawing board yet again. I hate the fucking drawing board. The drawing board can bite me."

There was a long silence as the witch picked up her headphones from the floor and then sat down in her chair. "Look, if it will make you leave me alone, I did…kind of put a hex on Autumn."

Harper sighed and ran her fingers soothingly through her hair a few times. "I'm going to assume it was not of the chest-bursting variety."

"It was a low-grade avoidance hex. I didn't even feel comfortable hitting her with a memory wipe. There'd be no way of fixing things if I accidentally erased too much. So I just gave her subconscious a little push to give me a wide berth. Every time I saw her, it hurt. And that hurt made me want to lash out at her. At least this way, we could keep a healthy social bubble. No more arguments, no more drama. But I swear, that's it. The rumors I've been hearing about what happened to her? That's some high-level shit. And not my style anyway." She leaned back in her chair, draping her headphones around her neck and burying her hands deep in the pocket of her hoodie. "Some stupid part of me always hoped we could still figure it out someday. Killing her would have been really stupid. Can't hook up with a girl that's not alive anymore."

Harper sighed weakly, worn out from both the adrenaline spike and then the energy needed to push it back down. "You've got to give me something here. Is there anyone you can think of that would be able to corroborate your whereabouts the night of her death?"

"I get loud when I'm gaming. Especially online. Talk to my neighbors. I'm sure they'd be only too happy to bitch about me." Lakshmi gestured to the walls of her dorm. "I give you full permission to interrogate them to your heart's content."

"How gracious." Harper pushed herself back up to her feet and started for the door. "Look, Lakshmi, I'm s—"

"I know. I know, you're sorry. You can make it up to me by never coming back here. I'd rather not think about Autumn Temple for a while. In case you hadn't noticed."

As promised, the residents of rooms 201 and 205 were quite eager to complain about Lakshmi's volume. And both of them agreed that she had most definitely been getting into a screaming match with someone around the time Autumn would have died.

It was still possible that Lakshmi had done something to Autumn to hurt her remotely. But she still would have needed to leave at some point to clean up the scene of the crime in person. And by her neighbors' accounts, that gaming session had gone on long enough that each girl was thinking about raising complaints to their RA.

You couldn't call it an airtight alibi. Harper stood in the hallway, staring at Lakshmi's door, willing herself to knock for yet another disturbance. There was no way in hell it would go well.

The phone in her pocket emitted a pleasant little ring. She might have considered the interruption a blessing if it weren't for the name she saw on the screen. "Dammit. Esther." She opened the text to see what it said.

Meet me by the fountain.

Dry. Clinical. Terrifying. Harper swallowed the lump in her throat and began her death march down the stairs and out of the dorm. Her follow-up interrogation would have to wait. The door opened out onto the quad, and she could already see Esther on one of the stone benches surrounding the water feature. Her face and posture were completely unreadable, which didn't do much to keep Harper from assuming the worst.

Her approach was timid, like she was some skittish little squirrel investigating the possibility of a snack. She did eventually take a spot on the bench, making sure to put more space between them than she otherwise would have.

It was a few seconds before Esther spoke. Agonizing seconds. "All right, here's the deal. There was a lot of debate between everyone. They're not all happy about it. But they did reach a consensus, eventually. You come to the meeting tonight."

Technically, that was mostly good news. But her voice was still hard, her pitch low. Harper wondered if this group chat didn't include several lines of Esther saying what a terrible idea it was. And talking to all her friends about how Harper was an asshole. And how much she hated her. And that she was a big stupid dummy who should just go away forever. You know, the way she definitely talked. That was a reasonable fear that a normal person should have. "I feel as though there's a catch."

"You would be correct. If you want to attend, you have to participate. Sharing isn't usually mandatory, but it will be for you. Dig deep, find something about yourself that scares you, that you're trying to change. Because you're going to need them to trust you if you want even a sliver of a chance at getting information from anyone."

"Be repentant, got it. I can do that."

Esther didn't say anything, but the face she got in response spoke volumes. Well, not volumes. But there were definitely two words there: *Can you?*

The Repentance Club met in a room on the second floor of the student union building. While Esther was busy opening up a folding table and burdening it with snacks and drinks, Harper poked around the room. There were framed photos all over the walls from the college's past. Black-and-white pictures depicted buildings that were no longer around, faculty that were probably no longer alive, and students who had long since gone on to fruitful lives.

"Hey," Esther said softly, breaking her out of her investigation. She was still acting rather stilted and distant, and while Harper knew she had every right to do so, it was still painful. "I need to put out all these chairs. Help a sister out?"

"Think I can manage that." Harper followed her over to a nearby closet filled to the brim with plastic folding chairs. While Esther retrieved them one at a time, Harper began taking armfuls in a single trip, fluidly popping each into place.

She knew it was a dumb ploy, a bit of playful flirtation to show off a little while being helpful. And she could have sworn she saw a small smile grace her lips finally. That was something worth celebrating.

Once Esther seemed satisfied with the concentric circles of chairs, Harper plopped herself down in a random spot. Esther planted herself a few seats away.

Slowly, students began filtering in through the door. It really said something about the school's mass variable glamour that you couldn't tell a single one of them was anything other than human. Harper nodded politely to anyone who happened to glance her way. After all, they were at least prepared for her presence. The fact that any of them even did her the service of a smile gave her a sliver of confidence. But that didn't stop her heart from hammering in her chest, or the slight buzz in her head.

Once all the chairs were filled, plus a few more pulled out last minute for latecomers, things got underway.

Esther cleared her throat softly, but judging by how quickly everyone shut up, you'd have thought she were banging a gavel. God, she commanded so much respect everywhere she went. It was incredible. "All right, looks like just about everyone is here. Um, so, as you're all aware, we have a guest with us tonight. Harper is here investigating—Well, she's looking into...into what happened to Autumn."

A few heads nodded along gravely. Some of the students glared in Harper's direction, though most of them were avoiding looking at her altogether.

"She's a hunter, but I can vouch that she's got the best of intentions, or I never would have let her set foot in this room. And she's agreed to tell her story, the same as any of us would. Which means she'll get the same respect." She looked directly at Harper and gave a small head tilt.

Time to do this. Just speak from the heart.

Super easy. Super-duper easy. Anyone can do it.

Harper stood and cast off her leather jacket, placing it on the back of her chair. Maybe it wouldn't mean anything to the rest of the room, but it felt like a good first step, to get her armor out of the way. As she spoke, she started rolling up the sleeves of her flannel.

"Every now and then I think about when I was six. My parents were helping this family of satyrs. I think mom said they were dealing with a curse, I don't really remember that part too well. Anyway, they had a daughter about my age, so they told us to hang out while the adults took care of their adult thing." She chuckled softly and shook her head as she remembered herself as a stupid little egg. "God, I had the hugest crush. Her horns were just coming in, and she kept her hooves so shiny. I asked her all sorts of questions about her life, but she didn't seem to mind. She even activated the glamour in her ring to show me her human disguise. I was this stupid little boy with a crush, so I tried to be all precious and said, 'You look better without it,' or something equally cheesy."

She thought she heard a chuckle or two, though she couldn't place whether that was good or bad, so she just pressed on. "I… lost some of that a few years later when my training began. Mythics became something I studied abstractly. Biology and physiology, psychology, strengths and weaknesses. But never the stuff I wanted to know. No sociology, y'know? When I was twelve, we started training with weapons. By sixteen, I was joining my parents on their hunts. And a few days ago, when I turned twenty-one, I took on my first job alone. While I was busy tracking down a vampire in Chicago, Autumn Temple was receiving a mysterious phone call that drew her out to the woods. And when I was trying to hit on his latest victim, she was being killed."

A quick glance around didn't show any guilty faces. Nobody fidgeted when she mentioned the phone call. They all just looked sad. One or two faces might have been showing sympathy, but she didn't want to get her hopes up. A few looked angry, and they had every right to be. She didn't have the heart to look and see what Esther was feeling. "That vampire…he was a bad guy, objectively. He killed people, and sired a few before leaving them alone. The guild was looking after them. So I'm glad I stopped him. But...killing him came easy. Way too easy. I'm trained to hurt people. And I wish I wasn't, sometimes. I wish it felt harder, having to do that. I wish I was more like that younger version of me, who got to actually hang out with a girl and really get to know her. I wish 'hunter' wasn't a word that made all of you look so nervous. But that's...all in the past. I can't do anything about that stuff now. But maybe there's still time to change. I really fucking hope so."

She was shaking a little as she sat down. Just a few hours ago, she had been so close to attacking a girl whose only crime was being bad at taking rejection. And sometime in the near future, she would have to confront whoever had killed Autumn. If she really tried, maybe she could be better. That sounded nice.

No one applauded. Harper was pretty sure you didn't clap in support groups. But they had allowed her to come here and say what she needed. That was more than she deserved.

After a few beats of silence, Esther spoke again. "There's always time, Harper."

She could just make out a few heads nodding around the room through her kaleidoscoping vision. Shit, she was tearing up. Harper hastily nodded back and tried to subtly wipe at her eyes. The guy sitting next to her gently put a pale hand on her shoulder. He smiled, revealing a small flash of fangs.

It wasn't much. But it felt immense.

"Who would like to speak next?"

Even after the official meeting had ended, most of the students stuck around to chat. Everyone had broken off into their own little clusters, and Harper was left alone leaning against the wall near the refreshment table. Hunter instincts prompted her to stay just in case anyone wanted to talk to her, even if another part of her wanted little more than to be an invisible observer. With great reluctance, she picked up a two-liter of generic-brand pop that was somehow warmer than room temperature and poured a small amount into the flimsy plastic cup. She at least managed to get a full sip in before deciding the exercise was best forgotten entirely.

Suddenly, someone sidled up next to her and cleared their throat, and she turned to see the pale-skinned kid from before. The vampire. "It's Harper, right? I'm Andre. I just...W-W-Well. It was really cool that you took the leap and told your story tonight. It's not easy."

It wasn't until he spoke that Harper realized the other reason he'd seemed vaguely familiar. This was the stuttering kid she'd met just before going to speak with Imogen. Harper held her breath and waited to see what else he had to say.

"Anyway, that guy sounds like a huge d-d-douchebag and I'm really glad he's not around anymore. All of us here are trying to d-do better. Just because you're not a mythic doesn't mean you d-don't belong here. Maybe once you've found Autumn's killer, w-we can talk more. Sociology, and all that. It's nice to know there are hunters like you out there."

Some part of Harper had really been expecting at least one person to come up to her and explain in a hushed tone that they didn't appreciate her being here and that maybe she should get the hell out before they turned her inside out. This guy was so kind and gentle that it really threw her for a loop. "Um, thanks, man. That's—Thank you."

That seemed to be all the courage he had in him. "Right, well that's all I w-wanted to say and it was nice to meet you and have a good night!" He quickly scurried off to go talk to a girl that had spoken after Harper did: Grace, a succubus sorority girl who had drained more than a few souls in her search for true love. Pretty tragic.

Really, all of this was. Glancing around at everyone, it was obvious to Harper that this night was a dead end. Yeah, she was glad to have gotten some stuff off her chest. But beyond that, nobody here could possibly be a culprit. They were just a bunch of kids, scared of the damage they could do. She didn't even have the heart to do any questioning. It would have gone nowhere, it would have made enemies, it would have upset Esther. Take your pick.

Harper dropped her cup of warm pop in the trash and nervously shuffled her way over to Esther, who was just finishing up her conversation with a girl in a wheelchair. She was a mermaid who had caused a yacht full of frat boys to run aground just a few years ago.

"Seriously, nobody here is going to judge you for holding on to that grief for as long as you need. It's terrible, but sometimes it's just an important part of the process of growing. You're allowed to feel bad. Just don't let that feeling consume you and become all you are." She turned and noticed they had a new presence in the conversation and nodded her head subtly, then glanced back at the mermaid. "Hope that helps, Chelle."

"More than you know, Esther. You're amazing."

She just smiled beatifically and shrugged her shoulders. "I'm really not. Good night." Finally, she brought her full attention back to Harper. "So," she began, and then immediately left the thought hanging. And it was a thought that Harper did her best to translate in her head.

So. Just like I knew would happen, we got nothing from this. These are good people who are just trying to make up for some past mistakes, or are terrified of making mistakes in the first place. But, also, maybe you got a little bit of repentance yourself, and that's probably kind of a relief. So I don't necessarily regret bringing you here. But maybe now we can get back to the real investigation and find someone who could actually be guilty.

"So…" Harper said. She didn't find it any easier to voice her own thoughts at the moment. Her response hid yet another unspoken paragraph.

So. You're absolutely correct, vis-à-vis these people and their innocence, and also with regards to the fact that maybe I needed to say some stuff out loud that I've never said before. And yes, we should really get ourselves back on track somehow. But that's easier said than done with how few leads we have. This is a mess.

"Um," Esther said softly, not really making direct eye contact at the moment. "I'm still knee-deep in a research paper. I should clean up here and head back to my dorm for the night. Are you okay with that?"

Harper shrugged, still feeling a bit ashamed and embarrassed about strong-arming her way into this meeting when she didn't need to in the first place. "If you've got stuff you need to take care of, go for it. I'll find something to do with myself. What's that thing my mom always says? 'No rest for the weary'?"

There was just a hint of a warm smile on Esther's lips, finally. God, that was good to see. "I thought it was 'no rest for the wicked.'"

"Yeah, I guess maybe that's a bit more accurate at this point," Harper said bashfully. She crossed her arms and shifted her stance slightly. "Look, I'm really sorry about all this. I should have just trusted you. But I'm glad I at least got to voice some… stuff. And maybe everyone got to see that we're not all bad."

"Humans or hunters?"

Harper just shrugged with a weak smile. "Yes?"

"Hah, yeah. Rome wasn't built in a day, and trust can take a lifetime. But maybe this was all for the best in the long run. Or at least I hope so. Good night, Harper." There was the briefest moment of possibility for something else as Esther went to lean in closer, perhaps to close the distance between them for a handshake or even a hug, and Harper held her breath in anticipation. But Esther stopped herself and instead gave a little wave.

Definitely deflated but respectfully resigned, Harper matched her energy and returned the awkward wave. "G'night, Esther. And thanks again."

CHAPTER TEN

Harper left the student union in a haze of tangled emotions. Her appearance at the Repentance Club had inexplicably *not* ended in total disaster. That Andre kid had gathered up the courage to give her a supportive word, which was sweet, but stupid. It was more than she deserved. Hell, she was fairly certain what she deserved was to be yelled at and chased out.

More than that, though, there was a sense of belonging in there. Not the starry-eyed hopes she had of being welcomed into a community of mythics. This was deeper than that. She was in a room full of people who all had struggles within themselves, between the desire to do good and the urge to do harm.

And, of course, there was the messy situation with Esther. Things had been going all right, but then she followed through on a lead from Imogen and it had ruined the vibe between them. After the meeting, it seemed like she was starting to warm to Harper again—slowly, anyway, which was better than not at all. But she wasn't sure that they'd really be able to move past her presumptuousness.

Things were complicated at the moment, and Harper wasn't totally sure what to do with herself. As if on autopilot, she hopped into Lilith and started driving. It was only when she pulled into the tiny parking lot that she realized she'd brought herself back to The Landlocked Atlantis. A bit of comfort food did sound pretty good.

Harper slid into the same booth she'd been sharing with Esther, because it was turning into a habit, and suddenly had to do a double take. Carol was still here. Was she working a second shift or something? Not that you would have been able to tell by looking at her. She seemed to be glowing just as much as usual. Carol even wore a pleasant smile as she came over to the table. "Hmm, Esther's friend, without an Esther. Everythin' okay, hon?"

She did her best to give a smile in return, but it wasn't really happening. "Oh, I never gave you my name. Um, I'm Harper. And yeah, I guess you could say we had a…a fight." She shrugged her shoulders and ran her fingers anxiously through her hair. "It was bad, and it was definitely my fault. And I think I've managed to screw up my hu—" She stopped herself, but it wasn't easy. Carol just had this aura about her that made you want to be blindingly honest.

"Your hunt?" Harper's face must have been projecting her full range of emotions in that moment. Carol just winked at her. "That poor girl gets murdered and suddenly you show up. C'mon now, Harper. I've been around the block more than a few times. It takes a lot to put one over on me. Now, you orderin' something, or did you just come here to chat?"

Right, this was a diner, not a therapist's office. "Yeah. I'll just—I'll take a burger. Um, and can I get a pop with like…extra ice? Please and thank you?"

"You got it, sweetie."

While the waitress was gone, Harper tried to shore up her mood by focusing on the hunt again. She hadn't gotten much from the theatre kids. Even Lakshmi, arguably her biggest lead, had ultimately led nowhere. She'd at least learned that Imogen was a fellow hunter, but otherwise that journal thing didn't really pan out. The support group had been a bust. A big bust. A big huge stupid dumb bust.

Get it together, jackass.

There was still the mage angle. That was something. Though she wasn't looking forward to knocking on doors to pester each of them about what they were doing that night. Nobody liked to be interrogated, not even the innocent.

But beyond that, she was running low on things to work off of. Dead ends, no matter where she turned.

Carol returned with her meal, much to her relief. Maybe getting some damn food in her belly would make her less moody. "Ahh, thank you, you're an angel."

The woman smiled conspiratorially. "Not quite. But it's a decent guess." Surprisingly, she wasn't going anywhere. Carol continued to stand there casually, giving Harper a moment to take a sizable bite from her burger. "So, you're lookin' into what happened to that poor girl?"

She nodded and hurried to chew through the food. "Mm-hmm. How do you know all this stuff anyway?"

"Ain't just the college kids that're special. Without that big ol' glamour of theirs, I'd look a good deal more…rotten."

A zombie. That made sense. She didn't need sleep, and she couldn't get tired. So Carol could work as many shifts as she liked. And she clearly liked her work, liked being around people. "But how—"

"Calf brains," she answered before Harper could even fully voice the question. "Now, I can tell from the look on your face something went a bit sideways."

"'A bit' is putting it mildly. Sideways, upside down, inverted, and inside out. It's all over the place."

Carol crossed one arm against her chest, tucking her chin into the other hand. "Y'know what I always did whenever things went every which way but right? I'd talk to my mom. Ain't nothin' quite as nice as that."

Harper felt foolish for not thinking of the most obvious solution. She'd always gone to her mom when things imploded. Why should that change now, just because she was working on her own? She wasn't *actually* alone, not by a long shot. "Yeah, thanks, Carol. I really appreciate it."

The bells on the door rang out, announcing the arrival of another customer. The waitress gave her a warm smile. "I'll let you enjoy your meal in peace. Oh, and hey. Don't you worry about little ol' Esther. That girl's got the kindest heart I've ever seen. She just needs some time to fuss and fume. You'll see her again."

She really wanted to believe that. And Carol sounded so certain, she very nearly did.

Outside the diner, Harper sat on Lilith's trunk and dialed up her mom.

"Harper! Hi, sweetie, what's up? How're things going down there?"

The sigh left her so automatically it was almost scary. Harper idly scratched at the shaved side of her head. "Uhh, not ideal. Tons of dead ends. I'm sure Dad told you about the weird nonscent thing. Evidence points to a mage. But short of just wandering around asking everyone if they know any evil wizards, I'm running out of things to work from."

"Hmm…" She could just imagine that little thoughtful pout Calliope always got when she was contemplating. "That does all sound a bit frustrating, Harper. But…Well, if you don't mind me saying so, it kinda seems like there's more to it. Maybe start from the beginning, hmm?"

Leave it to Mom to be so observant. "Y-Yeah, okay." She did her best to summarize the events of the last few days. With her father, she tried to focus on the events in an objective way, giving him the facts and her observations. But she knew her mother. The woman wasn't asking about the details of the case just to provide insight. No, she wanted to know how her baby girl was doing. Which, of course, meant making it obvious to the woman just how twisted up she'd let herself get over a girl she barely knew.

To her credit, Calliope didn't needle her about her silly crush. She just cooed sympathetically. "Being a hunter, it's not a life known to make you a lot of friends. And that goes double for mythics. The fact that this girl gave you the time of day in the first place says a lot about how approachable you can be. For her to try and help you so much, she must be a wonderful person."

Harper looked up at the stars overhead. "Exactly, and now I've made her mad. One of the only people around this school who was fully and completely on my side, and I managed to piss her off. It feels like I'm bungling this whole damned thing."

"Because you're all locked up in your own head, Harper. This stuff is messing with you. And I think you're right, sometimes it's good to distract yourself with work."

She massaged her forehead a few times. "I'd love to, but I've run out of worthwhile leads. And the one I do have requires working with a girl who maybe isn't too fond of me right now. I'm just...not sure what to do with myself right now."

"Aww, have you forgotten the first rule of the hunt already, dear?"

There were an aggravating number of "first rules of hunting," and they changed depending on who you were talking to. But Harper didn't feel like getting off on a tangent about that, so instead she just admitted defeat. "I guess I must have, Mom."

Calliope chuckled on the other end of the line. She was probably beaming. The woman was always beaming. "I'm just teasing you, ya goof! I know that's a loaded question. Anyway, when all else fails, I say go for a walk. You can call it patrolling, or pounding the pavement, or even just clearing your head and getting some air. But the goal is always the same. It's going back to basics, trying to shake out the cobwebs and just examine things again. Look for a new angle, or let your mind wander and see what your subconscious can come up with. You're not lost, it just seems that way."

Her lips curled up into a smile despite her best efforts to remain despondent and hopeless. "Thanks, Mom. You're the best."

"I know," she replied cheekily. "And so are you, sweetie. Now go out there and make us proud. Just like you always do."

Malcolm-Baptiste was a different place at night.

During the day, there were students everywhere, constantly moving, and all the buildings were filled. Even without classes happening, there was still constant activity. There was steady traffic coming and going from the dining hall, the library, and the student union.

But now, that activity was much more contained in specific pockets. There were dorms where students were working, or more likely slacking and sleeping. And of course the frat houses, most of them abuzz with parties that occasionally spilled out onto the lawns. But in other places, the school was silent as a graveyard. Sure, there were lights everywhere, but they couldn't chase away the gloom in certain corners. If anything was going to happen, it wouldn't be in the light. Harper stuck to the shadows, looking for something, anything.

The first few times a stumbling, drunken idiot entered her range of awareness, she had a momentary panic attack. But before long she'd managed to discover the rhythm of their movements and learned to let it fade into the background. Besides, they were usually loud and shuffling. She was looking for the suspiciously quiet, the eerie, and the unsettling.

These things were, it turned out, in very short supply. Despite there being a killer on the loose, there just wasn't that much to see.

At one point, Harper spied someone in a long coat with a hood pulled up over their head. But that was the most cliched suspicious thing ever. Besides, it was officially fall now, and some people couldn't handle the dropping temperature.

Patrolling for a few hours wasn't terribly exciting, but it did get exhausting, so Harper looked for a place to sit down. There was a bench close by, but it was occupied. She thought about moving on, until she realized who the occupant was. "Oh, Andre!" She'd been hoping she might be able to say something a bit more coherent to him after his kind words to her earlier that night.

She sidled over and sat down next to him, clearing her throat softly, searching for the right words. "I just wanted to thank you again for actually taking the time to talk to me after the Repentance Club. I know I really barged my way in there, and maybe not everyone was so happy to have me there. Having a friendly face and a kind word helped a lot. Made me feel a little more welcomed, like I wasn't screwing everything up."

He didn't say anything right away, which was fair. He'd clearly been pretty nervous before, and that wasn't likely to have gone away in just a few hours. But another few seconds passed, and he wasn't even fidgeting or looking in her direction. He almost seemed to be napping or something. "Andre?"

She reached out and knew long before she ever made contact what she was going to find. Instinct could be a powerful thing. But she let the moment play out the way it was intended, to honor the dramatic tension, or maybe just to keep alive the stupid sliver of hope that her instincts were wrong. Her fingers brushed against his shoulder, intending to shake him gently. That little bit of force was enough to unbalance him, and he fell down to the ground. Lifeless. Or, more accurately, un-undead.

With a gasp, Harper dropped down next to him on her knees. She cradled his body and began searching him over for injuries. He wasn't a pile of ash, so he hadn't been staked, but she checked his chest just for posterity anyway. His head was still very much attached, so no decapitation. There weren't a lot of ways to drop a vampire, and she was having trouble finding the culprit. It was only when she tipped his body just right that his especially pale skin caught some distant light and she saw it.

Two small wounds in the neck, maybe an inch apart. Andre had been killed by a vampire.

Talking to no one in particular, Harper gave voice to her sheer confusion. "What the hell is going on here?" Fishing out her phone, she held it up with the screen facing toward the wounds so she could get a better look at it. This didn't make any damn sense. There were only two reasons vampires ever drank from one another. The most common was the sense of intimacy it created between lovers. But they could also technically do it for food. It provided minimal nourishment and really only happened if one of them was starving to the point of madness.

But on a campus this diverse, surely there had to be a hundred better targets—just pop over to a frat party and snag someone there.

There was something else, too. The bites looked weird. It wasn't like Harper had an encyclopedic knowledge about the shape and size of vampire bites, but this one seemed off in a way she couldn't yet determine. There was a chance—and a not insignificant one at that—that this was yet another attack masquerading as something intended to throw off anyone trying to investigate.

But that didn't narrow it down. She could examine Andre's body until the sun came up, but she wouldn't get any closer to figuring out who had done this.

Much to her chagrin, she called 911.

The good news was that Harper didn't have to outright lie to the sheriffs. Parts of the truth were completely reasonable. She was visiting the college and had decided to take a walk around during the night to get some air, vibe-check how safe it felt after dark, that kind of thing. They had her contact information and promised to be in touch if they needed anything.

Of course, this level of flashing lights and people in uniform inevitably drew attention from students, who immediately saw Harper standing around near to the dead body of one of their classmates. The same Harper that was already the subject of several rumors around campus. And the same student that she'd been seen talking to only a few hours ago.

It was a bad look.

Once Harper was able to get away from the authorities, she found somewhere quiet to make some phone calls.

Scrolling through her phone's contacts, she eventually found the one she wanted and punched the worn-out little OK button. Exactly three rings later, she heard the telltale sound of a bong, followed by a scratchy voice. "Harper Zeale. You son of a bitch."

"Seriously, Trent, are you gonna greet me like that every time I call your ass?"

"I'll stop saying it when it stops sounding awesome. And what did I tell you about using my real name?"

Harper gave a long, drawn-out sigh. This was so stupid, but if she didn't indulge him, he'd never do what she needed. "Sorry, Umbra. Look, I need some help with something."

"Of course you do, or you wouldn't be contacting me. So what's up?" Trent, or rather Umbra, was a fellow guild member. He was an expert Key, and a massive pothead. But the latter was allowed so long as the former remained true.

"Two deaths in Kitezh, Illinois. First is Autumn Temple, second is Andre—though I don't know the last name yet. Temple died a few nights ago, Andre's being brought in as we speak. I just need to know if the county coroner notices anything especially weird about either of their deaths. Well, beyond the fact that one of them had her chest opened up and the other was a vampire apparently killed by another vampire." It wasn't an easy job she was dropping in his lap. He had to sift through some poor idiot's notes for the needle of bizarre in a haystack of uncanny. But there was a reason she called Umbra when she needed this kind of thing done fast and efficiently. "You got all that?"

"I do indeed, Harper. If I have anything, you'll know by tomorrow."

"Thanks, dude. Sorry to bring this to you at such a weird hour." She mostly said that as a courtesy. Harper knew damn well that Umbra had never and would never maintain anything resembling a normal schedule.

He just scoffed. "Please. Might as well be daylight as far as I'm concerned."

With a sigh of relief, she hung up on that call and took a beat to collect herself. This next one was going to be rough. After choosing the contact, she brought the phone back to her ear, noticing a slight hitch in her breathing as she did so.

"Harper? It's like midnight. What could be so important?"

"Esther, I'm so sorry. Uh. I was walking around the school. I found Andre. He's…" She really didn't feel like dealing with any semantic confusion and picked something a little bit less loaded. "He was attacked. He's gone, Esther. Someone got to him. And it's probably going to get pretty bad for me. I was one of the last people to talk to him. I'm the one who found him, and a bunch of people saw me talking to someone from the sheriff's department, and—"

There was sniffling on the other end of the line, but then Harper was a little surprised by the firmness when Esther spoke again. "That's bullcrap."

"What?"

"There's no way in hell you would have done that. You're a lot of things, Harper, not all of them good. But I heard you talk at the meeting. You're not a cold-blooded killer. This wasn't you."

She couldn't help but give a dry little chuckle at Esther's semi-affirmation. "You still willing to back me up when everyone gets out the torches and pitchforks?" She realized only after she said it that this was probably the most ill-conceived allusion she could have used. Too late now, though.

"You find out who did this to my friends, I'll stand next to you no matter what." There was a long shaking sigh, and when she spoke again, Esther no longer sounded so confident and strong. "I think I'm going to need to have a good long cry about this. And you're gonna need your rest too. 'So do not worry about tomorrow, for tomorrow will bring worries of its own. Today's trouble is enough for today.'"

Harper smirked. "You figure out how to actually do that, let me know. Because I will never stop stressing out about tomorrow. 'Tomorrow and tomorrow and tomorrow.' See? I can quote the Bible too."

She was surprised to hear a faint chuckle. "That's Shakespeare, Harper."

"I'm tired and stressed. So sue me," she said, allowing herself just the tiniest of smiles. "See you tomorrow."

Carol had been right. Esther really did come around. That vote of confidence did a lot to keep her from sinking into despair over this new development. If she'd stuck around campus instead of moping at the diner, she might have caught this in time. What could have been an excuse to despair instead lit a fire under her. There was nothing else to be done tonight. She was loath to admit it, but only the sloppiest killer would go for two victims in one night. And she wasn't dealing with an idiot. This asshole was smart and cruel.

Harper decided to learn her lesson and not force herself to run on zero sleep for a day and a half again. She was going to put an end to this, and she needed to be at her best to do so. As she made her way once again to find Lilith, she remembered one of the last things that Andre had said to her. He wanted to get to know her, and to let her know him in return. That had been taken away from her. An innocent person had been killed for no reason.

She would make this bastard pay.

"I take it this is not you calling me to say that you're making your way home with that case of beer?"

Harper rolled her eyes and sat down on her creaking motel bed. "Unfortunately, no, Nat. Believe me, I wish that were true. It would be far more enjoyable than sitting in this dingy room and trying to find something other than static on a television from the mid-nineties."

"Ooh, hear that, Katie? We rank higher than a small-town motel. Really moving up in the world."

"Aww, come on, I bet we're higher up than that," came a second voice from the other line.

"You think she'd still be saying that if she were at a party? Come on, Harper, fess up. I bet there are all kinds of hijinks you could get up to down there."

Harper couldn't stop herself from scoffing as she stretched out across her bed and stared up at the stucco ceiling. "The only reason I've gone to any gatherings of students is to question people. And I wouldn't call interrogations in a theatre green room or a support group meeting 'parties.'"

There was a light tongue-clicking from Katie. "Wow, you really are scraping the bottom of the barrel there, huh? What were you doing looking for killers at a support group? What kind was it?"

For a moment, she focused on the chaotic pattern above her and gnawed on her lip. "All right, look, it's been driving me crazy and I have to tell somebody about this place. But you cannot let this get back to my parents. I'm serious. This is pinky-swear territory."

Katie gasped excitedly. "Of course! On threat of torture. Now spill."

"We've been keeping each others' secrets since we were toddlers. We're not stopping now." She could picture Nat's serious face and grinned. She had missed this, even if doing it over the phone didn't quite compare to the real thing.

"There's more than just a werewolf here. The entire school is all mythics and magic humans. Oh! And the president is a former hunter. Seriously, it's incredible. I've met a banshee, a pixie, an alchemist...They're all just here being normal and going to classes and shit."

"Whoa. Total YA novel territory," Katie cooed.

"I can see why you don't want your parents hearing about that," Nat said seriously. "They'd probably have to report it, and then it would be a whole...thing. Don't worry, your secret's safe with us."

"Wait, you're not in any danger, are you?" The concern in Katie's voice was touching.

Harper smiled fondly and shrugged. "Only from the actual killer. And myself, if I ever succumb to the impulse to bang my head against a wall in frustration. It's just a regular old school otherwise. A bunch of nerds studying nerd stuff."

"What I'm hearing is you fit right in," Nat said. Harper chose to let that slide. Nat wasn't completely wrong. She wasn't completely right, either. Too complicated. "So then what's the deal with the support group?"

"Right, the werewolf—Jesus, Harper, she has a name. Esther. She made this club so students with dangerous impulses can talk through all their baggage."

Katie gasped again. "And they just let you waltz in there?"

"Not exactly. Esther got real pissed at me when I first asked. She only let me in if I agreed to speak."

Nat went straight for the jugular. She had a nasty habit of doing that. "God, Harper, you really do have a way of sticking your foot in your mouth. Especially around pretty girls. Is she pretty, Harper? I bet she's gorgeous, if you fucked up that bad."

All she could do in response was give a long, exhausted groan.

"*Extremely* attractive. Noted."

As savage as that was, there was something comforting about it too. She'd shoved almost her entire *leg* in her mouth with Nat. You couldn't break up with a girl in a community that small and not have everything get awkward. The fact that Natasha was able to give her a ribbing again meant things were getting patched up.

"Be nice!" In swooped Katie to save the day. "I'm sure Harper will make it up to her pretty friend." Scratch that. Katie was getting licks in too.

"Well, that's my cue to hang up before you two can start twisting the knife."

Both of her friends were giggling, and she eventually relented and joined in.

"Sweet dreams, Harper. We believe in you!" Bless Katie. That girl could light up a room through the sheer force of her positivity.

"And thanks for checking in again. Now I know you're not dead yet, and we got some sweet secrets to boot." There was a beat, just long enough to be significant. "Stay safe out there."

"My promises of beer and hangouts are solemn and iron-clad. A squad of assassins could not keep me away. Good night. Dorks." She flipped her phone closed and resumed staring at the stucco above.

She could already tell tomorrow was going to be a long day, so she burrowed her way under the covers and shut off the bedside lamp. Exhaustion pushed her into the arms of sleep in record time.

CHAPTER ELEVEN

The campus was quiet that next morning. With a second death shaking Malcolm-Baptiste, there were no doubt plenty of students who were opting to stay hidden away in the relative safety of their rooms. It was eerie, in a way. The sun was shining bright in a beautiful blue sky, and two kids were dead. Birds were chirping from nearby trees, and terror gripped the heart of a tiny liberal arts college. Somewhere nearby a cricket was playing its song, and a killer was planning their next attack.

Harper stepped in front of Randolph Dormitory and fired off a quick text to Esther to let her know that she was around.

"Yo! Hunter!"

Harper's shoulders tensed up as someone called out to her from across the quad. Things were already off to a bad start.

She turned around, shocked to see Izzy striding toward her, face twisted with fury. Zooey was hanging onto her arm, weakly trying to pull her back. "Babe…" the pixie pleaded softly.

Sighing, Harper attempted to bring down the aggression a bit. "C'mon, we really don't need to do this." She looked around her, praying that no one else was nearby. To her distress, she could see a few people lingering out near the student union who had turned their heads to see what the yelling was about.

Izzy obviously didn't give a shit about anyone else. She just continued on her warpath. "Actually I'm pretty fucking sure we do," she said, closing the distance between them and getting uncomfortably close to Harper's face. "What's this I hear about you killing Andre?"

With a groan, she tried to figure out how to properly explain this situation in ten words or less. Yeah, she figured someone would make a run at her. She just hadn't expected it would be the banshee. Though maybe she should have. "I found him like that. He had bite marks in his neck."

"You're telling me a vamp killed a vamp? That's bullshit."

She threw up her hands in frustration. "Of course it's bullshit! And I'm trying to figure out why someone would make it look like he was killed by one of his own. But I can't do that if I'm getting jumped by half the student body of Malcolm-Baptiste College."

"And how long before Esther is the one getting hurt under mysterious circumstances? We never should have let an outsider normie help solve Autumn's murder. Here's an idea—how about you disappear and run back to your little family of monster-killers?" She dropped her voice a bit lower, and it came out much scratchier than before. "Or maybe…I disappear you myself." Suddenly, Izzy began drawing in breath, and her eyes got the faintest hint of a glow to them. She was preparing to howl.

Instincts kicked in and Harper's hand went down to her side, opening the sheath and drawing her knife in a flash. She had no interest in killing her. She actually quite liked Izzy, in a way. She was honest and straightforward, so you could trust her to mean what she said and say what she meant. But Harper's muscle memory didn't care about silly things like that. A supernatural threat was right there, and it had to be dealt with.

The moment, though it couldn't have been more than a few seconds, seemed to go on forever. The two of them stood there, each contemplating how ready they were to actually do this. Izzy sure seemed certain. And Harper knew that she could do this—physically anyway, though emotionally was another matter entirely.

Nobody said anything, nobody moved. Just three people, the air thick with tension. Izzy holding her breath, eyes glowing white. Zooey pulling her arm. Harper standing poised with knife in hand, the blade inches from Izzy's neck.

The front door of the dormitory suddenly opened and Esther poked her head out. Her eyes were still red, her eyelids puffy, and she couldn't completely contain the occasional sniffle. She hadn't been kidding about needing to have a nice long cry. "Oh, hey, Zooey, Izzy. What's—" She saw the knife in Harper's hand and gasped.

And just like that, Izzy released the breath she'd taken in, and her eyes stopped glowing. She glanced down at the knife in Harper's hand and tilted her head, pursing her lips, brow furrowing. "Yeah. Exactly what I thought. You're just looking for an excuse."

Reality slammed into Harper, hard, as she realized what she'd done. Twice in the span of maybe twelve hours, she had very nearly brought herself to do something awful in the name of this fucking hunt. Something irreversible. "I—" The thought went unfinished. Harper just turned and booked it across the lawn.

This wasn't some logical retreat, she just needed to get the hell away from there before she had to properly confront the nature of that encounter. She just kept moving, stumbling away from campus. She was headed off into the woods, which seemed as good a place as any. No one was going to be out there. She could be alone, somewhere that she couldn't do any harm.

For no reason that she could fathom, her feet carried her to the tree that she'd occupied her first night in Kitezh. Harper hauled herself right back up onto that tree branch where she'd spent several hours watching a werewolf she didn't know sleep on the ground. Perhaps she was trying to reverse time and undo this mess. Or at least trying to return to a point when she still had an objective view of things, a point when all this seemed so simple. Maybe if she had just not fallen out of the damned tree like an idiot, everything would be different.

As she settled with her back against the trunk and went to wipe her face with the back of her hand, Harper realized she'd been crying. No, not just crying, but full-on snot-nosed bawling. "Shit." She hastily began wiping harder, to erase away all the sentimentality. But no matter how hard she tried, she couldn't go back, and she couldn't brush it away. She was here, she was in it now. She cared about these people, and she wanted them to care about her too.

Izzy was almost kind of a friend. She was certainly a decent person. And Zooey and Esther, they were both so sweet and didn't deserve to see her like that. And Rowan had been that perfect blend of a charming asshole that you just had to appreciate them. And poor Andre...

No, there was no going back.

Looking down, Harper saw her knife in her other hand. She thought back to when she first received it, feeling so badass, so powerful. This was her baby, her treasured item. And more than anything right now, it felt like a fucking *burden*. She'd used it to kill one mythic and threaten another. In a moment of anger, Harper had almost used it against a witch whose only obvious crime was being kind of a bitch. Her knife was a means for violence and destruction, not some cool plaything. It felt heavy in her palm, weighing her down, making her lazy.

How the fuck was she supposed to earn anyone's trust when her immediate impulse was brutality? Harper was sick of looking at it, tired of the weight. In a fit of frustration and anger, she hurled it down at the ground where the blade buried itself in the dirt.

There was a moment of relief once she had released it. But that was short-lived. Discarding her friend also felt a little like ripping out a part of herself. Her sobbing returned with a fury. Harper's body trembled and she hugged herself tightly.

"Harper?"

She looked toward the source of the voice and saw Esther staring up at her from below. As fast as she could, she whipped her face away and began wiping at her eyes even harder than before. "Gah, h-hey. Uh, hi. Sorry about…that. All that." She began to laugh, just a few small bursts, ragged and trembling. "That was bad. I'm…kind of the worst."

"You're not. Izzy told me what happened. Reluctantly. Zooey's currently in the process of chewing her out. Which is good, because if she didn't, I would have. It was incredibly stupid of her. But you—"

"I drew my knife on her, Esther!" She raised her voice enough to disturb a bird hiding in a nearby tree, and it hurriedly took flight. "It doesn't matter if she was just posturing or actually wanted to attack me. The knife came out, which means that some part of me—no matter how small—was ready to end her life. I never should have done that, I should have found some other way to defuse the situation. My dad may have trained me to fight, but my mom *always* emphasized finding an alternative. I should know better." She swallowed a lump in her throat. "I know what you said last night, but the thing is…I'm still a killer. I've killed before. I probably will kill again."

"I'm not saying I like it or anything. But I also recognize that you deal with a lot of dangerous situations. Sometimes you have to…Look, I'm not naive." She sighed and sat down on the ground directly below, resting her back against the trunk of the tree as well.

Slowly, Harper rubbed her right arm with her left hand, staring at the foliage around her. "You know, at the meeting, I realized something. I needed to be there. I may be an outsider, but I do have something in common with those students. I'm dangerous, and it takes a lot of concentration to be…not that. I didn't have to 'dig deep' to find something about myself I don't like. That's surface level, and I think about it constantly. Shit like that? When I feel my hand twitching eagerly to do something so terrible without a second thought? It eats at me."

There was a beat while both of them let that hang in the air. Eventually Esther gave a sigh and nodded slowly. "God, Andre. I can't believe it. He was such a sweetheart. His speech therapy was really coming along. Everyone knew how hard he was trying to put himself out there and be approachable. And someone just…did that to him. Cut all that potential short. Left him out, like…" She sniffled again but had apparently already cried herself out too much to start sobbing now. "Like they were proud of it. It's awful. I want…"

Harper figured she knew where this was going. She'd been there before. Shit, she was still there. "Yeah. You just want it to be over. And it will be. We're so close, like I can see the outline of something."

Esther's voice came out with just the slightest hint of a growl. "No. I want to do terrible things to whoever did this. I have spent so many years trying to push down those instincts. That's why I started the club in the first place. And someone is going a long way toward undoing all that work. Making me want to… to rip their throat out." That soft growl started to grow, and she quickly swallowed it. Esther brought her knees up to her chest and hugged them tightly. "It frightens me."

Finally, Harper pushed herself off the branch and dropped to the ground next to her. She crouched next to Esther and looked at her intently. Neither of them was in the best place right now. Trying to offer her comfort, it was the blind leading the blind. "Okay, fair point, that's pretty frightening. But anger can be normal and healthy. Isn't part of the process to move from pure repression to some kind of acceptance?" She was having a difficult time, figuring out how boundaries worked at the moment. The two of them had danced around a lot of stuff in just a few short days. So she settled for just putting a hand on her shoulder.

Esther laughed at that, almost barking it out. "Hah! That's funny, telling a God-fearing girl not to repress. You have no idea how…*tightly* I have to arrange everything to make it all— to make it all okay. So don't come around here acting like—" Suddenly she raised her head up, eyes focusing again, and she gasped dramatically. "Oh Lord, Harper, I am so sorry. That— You shouldn't have to see that."

Boundaries be damned. Harper sat down next to Esther and wrapped an arm around her shoulders, holding her lightly for a moment. "I'm not gonna pretend to understand what basically any part of your life is like. But I know a thing or two about repression. And yeah, when you've got dangerous instincts, it's totally fair to want to keep those in check. But not all instincts are bad. You've just got to figure out which are which."

Yeah, that's good. Seduce the nice Christian girl into "not repressing so much."

Shut up, that's not what this is about.

Okay, but it kind of is. Tell me I'm wrong.

You're wrong. When all this is over, we'll probably never see each other again.

We could, though. And even if we don't, at least she'll come out the other side of this a little stronger.

Well aren't you magnanimous. You predictable bitch.

Esther laughed again, gently, but also far more dry. She looked lost. "Easy as that, huh?"

"Didn't say it was easy," she said with a shrug. "I'm not some guru on the subject or anything. But I know that if I bottled up certain parts of myself, I'd be a miserable wreck constantly. So I embraced the things that felt good and right, and now I'm just a normal wreck. Hell, on good days I'm a happy wreck. You've got something about yourself you need to work on. So do I, obviously. Join the club. Er, no pun intended."

The two of them sat there staring at one another in silence. Harper slowly let her hand drift down, experimentally rubbing it against Esther's back. She watched her face go on a journey through several different emotions, unable to parse what any of them might be, before landing on a weary smile. "Thank you, Harper. Really."

That was about all the energy Harper had for this little seminar on self-improvement, so she forced herself to try to get back to the matter at hand. It was not a successful attempt. "I wanna say that we should try and get back to figuring out who did all this. But God, I don't know, it's all gone really fucking bad. It wasn't that long ago that Izzy trusted me, and now I'm persona non grata as far as she's concerned. How much worse is it going to be around the rest of the school?"

"I don't mean to be that girl, but...even Jesus had a tough time when it came to public opinion. It doesn't matter if everyone likes you and thinks you're a superstar, or if you're hated and suspected. Y'know? You still have to do the right thing. No matter what. You have to try." To drive the point home, Esther reached over beside her and cautiously pulled the knife out of the earth. It clearly made her nervous to even be holding the thing—though whether that was because it was a weapon or because of the silver, Harper couldn't be sure.

With a shaking hand, Harper took the knife from Esther, sliding it home in its sheath. It was strange; taking it back felt like a piece of her had been rightfully returned. But that also meant the return of that damned weight. "Yeah. The job's what matters," she said, unable to disguise her discomfort. "Um, well, we still need to follow up on that info Rowan gave us. I took a run at Lakshmi, unsuccessfully." Once again, a memory from the previous day flashed in her mind. One hand pinning the witch to her chair, the other poised to draw the blade. She wouldn't do that again. She had to be better than that. "But there are still other mages on campus. We just, y'know, have to track each of them down and question them. Super simple."

"Right!" Esther perked up a little bit. "Actually, that reminds me, I talked with Rowan a bit about that. They helped me put together a list. Uh, if you…wanna come back with me to my dorm? We can go over it and make a game plan."

"Yeah. Yeah, that'd be good. Lead the way."

Esther's room was neat and tidy. Impressively so. The desk was efficiently organized, with pens and pencils each getting their own upright holder. Esther's bed was perfectly tucked in, crisp and picturesque. There was a poster on the wall for a band Harper didn't recognize. Granted, her knowledge of music was as woefully out of date as her fashion sense or her technology preferences. The only thing that stood out was the pile of used and crumpled tissues next to the small garbage bin. Clearly the girl had attempted to hastily trash each one and failed consecutively, too distraught to fix it.

Her idle investigation was interrupted as Esther extended a piece of loose-leaf paper to her. She took it from her and smiled. "Seriously, this is great. Thank you." It was both a relief and a disappointment to see that none of the students from the theatre department were present on the page. It was good to have all of them officially crossed off her own list of suspects. But it also meant she'd wasted a lot of time interviewing all of them. She ran her finger down the page and noted a few additions beyond just a list of names. "What's the rest of this?"

"I didn't want to waste any extra time. Anyone that has an X next to their name, they're almost definitely not the one involved. Like Beckett there, he's the technomancer we mentioned the other day. All of his magic is based in machinery and electronics. He's not gonna know the first thing about disguising smell. There's a couple people with squiggles by them. They're people I know personally and couldn't imagine them doing something so awful. They could still be guilty, but it's...dubious. And the stars indicate anyone that could notably fit the bill."

"Huh. You put a star next to this professor. What's their deal?"

Esther got a little smirk, and it seemed like maybe the distraction really was helping. "Rowan seemed especially certain about that one. But I'm pretty sure that's just because Professor Harvey gave them a bad grade on their English Lit final last semester. But their supposedly airtight justification is that he's an illusion mage, which would be a useful school of magic if someone wanted to hide their movements. It's worth checking out, at least."

Taking into account all of Esther's symbols, there were still at least a dozen people that could potentially be involved. She gave a small stretch. "Well, then, better get to it. Not much else to do while I wait for my friend to call about the coroner's reports. You coming with, or do you need some more time?"

"No," she replied firmly. "No, I have to keep doing this." God, this girl was unflappable. Suddenly she looked at Harper more intently. "What about you? Are you going to be okay? Things got pretty rough for a minute there."

She just smirked and shrugged. "No idea. But you're right, I have to do this too. Before anyone else gets hurt. That's the job."

Esther put a hand on her shoulder and massaged it gently with her thumb as the two shared a silent moment. After a few seconds, she caught herself and pulled her hand back. "Okay, then. Let's go knock on some doors."

Getting information turned out to be just as difficult as Harper feared it would be. Of course there was already the usual resistance anyone got from a random person knocking on their door to ask them about the "dearly departed." Making matters worse, word was already getting around that the human visitor was actually a hunter who had more than likely killed Andre—and maybe Autumn too.

"Fuck off, hunter. You've done more than enough damage."

"You gonna ask me to join your little guild? Don't bother, I've already seen what you people believe in."

"If you don't leave in three seconds, I'm sending a magic missile straight up your ass."

The only reason she got even the tiniest scraps was because of Esther. It wasn't just that she seemed to have a deep well of resolve—deeper than Harper had expected. No, she also had pull around the school. Anyone who knew her respected her. And she never threw that weight around. She didn't call in favors, or give people knowing looks. That would have been smug and insufferable. She simply existed in such a way that people felt compelled to open up a bit.

But opening doors was only part of the equation. The other half was *supposed* to be the useful answers you got on the other side of that door. And the answers were in much shorter supply. They got more or less the same reply no matter who they visited.

"Autumn? Yeah, that girl was awesome. She let me bum some weed when I ran out. Wait, you're not gonna tell my RA, right?"

"Of course I knew her. Everyone did. She was a diva-princess-starlet-angel. Guys wanted to be her, girls wanted to be with her, fish feared her. Everything's a little more gray with her gone."

"Yes, I had Miss Temple in a few of my courses. She was never a particularly exceptional student, academically, but she always gave it a hundred percent. Now if you don't mind, I've got an appointment in ten minutes."

Harper was lying on her back in the middle of Esther's floor, hands resting on her stomach. Her host was seated cross-legged next to her, rereading the list for the eightieth time. "Either my bullshit detector is broken—fat chance—or literally nobody is guilty. Which is impossible. Like, someone had to do this. I'm missing something." Kicking her legs out a few times, she dug the heels of her palms into her eyes. "Uugghh, I guess we could try talking to some of the vampire students on campus? But they're gonna be even less friendly than the mages. What do I do?"

There was a vibration in her pocket, and Harper prayed it was the only thing that mattered right now. The familiar name on the screen gave her a flash of hope, and she couldn't have pressed that green button any faster if she tried. "Umbra." She didn't even bother to needle him about his stupid name.

"Quite the quest you sent me on, Zeale. But I come bearing goodies."

"Sweet baby Jesus, thank you. What've you got?"

"Okay, so this is…pretty fucking weird. There wasn't anything usable on the coroner's official report, unfortunately. But, the guy did say some stuff during his recording of the examination that I don't think he wanted on the record. He clipped it into separate audio files, then dropped them to his personal cloud storage."

"Cloud?" She really hated whenever people said something she had no frame of reference for. Umbra might as well have been implying that he'd stored some computer stuff on a literal cloud.

"Dammit, Miss Brick Laptop And Flip Phone, I want to rag on you for that so badly but I need you to hear this. I managed to pull the sound files and emailed them to you if you want to listen in yourself. Basically, all the damage on both students started *internally*. On this Autumn girl, he says it looks for all the world like her rib cage was opened from the inside out. Like, based on the way the rib bones broke and shit. He even suggested the heart might not have been taken at all. Like maybe it was the bomb that blew her apart. And Andre? Well, to quote the coroner, 'It's almost like the blood was actively trying to leave his body of its own volition.' Absolutely wild shit on this one, Harper. I don't envy you one bit."

There was a picture forming in her mind, but the pieces didn't quite fit yet. If all that stuff was true, then she had just massively narrowed down her suspect profile. In fact, there was really only one remaining option that fit the bill here—a blood mage. But that obvious answer also complicated things. Nobody started out going down that path. You ended up there after making a dark choice, and then working like crazy to master a notoriously difficult and deadly school of magic.

Umbra continued, "Oh! Totally unrelated, but I also dug a little bit into the school, just to be on the safe side. Place is completely clean, totally legit, certified and all that. Y'know, aside from the entire student body being what they are."

"Right. About that, can you please keep that under your black and/or white hat for now? The last thing I need is a bunch of guild Shields storming the place."

"Sure, sure, whatever. I'm no narc. But check this out—the president is a former hunter."

She clicked her tongue softly and sighed. "Yeah, I talked to her a little bit about it the other day. She wasn't a full hunter, just married into the guild and joined up then."

"No, like, I cross-referenced her name with our records because it sounded super familiar. This Imogen chick, she was a big deal back in the day. Her husband was a pretty competent Shield, but she was a top-tier Stave. One of the more powerful mages to have worked with that district."

"Why the hell wouldn't she tell me—" That was about when the big, obvious freight train hit her going top speed. "Umbra, you're incredible. Thank you."

"Wow, that was surprisingly sincere. You okay there?"

"Yeah, I think I've got everything I need. Things are about to get real complicated, and I don't have the time to snark at you."

"But you always have the time to snark." He sounded legitimately disappointed, which was kind of sweet. "Fine, I won't keep you. Whatever's going on, give 'em hell."

Esther waited patiently until the call was over but had been giving her more and more concerned looks as it went on. As soon as Harper hung up, she shuffled closer. "What is it? What's going on?"

This wasn't going to be easy. "I think...Well, Dr. White... It's possible Imogen did it. Did all of it." Harper sat up properly and leaned her body against Esther's desk.

"I'm sorry, you'll have to forgive me, that makes no sense." Esther tossed her notebook aside, got to her feet, and began pacing her room anxiously.

All Harper could really do was shrug her shoulders in response. "She's a former Silversmith, and a powerful mage. She definitely has the means, not to mention the experience and wherewithal to kill a supernatural being. Autumn and Andre both knew her, they worked in the admin building under her."

"That's just—No. Not Imogen. She has no reason to." Esther continued to shake her head frantically, still pacing her room from one end to the other.

Scratching her neck slowly, Harper decided to just lay out the woman's secrets. "Her husband was a hunter too. More than likely killed in the line of duty. She probably has a vendetta against mythics."

"No, no, she was president for years before I got here. But this is the first time anything like this has happened. The last student death we had was my freshman year, and they died in a car accident while on spring break in Maui. Why would she wait so long to do this? It just doesn't track."

She didn't doubt Esther's certainty, but everything else lined up. "Look, both of them were almost definitely killed by blood magic. It's one of the most notoriously difficult schools of magic there is. It takes years of experience and a ton of control. That officially excludes Lakshmi. She's too young. Besides, there's no way she could have perfected blood magic with how many video games she plays. I would bet anything Imogen's either the murderer, or there's something major she's not telling me. I have to do this."

Frowning, Esther took a few steps toward her. "At least let me help confront her. You shouldn't have to do this alone."

Finally standing up, Harper shook her head firmly and planted a hand on Esther's shoulder. "We're at the point of no return here. You need to get back to your regular life now and let me deal with this."

Surprisingly, Esther knocked the hand from her shoulder and shoved her in the chest. "I'm not just some princess who has to stay back in her castle for her own safety. I can turn into a giant wolf—"

"On full moons, and there isn't one tonight. Besides, I'm not saying you're helpless, but you are a *college student*. I'm trained in this stuff, I'm armed, I can handle myself."

"You're not listening, I—" God, she really did not want to hear "no" for an answer. But with two students already dead, Harper just couldn't have this girl's death on her conscience.

"I can't keep bouncing this back and forth with you. I have to go drop the bait and then prepare. Focus on your essays and whatever. Let me do my job." She turned and started for the door, not bothering to hear whatever else Esther might have had to say. Any further arguing and Harper might have caved. Again.

No, she had to do this alone.

CHAPTER TWELVE

"Imogen White. God, that must have been fifteen years ago now. And you're sure?" Harper thought she detected the slightest hint of pride in her father's voice once again. She had to admit, this case really seemed to be easing any of his worries that she might not be ready. That was something worth celebrating.

She heard her mother's voice next. "Yeah, honey, I certainly didn't get a bad vibe off her at the time."

"Fifteen years is a long time, Mom. Plenty of time to go crazy and start a murderous rampage." Harper paced the wooded clearing, idly kicking aside an empty can and watching it skid along the dirt.

Her father cut back in. "It's also a lot of time to get rusty. Or to perfect some especially nasty magic. You're going in with a lot of unknown variables there, Harper."

"Two students dead, and there could be more any moment. If I'm wrong, maybe she'll be mad at me, but maybe she'll also help me find the real culprit. And if I'm right, I have a chance to catch her off guard and end this now."

"You've never fought a fully fledged mage before, Harper," her mother said with a tinge of desperation. "We can be there in no time to back you up."

Logically, she knew that with her parents there, she'd have a much better chance of wrapping this up. But there was a huge difference between calling them for advice and asking them to clean up her messes. If she needed that much backup on only her second hunt, could she really call herself a proper hunter? Besides, if either of them got hurt here and another job came up, they'd be unable to take it. All because she was a little scared. No, at some point you had to prove yourself. "Thank you. But the sooner I do this, the sooner the problem is solved. Waiting for the cavalry means wasted time. Two deaths in just a few days. The body count will keep growing if I don't deal with this now. It's going to be fine."

"If you're sure," Calliope said, sounding less than convinced.

"You'd better call us the moment you get in over your head, Harper," Sebastian added quickly.

She nodded, figuring that stupid bravado probably wasn't a solid long-term attitude. "All right, fine, start gearing up. If you don't hear from me in two hours, get down here and clean up my mess."

Her father sighed. "Fair enough. But don't take any unnecessary risks." There was a beat, and then much quieter, Sebastian added, "I love you, Harper."

She smirked to herself and nodded. "I love you too, Dad. Go on. I'll call you when it's done."

After hanging up, Harper fished out Imogen's business card. She wondered idly if this was the number for the burner phone she'd given those poor students to summon them to their fates. Or maybe she had deigned to give Harper her real number. It hardly mattered now.

The phone rang a few times before going to the automated message for the voicemail. She waited for the beep, then put on her best rushed voice, breathing heavily for added effect. "Dr. White, I think all my digging has finally unearthed something major. Look, I'm going to need your help on this. Meet me in that clearing where all the students party as soon as you can. I'll explain everything then."

Harper closed up her phone and paced the clearing. The bait was set. Her fate was locked in. No matter how guilty or innocent Imogen was, this was bound to end explosively. But that was the job. You put your life on the line every single day, and death was always a possibility.

Right, death. Her parents weren't likely to tell Natasha and Katie everything, and they deserved to know. Pushing down the growing nerves, she typed out a few words, then deleted them and started over again. It took a while, but she finally had something that felt like a worthwhile message, in case it turned out to be her last one.

> *bad guy is a scary mage*
> *showdown time*
> *i love you both <3*

That was everything. All that was left to do now was wait. In the meantime, Harper started training.

She fetched a sheet of paper and her crossbow from her messenger bag and put together a quick bullseye, attaching it to a nearby tree with a spare piece of ammo. Harper stood back a fair distance and leveled her weapon, then started unloading bolt after bolt into it until she was satisfied with her grouping. Once she ran out, she yanked each one out and started over.

After that, she moved on to refreshing her knife work. Harper ran drills endlessly until her arms and wrists started to ache. Flipping, palming, slashing, stabbing, hilt-striking—she worked through every form a million times over. "Hmm. 'So. Imogen. Looks like someone's a dirty, fucking liar.' God, that's so weak. Makes me sound like a middle schooler. 'Dr. White, I presume?' Ugh, no, I already know who she is. 'Tell me the truth, Imogen. Or you're going to regret it.' Wow, how intimidating. She'll be quaking, I'm sure."

This sad display continued for quite a while, and she still didn't settle on what she was going to say.

Imogen finally showed up, wearing a long coat with the hood pulled up over her head. It took Harper a moment to realize she'd seen that look before. The figure stalking campus last night that she'd chided herself for suspecting. Dammit, if only she'd followed...

No. Too late for that now.

Pushing herself off the tree she'd been leaning against, Harper approached in a way she hoped was secretive. "Dr. White, thank God."

"You said you found something?" The president sounded rather eager. That could have simply been the voice of a former hunter and school administrator who wanted all these murders solved. Or it could have been a woman who wanted to know how Harper had bungled her investigation, and who she would be pinning everything on.

She wouldn't give her the satisfaction. "Come clean, Imogen. You didn't tell me the whole truth the other day. You were a fully fledged hunter *long* before you married Jackson."

Her face fell. "You're young, still learning how to do all this by yourself. If you knew how much experience I have, you'd lean on me too much. I didn't want to cramp your style." A stellar lie. Harper almost believed it, or at least she wanted to.

Trying to keep the illusion of camaraderie for now, she released a low sigh and shrugged. "Well. Thanks for that, at least. But I don't like being in the dark on stuff, no matter how good the intentions. Anyway, that's not why I called you here. Look, you've...you've got a blood mage on your campus."

The slightly contorted look of mixed emotions on Imogen's face as she pulled away her hood—that felt like the signal she needed. "You're sure?"

Harper leaned in a little closer. "I know. It's crazy, someone that powerful hiding out right here. And I'm sure you already know, no ordinary chump can manage something like that. You have to have years of experience, study, training, suffering, pain, drive. No, it's got to be someone older, so I'm thinking probably faculty. Right? That makes sense, yeah?"

"Could be a townie, though, couldn't it?" God, how had Harper fallen for all those lies before? She was so obvious now. Kind of sad, really.

"Could be. Could be the mayor, a bus driver, or a waitress at the diner. Could be a lot of people. But this all seems pretty contained. Had to be a faculty member. But that's where I ran into some issues. Only one professor is a human with magic experience, and he just does illusions. Seemed unlikely." With what she hoped was a stealthy movement, Harper reached down for the sheath at her hip. She popped the clasp and started drawing her knife. "But then I hear through the grapevine about the prestigious president of Malcolm-Baptiste, and her history as a Stave with the Silversmiths. Quite powerful. One who maybe has a grudge against the supernatural world for the death of her husb—"

Harper felt an unpleasant sensation in her gut. It was extremely painful, and it took her a few seconds to realize that she had been stabbed. Which was not ideal. Still, this wasn't Harper's first serious wound, and it wouldn't be her last.

Imogen's expression was still mostly collected, but there was an intensity in her gaze that hadn't been there a moment before. It was hard to look away. "All you had to do was *kill the damn wolf*, Harper. Or at least kill *someone*. God, why couldn't they just send a hunter with a bit of bloodlust? Why did it have to be a Knife with a conscience?"

Some of Harper's resolve did crumble for just a moment as the knife was pulled back out and she was able to get a decent look at it. Iron, veined with silver. A hunter's blade. Just like her own. And currently coated in her blood.

In an attempt to get some range on the woman, Harper stumbled away from her. She snatched up her crossbow from where it was resting against a tree and whirled around to fire a bolt straight into Imogen's throat. Even in pain her aim was good, and the thing should have hit its target perfectly.

But it turned out Trent's research had been correct. Imogen's magic wasn't just strong, her reflexes were instantaneous. She waved out her free hand, cloaked in a swirl of protective mana, and batted away the projectile like it was a particularly obnoxious gnat. The crossbow was clearly no good, so Harper closed the distance between them again, holding her knife in a reverse grip, ready to slash at whatever part of the woman she could reach. Her motions must have been just wild enough to catch Imogen off guard, because she did actually manage to slice through her sleeve and cut a pretty decent gash along her left arm.

"Ah! More tenacious than I gave you credit for, Zeale. But pluck only gets you so far. I'm about to take you to school." Dammit, this woman wasn't just more powerful, she was way better at the one-liners.

Harper's entire body suddenly went rigid, refusing to listen to a single command she gave it. Her legs locked up and her arms bent back to an uncomfortable angle. The sensation of ground beneath her feet dissipated as she was lifted up a few inches. Imogen was concentrating on her, with her free hand pointing palm-out in her direction. The veins in her eyes bulged slightly and blood was dripping from her tear ducts, her lips contorted into a manic smile. Unbidden, Harper's hand opened up, a finger at a time, until her beloved knife dropped from her hand down to the grass below.

There was a sickening, wet noise, and the pain in her belly got worse. Some part of Harper was vaguely aware of what was likely going on down there, though she couldn't currently get an angle to see it properly. Blood was, technically speaking, just goddamn everywhere in the body. And if you were skilled in manipulating the stuff, then your options were limitless. You could constrict all the muscles in someone's body, say, or perhaps open up a wound and make it far more lethal. Harper was an ant trying to fight a giant. This only ended one way, and that was when Imogen decided she was allowed to die.

Without even breaking her concentration, Imogen bent and picked up Harper's trusted knife, turning it over a few times. "Iron and silver. Everything you need to kill all kinds of monsters. And fairly unique, as far as anyone here knows. Once I drive this into Esther's chest, who do you suppose they'll blame?"

"D-Don't you fucking touch her," Harper struggled to say through her locked-up jaw. "She's innocent."

There was a deep growl from beyond the tree line, accompanied by a deep, sonorous voice that sent a shiver down Harper's spine. "For the last time—I'm *not* some damsel!"

Out of a nearby cluster of trees came a big blur of fur and teeth and claws. Esther, as it turned out, wasn't helpless, regardless of the moon's phase. Rather than being a full wolf, she was somewhere between a wolf and a human. She was massive still, easily six foot six while standing on her hind paws. Despite bleeding out, Harper's mind worked overtime to come up with an answer for this.

Werewolves had two states. They were human most of the time, and then on full moons they were big wolves. That was it. This in-between thing just didn't happen. Except it obviously did happen. Esther was proof of that. Was it some aspect of the curse? Maybe she was some particular breed that Harper had never heard of before. Or hell, maybe it had something to do with that childhood training she mentioned.

Maintaining her blinding speed, Esther slammed her shoulder directly into the president. Both knives went flying from Imogen's hands, and before she had a chance to go for either one, the werewolf drove a fist into her stomach. "Gah! Stupid of you to come here alone."

"Who said I was alone?"

The air was filled with a sudden ear-piercing screech. Harper was a little bit too distracted by the giant gaping wound in her side to be terribly bothered by it. Imogen, on the other hand, appeared to be having a very bad time indeed. Clearly the brunt of the sound wave was directed at her. Shortly after, the dark woods erupted in a bright flash of technicolor light, and the woman cried out in shock, most likely from being temporarily blinded. Only when the dust settled did Harper manage to make out the familiar silhouettes of Zooey and Izzy. What were they doing here?

With her concentration broken, Imogen lost her hold on Harper, who went tumbling down to the ground beneath. Her world exploded in pain. Instinctively, she put a hand to her side where the wound was, and she could feel just how wet and sticky it was with blood.

Most of her vision was suddenly filled with another familiar face, urging Harper to lie down on the ground. At least Rowan was kind enough to pick a soft, grassy spot instead of the bloody dirt. "No exacerbating. It's going to be hard enough to treat without you doing sit-ups." Rowan reached down to a satchel at their side and began retrieving ingredients.

Harper grumbled softly but otherwise said nothing.

A bundle of ground-up leaves and sticks or whatever was pressed into her side, and she was racked with yet another burst of pain. Her body reflexively began to twist and get away from the source of the hurt.

"Hey! What did I just tell you? No moving. This isn't instantaneous, I'm not using woobly healing magic over here. This is science."

"Okay, well, first…Ow. Your bedside manner leaves something to be desired, *doc*. Second, I'm never depending on you in a combat scenario again."

"At least we can agree on that. Tonight is a onetime deal. You find yourself infested with another case of death wish, leave me out of it. The only reason I'm even here is because nobody says no to Esther Talbot. You owe that girl your life, as far as I'm concerned." Rowan huffed softly as they started wrapping a bandage around her midriff.

From somewhere just outside her narrow field of view, she could hear the sound of Esther's voice, though heavily modified due to her transformation. It was pitched lower, gravelly, and maybe a little hot. "Rowan. She's trying to stop a madwoman. Give her a break."

"Yeah. I'm the big he—" Harper coughed up a bit of blood onto her shirt and was at once equal parts worried about the coughing up blood part and the fact that her shirt was getting more ruined by the second. "Hero. Ow."

"Right, well, Miss Big Hero, that's gonna close up the wound, but it's not gonna stay closed if you move around too much.

Remember, you're still a squishy human filled with blood. So I'd suggest maybe not engaging in a second attack on the lady who can control it with magic."

"But—" was all she managed to get out before she felt Esther's big, pawed hand pat her on the head a few times.

"Just stay here. Let me do this." That came out almost pleadingly. For a moment they stared into each other's eyes, until finally Harper nodded her head silently. It wasn't really accurate to say Esther smiled, but she did give an excitable little yip of delight. In a blur, she was taking another run at Imogen, who was still reeling from the pair of girlfriends simultaneously blinding and deafening her.

But all Harper could think about were those fucking knives. Sure, Esther wasn't a damsel, but she damn sure wasn't a warrior either. How many times would she be attacked before she crumpled? Five? Ten?

Besides, could any of them do what needed to be done? A fight like this required someone who wasn't afraid of getting her hands dirty. Harper may not have liked the terrible things she needed to do, but she would much rather take that burden than force anyone else to experience the guilt. Against Rowan's insistence, Harper turned herself over onto her knees and started pushing up to her feet, hand twisting up the earth and grass beneath her as she fought through the pain.

"Hey! You heard the girl, stay down!"

"Get out of here, Rowan. You did your job, don't stick around and get hurt on my account."

Surprisingly, they put a hand on Harper's shoulder and gave her some very direct eye contact. "If you go over there, *you are going to die*, and that will be the end of it. So long as you're alive, there's hope. So just stay here, you fucking *idiot*."

"Fine. I'll stay right here," Harper muttered with a grin. "But I'm not done with this bitch. Get me those knives." She pushed herself the rest of the way to a standing position, swaying weakly. As the world spun around her, she tried to gesture to the spot where Imogen had been cold-cocked and dropped the two blades.

Their brow furrowed slightly, but Rowan raised no objections as they stooped down to grab each one up, passing them off to Harper. "You got some kind of genius plan rattling around in that skull?"

"Genius? Never. But it's something." First, she made sure to secure her own knife in its sheath. The knives were technically identical, but there was no way she would ever let herself mix the two up. The day she'd received it, Harper proudly wrote her name out along the grip in permanent marker. After years of using it, the letters were still faintly visible, but even if they had faded completely, she knew the shape of those silver veins by heart.

Bracing herself against a nearby tree, she held Imogen's own stupid, inferior knife. She spent a moment weighing it, getting a feel for the balance. Hunter knives weren't exactly made for throwing. But it would do the job.

She looked out across the clearing just in time to see the giant werewolf girl throw an incredibly mean hook directly into Imogen's face. Still stunned and blinded, she could only stagger sideways a foot or two, and Harper saw her opening. Her lower body was aching, but at least her arms were still good. Mostly. She took aim, shifted her arm back, then stepped forward off the tree, wheeled the arm forward, and released. It wasn't a great toss, but a knife that heavy didn't need expert aim. With a satisfyingly wet slicing noise, the blade buried itself directly into Imogen's shoulder, just above the gash Harper had carved into her earlier.

Imogen gave a loud cry of pain, then growled and started drawing blood from her wounds. That was the trouble with a blood mage—the more they bled, the more ammo they had. She threw down a few drops of her own blood into the grass. Where it landed, it suddenly clotted and grew into basketball-sized chunks of gore—red and pulsating and utterly stomach-turning. They began rapidly replicating, expanding upward and outward into a wide wall of wet, spongy material that cut her off from her gathered assailants. From behind the barrier, they could see a dim flash.

Esther tore away chunk after chunk of the viscera. By the time she had demolished the hideous wall, Dr. White was completely gone. Seeing that the villain had been chased off, she whirled around with a howl of victory.

The next thing Harper knew, the massive werewolf was running her way, seamlessly transforming back into a human. A nude human. A laughing, nude human. Her arms wrapped around her and she pulled Harper into a hasty kiss. While the nudity certainly added a strange dimension to this, she was much more confused considering the last few days. Things had been rather...complicated between them.

"Did you see me?"

"Uhh. Yeah. Yeah, I saw. That was awesome. Um. Do you have clothes somewhere nearby, or...Like, do I need to loan you my jacket? Crap, it's a little coated in blood. My blood. Um."

Only then did Esther finally look down and realize what she'd done. She quickly let go and whipped around, facing away from everybody. "Forgot about that in the heat of the moment. Gimme a sec." She ducked back into the nearby overgrowth while Izzy and Zooey strolled over, both of them short of breath, clearly still running on adrenaline.

"Hey, Harper." Izzy hit her with a glare, but it slowly softened. "Look, uh, I wasn't really sure about coming out here. The only reason I agreed was because Esther was the one asking. And because she said we could get payback for what happened to Autumn. That girl, she's special. So let me be absolutely clear about something. You break her heart? I scream so loud your brain liquefies and melts out your ears."

Unlike the last time she got threatened, and perhaps because of how insane this whole night had been, she actually laughed softly. "Duly noted."

Just as suddenly, the banshee's eyes began to glow with a sort of soft, white light that practically poured out of them like mist. She emitted a low, anguished howl that seemed to go on for ages. For a moment, Harper feared that this was somehow related to the threat, that any moment a bit of brain matter might start to leak out her ear canal. Instead, it remained this sad, keening noise, and Izzy's face contorted into a look of pained anguish. The mist slowly faded along with the howling cry, but Izzy still looked so...sad. "Harper. I'm...Shit, I'm so sorry."

"Why? I mean, yeah, that was pretty intense but—" The answer hit her a moment before Izzy explained it. She was a banshee. That was a warning. "No."

"Your family. She's going after your family. If you don't do something, they're dead."

Esther had returned to quite the scene. Rowan was busy packing up their bag, muttering softly about Harper's death wish. Izzy, wiped out from the unexpected morbid wailing, had laid her head down in Zooey's lap to rest. And Harper was pacing nervously, shaking her head, trying to keep herself centered—and failing.

"It's just not possible. Imogen's powerful, but my parents aren't slouches. Dad's smart and competent, even if he is a hardass. And Mom's not a fighter, but she's one of the best druids in the state. No way." With panic continuing to set in inch by inch, she fumbled for her phone and started trying to call either of her parents.

"What did I miss?"

Zooey had to answer for her, since she was busy muttering to herself as each ring went by. "Harper's family is in danger. If we're lucky, Imogen's gone for her car and she plans to make the two-hour drive up to Harper's commune. Otherwise, she's powerful enough to warp herself there directly."

"Oh God, Harper, I'm so sorry," Esther said softly, stepping closer.

Running out of options, Harper switched over to her texts and began spamming Katie and Nat's phones.

SOS! mom and dad in trouble!
find them & get to safety!

Izzy finally pushed herself up to a seated position. "Look, banshee portents aren't set in stone. They're an art, not a science. They're, y'know, 'shadows of things that May be, not Will be,' or whatever. Ugh, Autumn would be so mad if she heard me butchering Dickens like that." She rubbed at her eyes a few times and tried to start over. "Still, I don't get visions of people just because they're in a spot of trouble. Currently, their chances are slim. So if you've got a plan, now's the time."

Harper spun on her heel and tossed her phone to the ground. Neither Sebastian nor Calliope was answering theirs. No replies from her friends. All she could imagine was the worst-case scenarios as Imogen killed her loved ones in the most violent and painful ways possible. "There is no plan! I'm fucked. If I go right now, drive as fast as possible, and *don't get pulled over*, I can probably manage…an hour and a half?" It all seemed utterly hopeless. "And even if I get there, and somehow they're still alive, there's no way the next fight goes nearly so well. Imogen won't pull her punches, and she'll probably just pop me like a balloon."

The anger and sadness were starting to eat at her more. Her eyes were burning and tears were streaming down her cheeks. No matter how much she tried to wipe them away, they wouldn't stop. And there was still a wound in her gut and she'd lost a lot of blood and…

Suddenly there were warm arms folding around her. She looked down at Esther holding her gently, not saying anything, just being there for her. It was a little overwhelming, but it was also just enough kindness to counteract all the negativity building up in her mind. The clouds parted, barely, and she could start thinking clearly. She gave her a squeeze of gratitude in return, and for a moment the two of them just stood there, sharing the embrace. "It's okay. I'm…gonna be okay." Somewhere beyond the break in the dark clouds of her mind, an idea shined through. A dumb idea. The only kind of idea she ever had, it seemed.

It wasn't easy, but she let go of Esther. She shed her jacket and flannel until she was down to her tank top, then retrieved her marker from her messenger bag. Imogen hadn't seen all of her tricks yet. This was an idiotic Hail Mary that could very well get her killed. But if it saved her family, she would do it in a heartbeat.

She fought against the slight tremble in her body, forcing her hands to remain as steady as possible. It took almost all of her concentration, but the last thing she needed was a pair of shattered arms on top of the wound she'd already sustained. For a moment, the world faded away and the only thing that mattered was getting this done.

There was a long silence while everyone watched her work. Eventually, Zooey spoke up, though it was barely a whisper. In spite of the low volume, the importance of the words managed to pierce Harper's concentration. "I…might be able to help. Get us there fast, I mean."

"Babe. No." Izzy looked at her girlfriend, shaking her head firmly. "That's a terrible idea for multiple reasons."

Harper looked straight at the pixie. "Terrible ideas are all we've got right now. Tell me."

CHAPTER THIRTEEN

Zooey spent some time scanning the open plot of ground where everyone was recovering. Her brow was knit together with intense concentration as she traced some invisible path, her open palms outstretched toward the ground. "It's around here somewhere..." Suddenly, she drew up short and bent down. With slow strokes, she brushed her fingertips across the grass beneath her. "There you are."

"What is she doing?" Harper quietly asked Izzy. She kept her voice low, not wanting to distract from whatever delicate process this was. While Zooey worked on her mysterious project, Harper continued to cover herself in glyphs with her marker.

Izzy was sitting upright, having finally recovered from her bout of prophecy, and watching her girlfriend proudly. "Finding a ley line."

Harper frowned, not even looking up from her distracting task. "I thought that was just garbage mysticism." Ley lines were a perfect example of human arrogance. The theory had a few different incarnations, but the basic idea was that there were imperceptible connections between various important landmarks, highways of magic or power that linked holy places together. But it was so anthropocentric, based completely in locations deemed important based on religious significance.

It was Zooey who responded this time, looking back over her shoulder with a little grin. "They had the right idea. But their methodology was all wrong. Honestly, we just call them ley lines because it's easier that way. In the Fae tongue, it's..." Here, she said something that sounded like complete gibberish to Harper's ears. "You could loosely translate it to 'thin places'? They're spots where the fabric between our worlds is easier to slip between."

Zooey turned back and rose gracefully to her feet. She thrust her hands forward and grabbed at the air, then pulled to each side as though she were opening a pair of curtains. Harper could just make out something beyond Zooey that hadn't been there a moment before.

She stepped to the side with a flourishing gesture toward a small rickety wooden fence, roughly ten feet long. It was the kind you might see at an old ranch or park, composed of little more than a few vertical posts crossed by two horizontal beams that gently rested in empty hollows bored through the upright pieces. In the center was a "gate," though this was little more than a few bits of the wood slapped together with hinges, with the most pathetic little horseshoe piece of metal that looped over the nearest vertical beam as a "latch."

Harper had been bracing herself for a grand reveal, but there was something about this moment that was both wildly fantastical and yet so understated. "And this is...a portal?" She turned her attention to her arms once again, triple-checking that all of her sigils were properly sealed and there were no smudges or gaps. Once she was satisfied, she climbed up to her feet, pleased to find there was now only a dim throbbing in her gut wound. Harper secured her flannel around her hips, then zipped up her jacket.

Zooey rolled her shoulders a few times. The gestures she used to summon the fence were simple, but perhaps the energy needed to perform them successfully was more draining. "It's a gate. Portal implies magic. This is...primordial. That gate will take us to Faerie, where time and space are a little more fluid. I make another gate there, and we arrive at your commune."

Yeah, this definitely qualified as a terrible idea. "Wait, when you say time is fluid there..." She suddenly imagined them emerging into a plot of land where a commune had yet to be built, or a desolate little ruin where the commune had once been. Neither option was ideal.

Izzy shook her head and gave a dismissive wave of her hand. "We're poking our heads into the realm for a minute or two at most. The effect is negligible for a jump that small. Plus, it's all relative. Five minutes in Faerie is basically five minutes here. But if you stay for a long, boring meal, that could be a week in real-time. You have sex in Faerie for an hour, that's barely thirty seconds out here. It's, uhhh, perception based. Relative."

Harper nodded, mostly following along, though she wasn't raising any questions partly because there just wasn't enough time.

Izzy snapped her fingers and gestured to the gate. "Oh! Uh, one other thing. When we go through Faerie, and then come back into the mortal world away from the college, we'll be outside the range of the school's glamour. Me and Zooey are gonna look like our real selves. So just like...y'know. Be cool."

Harper shrugged. "I've been involved with the world of the uncanny since I was a baby. It's fine."

She grinned and stepped forward, flipping over the latch on the gate. "No, I'm just telling you so you don't see how hot we really are and start crushing on us too." Harper didn't have a chance to fire back because Izzy was already stepping through the gate and disappearing from sight. There was no shimmer or glow. One moment she was there, the next gone.

Zooey followed after, turning to give a sweet smile. "See you on the other side." Just like that, she was gone too.

Now it was just her and Esther. Swallowing, she reached over and took her hand, holding it firmly with a nervous smile.

Esther smiled back, looking just as nervous. "Not leaving me behind again?"

"You've more than proved you can handle yourself. Besides, you all have a super important job, and I need to know someone is looking after those two idiots." Harper grinned, squeezing Esther's hand firmly one time before rushing through the gate with her in tow.

She'd been sort of bracing herself for sparkles and glittery plants and little jackalopes running around everywhere. Instead, it looked a whole lot like the woods they'd just come from. Harper might have been more disappointed if she wasn't so focused on getting home to save everyone's asses.

As promised, the other two definitely looked different. She could still see hints of their glamoured forms here and there. But Izzy was now significantly taller than she had been, and kind of...Well, it was like she was underwater despite clearly being out in the open air. Her purple hair was stringier and flowing around her, and her clothes were doing the same. Zooey was definitely smaller now, maybe four feet tall. Her skin was pinker in hue, and her hair was almost silver, with gossamer wings sticking out from her shoulder blades. Both of them now sported pointed ears and eyes that glowed ever so slightly.

"Damn, guess I have to go back on my word. You *are* hot."

"Told you," Izzy said with a grin as wide as a knife, displaying some pointed teeth.

Zooey shared an exasperated look with Esther, then reached for Harper's hand, looking up into her eyes. "This is really important, so quit flirting with my girlfriend for a second. When I make this next gate, you need to be thinking about home. No, not just *thinking* about it. You need to picture it, and all the people, and how they make you *feel*, and everything it means to you. Can you do that?"

Harper nodded. The commune was all she knew. Her parents gave birth to her, but everyone there had raised her. They were all her family. It wasn't hard to dredge up powerful feelings and memories, so she closed her eyes and focused on home.

Harper is fifteen years old and her father has just given her the blade. A knife for a Knife. The iron makes it heavy, and the silver veins running through it shimmer in the sunlight. He reminds her it's a tool first and a weapon second, and most definitely not a toy. She thinks it's the coolest thing ever, but she will never tell him that directly. It will take six years for her to understand his warning. It will take slightly longer for her to admit he was right.

Her knee is burning. She skinned it playing basketball with Katie and Nat. She knows she's supposed to be a big strong boy who doesn't cry from a stupid little baby wound, but it hurts. Her mother literally kisses it better, planting her lips against the scraped-up skin while casting a small healing spell to mend the boo-boo back together. It tickles a little, and she laughs as her mother places another kiss on her forehead.

It's her thirteenth birthday, and Harper hasn't been Harper for very long yet. Her friends give her the full run of this TV show on DVD. It's an older series about this girl who kills vampires and stuff, and she's super cool and the music is awesome and it gives her an idol she can look up to. Maybe someday she can be that cool.

The whole commune smells like smoke and barbecue, and somewhere in the distance Harper can hear the sound of everyone else finishing up their delicious meal together. Rick's pulled pork is something you should never miss. But she's snuck away with Nat, who is presently pushing her up against the outside wall of the dormitories and capturing her lips in a sloppy make-out session. They will date for twenty-eight days, three hours, and twenty-seven minutes before coming to the conclusion that it's detrimental to both of them.

Katie holds her hand after the breakup while Harper complains about how much it hurts. Her friend goes for a nervous kiss, and Harper accepts it because she's lonely and sad. They quickly agree it feels weird and bury that experience deep down. But the complications remain.

Harper's twenty-first birthday is weeks away, and she knows that if she doesn't make up with her two best friends, it's going to be really lame. So she bites the bullet and sits down with them, admitting she misses hanging out, and that she feels bad for how everything shook out, and they eventually hug and everything is okay. Except for the inevitable thick fog of tension that never quite goes away.

Harper has just returned from a trip to the thrift store. She has bought the only thing a try-hard sixteen-year-old ever truly wants:

a worn-out leather jacket that is woefully out of fashion and won't be back in fashion for several more years. But she puts it on anyway and struts proudly around her bedroom and stares at herself in the mirror excitedly. She'll never take the damn thing off.

When the gate appeared, Zooey looked at Harper in shock. This one wasn't like the first, not even slightly. All the pieces were composed of solid metal. Rather than bars or slats or chain-links, the fence and gate were crafted with intricate filigree of roses, swords, and glyphs. "It's never been that easy before. You must really care about this place."

"Let's just say if Imogen has hurt my family, dental records will be the only way to identify her." With that, she strode forward, grabbing the handle to throw the gate open, and stepped through.

The doorway placed the four of them a few hundred feet away from any of the main buildings, which Harper was grateful for. The last thing she needed was to walk out directly in front of Imogen and get attacked instantly.

Suddenly, Harper's phone erupted in a series of aggravated buzzes from within her pocket. She saw a flurry of messages from her friends, but still nothing from her parents. "Looks like everyone is alive. They're trapped in the dormitory."

"Yeah, I coulda told you that." Izzy gestured out across the commune grounds to where a giant cocoon of gore and viscera encased the entire building. "I'm going to assume that's it?"

"Yeah," Harper said. She couldn't keep the tinge of sadness out of her voice. This was all her fault. If she had let her parents come help, or just not rushed to confront Imogen so soon, maybe her whole family wouldn't be in danger now. She looked over at the pixie. "Zooey, I know I've asked a lot of you tonight—"

Zooey cut her off before she had a chance to apologize any further. "We're here for you. Just tell me what you need."

"Do a quick flyover, get a lay of the land. I'm going to be keeping Imogen busy and I won't be able to help show you around. Keep an eye out for any more gross shit where she might have someone else trapped. Once you're confident, come back and grab Izzy and Esther. Help free and protect anyone who needs it, especially my parents. I need them with me. I won't be able to last long."

Suddenly, Esther's hand was on her cheek, and Harper looked over to see those umber eyes, wide and pleading. "You better come back alive. I'm not done with you yet."

"You got it," she said with a grin. Glancing between them, she gave one more serious nod. "Stay safe, keep out of sight, and look after my family. I'm trusting you." With that, she began the trek into the main part of the commune, limping bravely toward her doom.

It took a little longer than she was used to. With every step, she was aware of the wound in her gut that was still trying to heal while she kept aggravating it. But slowly Harper did manage to hobble her way out into the very center of the main courtyard. She called out, straining her voice. "Idgie? I'd like a word with you, darling. I feel like we have some unresolved tensions that need sorting out!"

Strutting out of a nearby cabin, thankfully unoccupied, was Imogen White. She looked to be unraveling in every sense of the word. She was in significantly worse shape than the last time Harper had seen her. The woman's hair was wild, and parts of her clothing were ripped. She'd sustained a few wounds during their fight in the woods, but there were considerably more than when Imogen had disappeared. Harper's parents must have done a number on the woman, so where were they now?

Imogen's bleeding eyes scanned the horizon until they finally landed on Harper. Her mouth spread into a wicked grin. "You know, I've been racking my brain, trying for the life of me to remember—"

"Really?" Harper groaned. She wasn't exactly in the mood for a bad-guy monologue at this point.

"I just can't recall any little girl running around playing hero when I visited. I wasn't here long, but I'm sure I'd remember. But that's when it hit me. Sebastian and Calliope didn't have a daughter. But they did have a son, a ginger brat, following them around. Training to be a hunter. Hanging out with a bunch of girls from their little cult. Hated him immediately. Wanted to cave his stupid freckled face in. What was his name? Ga—"

"You literally stabbed me not even an hour ago. You think misgendering and deadnaming me is what's really gonna hurt?" Harper lifted up her crossbow and took a quick potshot at Imogen.

The woman extended a ribbon of blood to knock it away, laughing softly. "You're going to have to do much better than that." Her lips formed into a pretty pout. "Oh, but you probably can't. Not a lot of options for you. Shoot me with your little crossbow? Stab me with your little knife?" More crimson ribbons began whirling around the woman, significantly increasing just how imposing—and unhinged—she looked in that moment. She laughed, practically cackling.

While she attempted to restart her monologue, Harper loaded up another bolt into her weapon and leveled it at her again. "You'd be surprised. I do have a few more arrows in my quiver. Or—Ugh, whatever! You get the idea."

Imogen cracked a smile—and here the verb *cracked* felt especially useful. "You really are terrible at banter, aren't you? Perhaps we should just get to the part where I kill you."

"Good luck with that." Harper took careful aim, giving her opponent plenty of time to respond. Okay, she told herself as she took a deep calming breath, this next part is going to be tricky.

Just like the last shot, Imogen was already preparing to block the attack. A cluster of gore slid around in front of her and took a shape vaguely reminiscent of a kite shield. "Again? Step up your game, Zeale!"

She just couldn't help herself. She grinned wide, maybe looking a bit manic herself. "I intend to," she muttered, mostly to herself, as she pulled the trigger. As soon as the bolt had been released, Harper dropped the crossbow and flexed her arm, focusing on the glyph she'd drawn along her inner forearm, hidden beneath her jacket sleeve. Lightning started arcing and crackling all around her, wild and difficult to control. While the woman's guard was dropped, Harper hastily gathered up the energy and hurled it right at her. Of course Imogen could still counter it; she wasn't some amateur. But countering a crossbow bolt and countering lightning required different processes—

like switching from solving a maze to solving a crossword. Different muscles, different parts of the brain. Each school of magic required different "muscles" to operate properly—and to defend against.

This was the part where the gambit officially kicked in. She dropped her crossbow, then unzipped her jacket and shrugged it off, revealing her stupid Hail Mary. It wasn't just a single glyph—there were dozens all along her arms. Each one was keyed to a different spell, a different school. Harper didn't have to worry about the metaphorical muscles. For her, everything came from the same basic instinct: focus on a glyph, yank a little energy out of her own body, and activate it. Granted, that meant this strategy could only hold out for as long as her body could. But she didn't need a long time, just a few minutes. The price would be minimal compared to the payoff...provided this worked.

Once she'd brought her blood-shield back down, Imogen got a look at what Harper had done to herself, and her eyes widened. "You're as crazy as I am."

"Maybe so." She focused on the symbol at her left elbow, launching a beam of blinding light directly at her.

Imogen roared, probably not too eager to lose her sight again, and created another blood-clot wall to stop it. Then she stepped out from behind it and gathered up some blood into a spear before chucking it in Harper's direction.

After an awkward pirouette to the side to avoid it, Harper realized that she was grateful for her intense training for the first time in several days. It might have ruined an interrogation and a friendship, but at least she was still alive. She shrugged her right shoulder to summon a wave of illusory copies of herself. None of them were especially convincing, but anything that bought her a few more seconds—or that pissed Imogen off further—was worth it.

Imogen focused her bloody ammo into a dense tentacle, slamming it down on one of the fake Harpers, causing it to dissipate in a spray of particles. She roared again and rotated her arm, swinging the massive tentacle horizontally.

The air around Harper was filled with a million particles of her own energy, succinctly representing just how much she'd expended on that useless distraction. But she didn't have long to think about that as she rolled to avoid the attack before pushing up to her feet with only minimal panting and a small reminder from her abdomen that she wasn't fully healed.

Harper braced herself for another swing, but thankfully Imogen pulled the blood back toward herself to prepare for a new volley instead. Harper siphoned energy simultaneously into her left wrist and her right biceps. From her left hand she coalesced a burning ball of magma and threw it, loosely aiming for Imogen's chest. As quickly as she could, she pulled the frigid energy around her right palm and flattened it out into a razor-sharp disk of ice and wheeled it at her in quick succession, aiming for her neck.

The concentration caused Imogen's face to contort as a splash of thinned blood doused the magma while a thick clot of blood stopped the blade of ice from striking any vital flesh. "This is just sad."

It didn't even seem worth retorting at this point. Banter would just take away precious concentration and energy at this point. Illusions and shields, acid and poison, the goddamn kitchen sink. Harper was going in like a street fighter tossed into the ring with a boxer, ignoring all the established rules of the sport and just throwing as many punches as possible. As she turned the ground beneath Imogen's feet into quicksand, she couldn't help but laugh to herself a little. *Hah...dirt magic.*

Mission technically accomplished—Imogen was looking exhausted trying to keep up. The problem was that Harper felt just as wiped out. In fact, it probably looked pretty damn sad as the two of them simultaneously slowed down, until it was just two women sluggishly slinging spells back and forth. "You'll... hah...pass out long before you manage to kill me, Harper. Give it up now, and I won't make you watch as I kill all these people..."

Don't have to kill you.

Just need to keep you focused on my pretty face, Idgie.

Trying to keep Dr. White on her toes, Harper retrieved her knife and decided to go for another toss. Her form wasn't as tight, and her aim wasn't as good, but she was also much closer to the woman now. The knife went a bit lower than she'd meant for it to, but it still buried itself in Imogen's thigh, causing her to drop to her knees.

Suddenly, a massive growth of vines burst up through the earth beneath Imogen, coiling around her until the woman was fully immobilized. Her arms were drawn out to the side, encased in vines and flowers that kept her from weaving any further spells. Some had even crawled their way around her throat and across her eyes. In her exhaustion, Harper momentarily thought, *Was that one of mine?* She couldn't remember branding herself with any druidic glyphs. Had she actually broken through and learned how to cast real magic?

Of course, a moment after that her eyes focused and she realized her mother and father were nearby. Calliope was holding out a hand and focusing on Imogen while Sebastian was striding closer with his trusty longsword at his side. Both of them were looking a bit worse for wear. But they were alive. She'd done it. Her plan had worked.

Those were her last few coherent thoughts before the exhaustion finally claimed her properly. Just as the darkness crept across her vision, she saw big, fuzzy Esther approaching her, sweeping her up into her arms before she could drop to the ground. "Nice catch…"

And then Harper promptly passed out.

* * *

Harper's danger-senses were tingling.

She strongly remembered being in the middle of a perilous battle. The details filtered back to her too slowly. Her aching body told her she'd used a lot of spells. Imogen had been flagging—they both had. And then suddenly, those vines.

"Mmnn…Mom…"

She heard a familiar, earthy giggle from nearby. "Not quite."

"Bwuh?" Her eyes fluttered open, and she did her best to take everything in. She was in her bedroom, sprawled out on her bed. Esther was sitting close by on her worn-out chair, presenting a very complicated mix of emotions ranging from concern to relief. "Isther. Ev'rythin' 'kay?"

She reached out, gently brushing Harper's hair. "Everything is fine. You passed out for a few hours. It's nearly dawn."

As promised, there was some faint light sneaking in through her window blinds. "Ugh. Wha'bout Imjen?"

"I can't say I really care about her at the moment. How are *you*?" She leaned in closer, gently running her fingers through Harper's hair more firmly, scritching at her scalp.

All her addled brain could think about was closing the distance to kiss those lips. That *did* actually happen last night, right? She was fairly certain she hadn't made that one up. But right now it was hard to tell. She at least managed to keep a lid on that impulse and instead just held out a weak thumbs-up. "Gonna be jus' fine. M'invincible. 'Nstoppable. A champ'yun."

"You may have saved the day, champion. But you're definitely not invincible." Esther's face fell a bit as she put her free hand against Harper's side.

She braced herself for more pain and winced preemptively, but nothing happened. Well, not nothing. Esther's touch was soft and gentle and warm and comforting and…Anyway, no pain. She made a mental note to thank Rowan. They might have been an asshole about it, but they were a smart, talented asshole.

Harper gently rested a hand on top of Esther's and spent a moment just looking up into her eyes. Yeah, that had definitely happened last night. She definitely wanted it to happen again. Was that stupid? It seemed like it was probably stupid. Esther had been put in danger. Wait, no, she'd put *herself* in danger. Not only that, but she'd managed to handle herself incredibly well. Even worn out and beat up, Harper couldn't stop the inquisitive streak. "You were…wolf."

"I sure was." Esther's tone was placating, almost infantilizing. It might have been insulting, but then she resumed her gentle hair-stroking and scalp-scritching, and Harper's brain melted a bit. "A few generations back, we discovered our particular curse came with certain benefits. You've already seen the nose sensitivity. But we also found ways to tame the beast. We didn't just learn to behave during the full moon. We can perform a partial transformation at will. It's way harder to master. Painful, draining. But it gets a little easier each time."

A little whimper escaped from Harper before she had a chance to push it back down. "Painful? Draining? You did it twice last night!" Ah, good, she was able to form complete sentences again. Just in time to turn into a brat. "You should have said something."

"I *did* try to tell you, if you'll recall. But you were so intent on completing your quest by yourself, I never got the chance. You're not the only one with a drill instructor for a father. He made me force out transformations again and again until I could do it at the drop of a hat without getting winded." She frowned and gave her a gentle pat on the head. "Okay, I'm deflecting slightly. Yes, it's still hard to do. But...you were in trouble. And I just kept thinking about all the terrible things that might end up happening to you. So I helped Izzy pull her head out of her... her butt. I grabbed her, Zooey, and Rowan, and went to back you up."

Harper gave the hand at her side a few gentle pats in return. "You saved me. Even when I pushed you away. That's twice now. What'd I do to earn that kind of loyalty?"

"It's not something you earned, Harper. It's something I've given to you because I believe in you. But as you've seen, it's also a burden. You're stuck with me now." Almost seamlessly, Esther laced their fingers together. "I guess I thought about what you said. About...not repressing. And knowing how to sort out which impulses are good. And I realized that my impulse to help you was more important than my desire to respect your wishes."

Speaking of impulses, Harper tried to find the words to address the elephant in the room. "Hey, so, can we talk about—" A knock at her bedroom door pulled Harper away from her questioning. She couldn't decide if she was grateful or pissed. "Huh? What is it?"

The door opened and Sebastian stepped in. He saw the way Esther was touching his daughter and seemed to grow instantly uncomfortable by a few degrees. And, oh, how Harper ate it up.

She grinned at him just a split second before forcing her face into a more innocent expression. "Hey, Dad. What's up?"

He cleared his throat and shifted his feet awkwardly. "We're in a bit of a strange position. Imogen White is putting up no resistance downstairs. But she's refusing to explain herself unless you're there, Harper. When you're ready, come to my office. I'm eager to know why she hurt innocent people and tried to kill my family." He gave Esther only the briefest of nods before exiting the room and closing the door behind him.

Esther waited a moment until they were sure he was gone, then began to laugh softly. "Okay, forget what I said. My father isn't nearly that bad."

Harper burst out in bright laughter, glad that her body had mostly healed and she didn't accidentally exacerbate her injury.

CHAPTER FOURTEEN

Fifteen minutes later, having scarfed down several granola bars and chased those with a few liters of water, Harper felt at least somewhat ready to do this. She was still in need of a decent meal, but that would have to wait. For now, she just had to suffer through more monologuing from Imogen White.

Her father had willingly given up his office to serve as the woman's temporary cell. It seemed stupid considering the number of weapons inside. But with a Shield and Stave on loan from the guild to watch over her, everyone seemed to think she was effectively dealt with. Sebastian said that she was being shockingly compliant.

That hadn't stopped the guild from putting several security measures in place. Imogen had a set of heavy-duty cuffs binding her hands behind her back, and a magic-nullifying band secured around her neck. As Harper walked in with Esther and her parents in tow, Imogen sat up with a pleased smile. Smug, in fact. If it weren't for the cuffs and the band, you might never know she had been defeated and arrested.

It took concentration to not get disturbed by that smile. Harper planted herself in one of the chairs across the desk while Esther took the other. Her parents lingered by the door, letting their daughter take the lead. "So, I'm told you didn't want to give anything away unless I was here."

"You're the woman of the hour. It's only fair that you get to hear all this firsthand."

"Okay. So…" Harper tried to come up with something to ask, but too many questions jumped to mind right at once. They all ran around, bouncing here and there, and she couldn't pin down a single thought. Fumbling for something to say, she went for the most unhelpful question she could conjure. "What the hell, Idgie?"

Shockingly, Imogen laughed at that and assumed a more relaxed posture. "First, you need to understand how my husband died, Harper."

"In the line of duty, right? He got killed on a hunt."

The woman gave a wry smile and shook her head slowly. "I wish. Perhaps I wouldn't be quite so bitter then. Jackson was killed by a *monster*," she spat out the word, causing Esther to flinch. "One that was supposed to be his friend."

That definitely made Harper hesitate for a moment. "A civilian? No…Someone being rehabilitated by the guild?"

Imogen winked playfully. As if the two of them hadn't been engaged in a damn wizard's duel a few hours earlier. Like they were old pals. "Bingo. A rage demon. He was learning to control himself, doing really well too. And then my idiot husband made some demonic social faux pas, shit-talking an infernal duke. And I guess you can take the demon out of the Pit, but you can't take the Pit out of the demon. He lost it, saw red, and attacked. And Jackson—" She stopped herself, choking up a bit, though Harper wasn't feeling particularly sympathetic at the moment. "Jackson was off-duty, and not expecting a fight. He got torn to shreds. And the bitch of the whole thing? After I received my condolences and insurance money from the guild? They went right back to helping that bastard."

"So, you went insane with grief and constructed some vendetta against all the occult beings out there, not to mention the Silversmiths, for destroying your life? You concocted some scheme to get yourself hired on at the college to enact your ruinous revenge?"

Surprisingly, Imogen's head canted to the side and she gave an amused, almost pitying smile. "Oh, Harper...I'm not some Saturday-morning cartoon villain. No. I grieved, of course, and then I slowly moved on with my life. I earned a degree in academic administration, I got a mundane job at a mundane school, and I was quite content with that. Eventually, I heard through a friend that there was a school in central Illinois in need of a college president. They needed someone...inducted in the world of the peculiar, so to speak. I applied. I got it."

It was actually Esther who posed the obvious question, sounding almost desperate as she did so. "You were moving on. You were okay. What happened to you?"

"When I worked at human schools, I saw students who could be kind and intelligent, but I also saw a lot of screw-ups. Kids who were selfish, thoughtless, and careless." Imogen shrugged. "It was unfortunate, but I got used to it, mostly. When I heard about this new job, I thought that maybe a school with such an idealistic mission statement would be more peaceful."

Esther sucked a little air in through her teeth. "Well, that's definitely not true."

"I got to Malcolm-Baptiste and saw the *exact same thing.* There was no difference at all. I suppose to some people, that might be a kind of relief—to think that a bunch of monsters really are no different. But over time, I just got more and more furious. Normal kids can't perform complex spells, drain all the blood from your body, or hypnotize you just by singing. Students with conditions like that? They should be *exemplars* of self-control if they want to play in the human world. And they don't. They just...*don't.*" Imogen sighed wearily and sank deeper into the chair.

"But I pushed my disgust down. If Malcolm-Baptiste wasn't what I thought it should be, then I just had to work that much harder. And I tried, I really did. I made myself available, I talked to students that I knew were especially troubled. I counseled and I nurtured and I really fucking *tried*. But years of effort without results can wear away at even the most resolute soul. I grew to hate them all. Even you, Esther." She muttered that last bit, and for the first time in a while managed to look appropriately ashamed of herself. "Students like you, and Autumn, were the shining examples. I saw what the ideal could look like, and I realized how unachievable it was. You're the exceptions, and you should be the rule."

"You—You were framing me. For Autumn's murder. To prove that even the 'ideal' could do something terrible. Trying to make it look like we're all one bad day from turning on each other…" Esther spoke softly, voice shaking a bit, and it took Harper a few seconds of watching her to realize it wasn't from sadness. It was that suppressed rage again. She wanted to fly across that desk and throttle the woman. "But why Andre?"

"The first spark didn't catch fire. Nancy Drew here didn't murder you when she had the chance. I needed chaos. I even told her about your little club, just to throw a wrench into the investigation." She winked at Harper again. It hurt, realizing just how easily she'd been played. "I needed everyone to see how terrible an idea that school is. So I shook it up for round two. Vampire-on-vampire violence. Get everyone questioning who could have done it, sow a little uncertainty and blame. I chose Andre because you can't get people riled up if you just kill some monster that deserved it. Then it's a lot of 'sad to see them go, but good riddance.' I wasn't counting on you being the one who found him."

Again, it was hard to feel terribly sympathetic for Imogen, though Harper did feel a surge of pride at having tossed the very same wrench right back into Imogen's machinations. It was a small comfort. "Your fault for lacking imagination."

"Obviously, I should have skipped ahead to the good part and razed that campus to the ground myself. I made it too complicated, gave too much of the game away."

"You would've gotten away with it too, if not for us meddling—"

Esther glared at Harper and shook her head firmly. "Not the time." She swung her eyes back around, boring a hole right into Imogen. "You've told your sad little story. Are we done here?"

"Hmm, I suppose that's all there is to it. I got old and jaded and angry. It happens to a lot of people." She gestured to Harper with a nod and smiled in a way that was frankly unsettling. "Especially hunters. I imagine you'll find out sooner or later. You'll lose someone, or maybe lose a part of yourself. You'll get jaded or scarred or heartbroken, and you'll always be just a little bit alone. And eventually, I think you'll understand. I hope I'm around to see that."

In a blur, Calliope moved from her place in the back of the room, closing in on Imogen and slapping her hard enough across the face to fill Sebastian's office with a deafening—and very satisfying—noise. Dr. White's head whipped to the side with the power of it, her cheek turning bright red. A spot on her lip had been split open and was now bleeding slightly. And, driving home just how broken she really was, Imogen began to chuckle as she casually licked up some of the blood.

"How fucking *dare* you try and fill my daughter's head with your bullshit? You don't see me or my husband going mad and murdering innocent people. You lost someone? We all have. Get over yourself!" She flexed her hand a few times and slowly took a step back. "Blaming a bunch of kids for being immature. You're so childish you act like this was all some natural progression, from hunter to murderer. You're looking forward to her breaking? I'm looking forward to her *shining*." Calliope didn't let Imogen get in the last word. She whirled around and stormed out of the office.

Sebastian gave a long, drawn-out sigh from somewhere behind Harper before addressing the large Shield in the well-pressed suit. "Make the call. Get her the hell out of here." He placed a protective hand on each girl's shoulder. "She doesn't deserve any more of our time. Come on."

In spite of what her father said, Harper did allow one last look at Imogen. She saw a sad, shattered woman that she had no intention of ever becoming. "Yeah. Let's get out of here." She reached out, and Esther took her hand without missing a beat.

Outside the commune offices, the three of them met back up with Calliope, who was still fuming and pacing in a small circle. In a show of affection between the two that Harper rarely got to witness lately, Sebastian walked right up to her and drew Calliope into his arms, hugging her tightly for a few silent seconds before sharing a shockingly passionate kiss.

Harper cleared her throat awkwardly and looked over at Esther to try to distract herself until they had finished. She got a sympathetic smile in return. Her impulse was to interrupt them, but it seemed like maybe her parents needed the room to decompress just as much as she did. They were only human.

Eventually Sebastian and Calliope did part, though he kept an arm around her, almost protectively.

It suddenly dawned on Harper that there was still one major thread left dangling. "So...what happens next? Like, Imogen has to pay for what she did. And what about the college?"

"Well, as far as *that woman* goes," Calliope said, barely suppressing her fury, "the guild will strip her of her ability to weave mana. If she stays compliant, she'll likely go through some very rigorous therapy for her grief, not to mention anger management. Some poor person will have to be her sponsor and keep her under close scrutiny from now until Doomsday. Ironic that the very rehabilitation process that she so loathed is now the only thing that will allow her to live."

Esther gave another subdued growl and looked at Calliope in disbelief. "That's it? They put her on a leash and hope she's learned her lesson? She killed two people!" She idly fiddled with the golden cross hanging from her neck, and the look of righteous anger slowly melted into one of grief and regret. "I just...Isn't there more they can do? Autumn and Andre, they deserve better than that." She clutched the cross tightly in her hand.

Not wanting Esther to get caught up in any desire for bloody justice, Harper squeezed down on her other hand. "The old guild might have done something more drastic. But we're trying to be better. It's the same thing we would do for dangerous mythics. Work with them, help them heal." As she said that, a memory flashed in her mind of the other night in that alleyway, of her knife going into Zachary's chest. *Trying* was the operative word. Violence couldn't always be avoided.

Sebastian nodded, glancing at the offices with a grim expression. "If she steps out of line, she'll be taken to a guild-operated holding facility. Hopefully that will help her see that Malcolm-Baptiste was practically a bastion of sanity." He looked back toward Esther and Harper, and for the first time in a while she saw legitimate uncertainty in his features. "Speaking of your school, that's a more complicated issue. The Silversmiths will have to contact the administration there and inform them of what happened. That's bound to create a wealth of new problems. Malcolm-Baptiste went to great lengths to ensure we knew nothing about them. People on both sides are going to be scrambling to figure out how to handle this without creating chaos."

"Yeesh. Makes me glad to be a grunt," Harper said.

"Well, we still have a few things to take care of. First—" It looked as though her father was about to say more, only to cut himself off with a monstrous yawn.

Harper's brow furrowed and she looked her parents over. Neither of them was in any condition to do much at the moment. After all, they'd taken just as much of a beating as she had. "*First*, you need to go rest. The guild can handle any major emergencies."

Sebastian initiated another silent battle of wits with her. Harper met his gaze evenly, staring him down. The man was practically swaying just trying to stand upright. A few tense moments passed, but finally he blinked and shrugged his shoulders in defeat.

She'd actually done it. She'd beaten him. So what if he was sleep-deprived and still nursing his injuries? Harper had won.

With a bashful smile, Sebastian hugged Calliope a little closer, pressing another soft kiss to her cheek. "You heard her, dear. It's time for these jaded, heartbroken old hunters to get some sleep."

Harper couldn't believe it. That was practically a joke.

"Will you two be all right?" Calliope looked back and forth between Esther and Harper, then down at their linked hands, and smiled gently.

Harper grinned. "Go on, you crazy kids. But you better be ready when the next mission comes around. No such thing as a break, not until you're dead."

Her father laughed at that. He actually laughed! This day just kept getting weirder. "Throwing my own words back at me. Good work, Harper. You're going to be just fine."

She stood with Esther, watching as her parents made their way back across the commune toward the dormitories. She took a few seconds to just breathe, not really processing the roller coaster of emotions until now. But before Harper was able sort out any of her feelings, her stomach erupted with a massive rumble that broke all the tension. "Holy shit. When was the last time I ate?"

"If you have to ask that question, it's been too long. Lord have mercy, you really don't take very good care of yourself when you're on the hunt, do you?" Esther squeezed her hand firmly and gave her an intense look with a hint of a smirk. "Sleeping like crap, eating random meals. That won't do at all."

"What?" Harper protested, but Esther was technically correct. She didn't take the best care of herself when she was on the hunt. The job came first. What she would inevitably discover was that Harper also didn't take great care of herself when she was off the clock, either. She could be kind of a gremlin.

"Don't bother denying it. You clearly get it from your parents." She giggled and glanced over to where the dining hall was. "Anyway, your friends have been looking after Zooey and Izzy. We should check in with them."

"Wow, Katie and Nat's first encounter with the supernatural and they didn't run off screaming? Should have given those two more credit."

"Judging by the way they were staring, I think they were more intrigued than scared. Uh, *very* intrigued, honestly."

Her feet were already propelling her forward at the prospect of seeing her best friends fawning over a pair of polyamorous mythics. "This should be good. Come on!"

"So there's this giant flash in the middle of the commune," Katie explained while gesturing wildly with her hands. "And out steps this woman looking kind of wild, with a knife jammed in her shoulder and blood everywhere. Sebastian had explained before that if anything ever went down, we just needed to get out of the way and let him and Calliope handle it. So we all scramble into the dorms to hunker down. She was stalking around, and suddenly we see your mom and dad walk out to confront her. Holy shit, Harper. I've never seen any of you in real action before. It was incredible!"

Nat chuckled and nodded. "Sebastian had this big fuck-off sword covered in runes. And Calliope summoned this…spectral wolf? He goes in for a big overhead swing, and the woman blocks it by ripping the knife straight out of her shoulder and growing a big blood sword out of it. Then she pointed at the wolf, snapped, and it just popped right back out of existence."

"It kept going like that for a while," Katie continued. "They'd pull off some incredible move, and she'd counter it. They fought her so hard, but once she'd managed to get that knife in Sebastian's sword arm, he was down. And your mom couldn't really stand alone against this crazy witch. Once the two of them were out, she dumped them in with us, at which point she covered the building with—" She quickly cut herself off, nearly gagging before reaching for her mug of cocoa to sip. "This…cocoon of clotted blood?"

"Absolutely disgusting," Nat cut in to add.

Izzy nodded in agreement before downing almost an entire mug of coffee in one go. "It was so much worse from up close."

"So my parents did all the hard work. Pretty sure that's the only reason I lasted as long as I did. An exhausted omnipowerful blood witch against little old me," Harper mused before shoving another hunk of steak in her mouth. She'd taken a cue from Esther's usual post-werewolf breakfasts and asked Rick to whip up a variation of the Full Moon Special.

Esther looked up from her mug of tea and smiled warmly. "Don't sell yourself short. I saw what kind of shape she was in once you were through with her."

Katie resumed excitedly, "Anyway. She had muttered something about looking for stragglers before she dealt with all of us. So we're freaking out, trying to help your parents with whatever first aid, water, and snacks we can cobble together from our rooms. Suddenly we hear this horrifying screeching noise that vibrates the cocoon, and this giant arm covered in fur and claws starts rending the blood open and we're all freaking out *harder* because, like, what if this is even more trouble? Only then this really cute girl with silver hair and wings comes poofing in, all like 'Be not afraid!'"

"Pretty sure I just said, 'Everybody calm down,' but sure," Zooey muttered.

Nat just grinned and shrugged, picking back up. "Once we managed to stop freaking out, they introduced themselves and helped get Sebastian and Calliope on their feet. They went rushing after the two of you—just in time, I guess. After everything shook out, and your guild locked her up, Esther took you to your room to keep an eye on you—precious, by the way—and these two have been hanging out with us."

And getting along swimmingly, it would seem, Harper mused silently. She had been watching carefully, and it didn't exactly escape her notice how much Katie seemed to be fawning over Zooey's wings, or the many glances Nat took at Izzy's sharp teeth.

Finally, her eyes flitted back over to Esther. Harper could finally just take a second to appreciate everything that had happened over the last few hours. After that first kiss with the werewolf, things hadn't really slowed down much. She pushed her plate aside, then gave a small tilt of her head and smiled at Esther. "Let's give them a little space, eh?"

She might have almost felt bad about being so obvious, if the other four weren't already lost in their own little world. Esther nodded her head enthusiastically.

Outside the dining hall, the two walked along, side by side. Harper eventually broke the tension somewhat by giving her companion a playful little bump with her hip. "Y'know, we haven't really talked yet about…what happened last night after that first scuffle." She gestured vaguely between the two of them. "Which, to be clear, very much in favor of! But it probably bears some clarification."

"That's fair. Um, truth be told, this is kind of new for me."

That was just vague enough to make Harper nervous. "Now when you say 'this'…" There could have been several different meanings behind that word. Attraction. Attraction to another woman. Attraction to a woman like Harper.

To her credit, Esther looked thoroughly embarrassed, hurriedly shaking her head. "No! Just…in general. Being close to someone. I've never, y'know, dated anyone."

Harper grinned reflexively. "Oh, we're dating, are we?"

"Gah! Potentially. I mean, I want to! Eventually." She sighed and stared down at the grass as they walked. "Honestly, I wasn't even sure what my chances were. Rowan made that joke about you and Dr. White, which made me panic and blurt out the stuff about the flag. And at the support group, you mentioned flirting with the vampire's victim. I assumed you had way more experience than me with…this kind of stuff." God, if only Esther could have seen what that moment actually looked like. Any attraction she was feeling would disappear in an instant. "And here's me, lonely werewolf girl. But I was running high on adrenaline last night and I just couldn't help myself. Glad you didn't seem to mind."

"Uh, yeah, I definitely did not mind. Hell, I thought I'd screwed up big time, butting my way into that meeting. Everything got all…weird. Also, y'know, almost getting into a deadly fight with Izzy. And telling you not to help me go after Imogen. And—Jesus, why do you like me again?"

Esther reached out and ruffled the long side of Harper's hair affectionately. She was apparently very fond of messing with her hair. Which was just as well, since it was a very easy way to make Harper melt. "Because you have a good heart, and a sharp mind. And some very attractive muscle definition." She muttered the last part a bit quietly, as her hand drifted down and rested softly on Harper's arm.

All Harper could really do in response was blush as the two of them continued to walk on with no particular destination in mind. She glanced at Esther again, her stomach twisting in on itself a little. She told herself that was just a lingering effect from being stabbed. "Well, we should probably go on an actual date before we say that we're dating. Y'know, for posterity."

"Of course. For posterity. To be absolutely certain. In fact, that's such a sensible recommendation, I think I'm going to have to insist."

As absolutely precious as the back-and-forth was, there was something Harper wanted more. "C'mon!" She grabbed Esther's hand, pulling her off the main path behind a nearby shed. "I want another pass."

"Another pa—"

Harper was already lifting up her hands to cup Esther's cheeks, pulling her in close, and capturing her lips in a desperate kiss. After so many days trying to play it cool, it was so good to just lean into it and enjoy herself for five minutes.

Suddenly she felt the pressure of a tongue brush against her lower lip, and she replied by opening her mouth ever so slightly, emitting a breathy moan while pulling their bodies closer together, wrapping her arms around Esther's neck. Her sense of time evaporated in that moment, and she could really only focus on the here and now.

When it became necessary to breathe again, Harper pulled away only the bare minimum. As she panted softly, she nuzzled into Esther's nose.

The affectionate nuzzling was returned for a few seconds, only for Esther to push right back up into another deep kiss. After another length of time that was impossible to measure, she felt teeth lightly sink into her lower lip, and Esther's hands dipped down before sliding up under her tank top. She slowly ran her fingernails along Harper's lower back and up her spine.

When that became too much, Harper once again paused the kissing to lightly brace her forehead against Esther's. An unbidden thought struck her while she was trying to catch her breath, and Harper began laughing to herself, giddy, just a touch unhinged.

Esther looked up into her eyes, face painted with concern. "What, what is it, what's so funny?"

Her laughter only continued to build. "Lilith!" she managed to get out between fits of giggling. "She's all the damn way back at your school. We—" Harper struggled to explain through her laughter. "We just left her!"

Once the surprise had passed, Esther began giggling along with her. The two of them pressed their foreheads tighter together, still occasionally bubbling up with delirious, exhausted laughter. "The poor thing! Probably wondering when her mom is going to come and pick her up. Hahaha…"

"Mmm, I hope Zooey isn't opposed to doing a return trip, or it's gonna be a long walk back."

Zooey did not, in fact, mind helping the two of them get back to Malcolm-Baptiste.

The four girls walked through the Faerie gate onto the quad near the fountain. A few students walking past looked on as though this was the most normal thing in the world. For them, it probably was.

Izzy stretched her hands up high over her head with a loud, high-pitched yawn. "Holy shit, wasn't expecting to be up all night. Thought I'd get to just punch that bitch in the face and then get some sleep."

Harper laughed bashfully and sighed. "Yeah, sorry for dragging you all into that."

Reeling back, Izzy slugged her in the shoulder. It was probably supposed to be playful, but she didn't bother holding back, so it definitely stung. "I don't know how many times we have to tell you not to apologize." Izzy's shoulders slumped and she looked down at the ground, kicking up a bit of grass and dirt. "If anyone needs to apologize, it's my idiot ass. I got all twisted up over Andre, and you were the only obvious target in my vicinity. That was fucking stupid."

"It was," Harper said, without bothering to hide her amusement. "But you made up for it. No point in dwelling."

A loud yawn erupted from Zooey. "This is all very sweet, but I need sleep. And you know I can't sleep without my bony body pillow." Not taking no for an answer, she latched onto Izzy's arm and started dragging her away with one last wave. "Thanks for everything, Harper. Don't be a stranger."

Huh. Weird, what little things could absolutely knock you on your ass. Like someone extending an olive branch and telling you that you actually were welcome in their community after you already assumed that you were only ever an outsider. Esther's hand squeezed her own firmly, and she looked over to see her beaming. "She's right, you know. You better keep butting in around here on occasion."

Glowing with embarrassment and needing something to do with her nervous energy, Harper walked toward her car with Esther in tow. "In case there's any more trouble. And no other reason." She laughed softly, trying to stay casual and charming to hide her nerves.

Judging by the look on Esther's face, her attempt to hide behind the usual facade wasn't working. "Hey. It's okay. You're allowed to come down here. You're allowed to want that. You belong here." Dammit, where was the playful banter? She could handle that, mostly. But something so sincere completely shut her down.

Flustered, Harper shut her mouth for the rest of their short walk. What could she possibly say to that? It would just be a string of excitable babbling. Only when they actually reached Lilith did she make another attempt at speaking. "So, uh. This is me. Time to get the old girl back to the commune. But…well. Don't hesitate to call or text." Jesus, how could she go from being the invincible, unstoppable champion to this awkward mess?

Esther laughed softly and gripped the bottom hem of Harper's jacket. The two of them marveled for a moment at what else Fae magic could accomplish, like mending and cleaning blood out of a beloved article of clothing. "Well, after all, we've gotta figure out what we're doing for our first…date."

Her face burned a little bit as she was reminded of their plans for the future. That definitely wouldn't be stressful in the slightest. "Yes! That is…a thing that we must do. And we will. Just as soon as I remember how to be a functional adult."

The laughter only doubled, and Esther pulled Harper in for a tight hug. "You're weird. It's cute." She held the hug for just a few seconds longer than necessary before releasing her. "Now go. Before I change my mind and tell you to stay longer."

"All right, all right, I know when I'm not wanted," she replied jokingly, pulling open the driver-side door before casting one last fond look at Esther. "Thanks for giving me another chance. And thanks for saving me last night. And thanks—"

Esther put a forceful hand to her shoulder, practically shoving Harper onto her seat behind the wheel. "I mean it, go!"

Cackling now, Harper fired the car up.

So much for a boring case.

EPILOGUE

It kind of sucked being on a boring job again. Though that was no longer because Harper sought some massive thrill the hunt wasn't fulfilling. It was because being out on the hunt meant she couldn't hang out with Katie and Nat, or go see Esther.

At least this job didn't involve some philosophical battle against a jaded witch, or a confrontation with the darkness of the human soul. A pack of hellhounds were terrorizing a small farm. That was simple, straightforward. Granted, she had taken more than a few bites and scratches in the ensuing fight. And right now all she wanted to do was get back to her motel room and bandage herself up, then catch a few hours of sleep.

So it was more than a little frustrating to roll up in the parking lot and see the light already on in her room and a figure inside waiting for her. Harper grabbed up her shiny new smartphone, tired of being badgered for living in a previous decade, and pulled up her group chat.

zealoushuntress: oh good someones waiting for me in my motel room
zealoushuntress: im sure this will go great
ManicPixieDreamGirl: Oh no! Please be safe!
KatieBean: you can just leave
KatieBean: hit da bricks
zealoushuntress: my stuff is in there!
XmetalXqueenX: oh no
XmetalXqueenX: theyre stealing your precious clothes
XmetalXqueenX: whatever will you do without all those identical flannels and tattered jeans
bannedshee: FUCK THAT
bannedshee: BUST DOWN THE DOOR AND SHANK THAT BITCH

Harper sighed softly. As usual, nobody was being especially helpful. Zooey was fawning and concerned, but "be safe" wasn't the most concrete advice. Katie and Nat were suggesting she just run away, which was practical but not possible for multiple reasons. And dear, sweet Izzy was at the other end of the spectrum—violence.

MyrtleStar: Babe.
MyrtleStar: Seriously.
MyrtleStar: It's not worth it.

Just because Esther was right didn't make it any easier. Getting new clothes was a pain, even if you ignored the aggravating dysphoria that cropped up while shopping. Money was hardly growing on trees around the commune.

zealoushuntress: but my stuffffffffff
zealoushuntress: whats the worst that can happen lol
XmetalXqueenX: you die??
nonegenderleftalchemist: No wait, Izzy's right
XmetalXqueenX: pretty sure that's the first time those words have ever been uttered
nonegenderleftalchemist: Do it, it'll be hilarious

Who the hell? Oh, right, Esther had invited Rowan to join the chat last night.

Harper tried again to get a decent look inside, but the curtains were drawn and she could only see the silhouette of the intruder. No way in hell was she going to let herself get chased off by some jerk with no sense of propriety. Breaking into her room was just rude. After all, Harper would never break into someplace she wasn't supposed to go. That would be wrong.

zealoushuntress: im going in. if you dont hear from me in ten minutes…im probably dead
zealoushuntress: and you better fucking avenge me
bannedshee: FUCK YES
MyrtleStar: *sigh*

Harper pocketed her phone and reached into her passenger seat, grabbing up her knife. They must have seen her headlights and heard the engine. The intruder was no doubt fully aware of her presence, so she didn't have the element of surprise on her side. The only thing she could hope for was that there was some way to talk them down before things got bad.

Blade at the ready, she walked up and tried the door, finding it already unlocked. Harper cracked it open a few inches and called inside, "Really not in the mood for a confrontation. So can whatever this is wait until tomorrow?" She braced herself and pushed the door open the rest of the way, finally getting a look at the guy. With the fancy suit and the slicked-back salt-and-pepper hair, she initially profiled him as a potential vampire.

How does that whole "permission to enter" thing work with a motel room? Does it have to be me giving it? Or was the guy at the check-in desk good enough to give him entrance?

But then she caught sight of the fancy leather briefcase sitting on the bed next to him, proudly emblazoned with a frankly garish and enormous guild crest in fake silver. "Oh."

"So enthusiastic to see a fellow Silversmith!" The mysterious visitor gave a chuckle, mostly amused by Harper's exhaustion and disappointment. "Don't worry, Miss Zeale, this won't take long at all." He stood up and flipped the latches on his briefcase, retrieving a manila envelope. "Fletcher Quinn, Greater Chicago Area guild admin. Here, this is for you."

As Harper took the folder from him and gave it a once-over, she couldn't help wondering if all the hunters from her dad's generation used these things. A sticker from a label printer was slapped on the cover that read *Bridge Offer*.

"What's this?"

"A Bridge Offer," he explained, unhelpfully. "Myself and some of the other guild administrators have been proposing a new position for our hunters. Malcolm-Baptiste College is not the only major discovery we've made over the last few decades. There are quite a few communities of supernatural beings out there that have been discovered by our people. We don't want to just march in and set up camp. That's a fast track to a bloody war. But we still want eyes on those situations with people that all of us trust—both humans *and* mythics. So we're deputizing Bridges to be liaisons with those communities on our behalf."

While he went through his little spiel, Harper idly flipped through the folder. She noted with no small amount of interest that there was a page included detailing housing and financial compensation beyond the usual per diem. The idea that she could live in Kitezh, still do her job, and make some actual money was kind of huge. But it was also a lot to have dropped in her lap out of nowhere.

She tossed it onto her bed and went to her personal first aid kit, pulling out the necessary materials and moving into the bathroom. At least she was nice enough to leave the door open to continue the conversation. "Mmm, believe me, I appreciate the offer. But I'm sure you understand I might need a little time to think it all over." She began pouring a mixture of antibiotic liquid and holy water on her scratches and bites. The stuff burned like hell, but it was the only way to make sure you didn't end up with either a mundane or supernatural infection.

"Oh, naturally, Miss Zeale. The proposal is nearly complete, but we needed to make sure we had at least some interest from our hunters before moving forward. As soon as we're ready to make the official offer, you'll hear from us."

She screwed her eyes shut as the substance bubbled up and the burning only got worse. Harper began wrapping some bandages around the various bites and scratches. "Ugh, yup. I shall—gah! I shall await your call with bated breath, good sir."

"Well, I'll leave you to it. No rest—"

"No rest for the weary. Yeah, yeah. Was there some kind of seminar on pithy comfort that I missed?"

"Have a good evening, Miss Zeale," he called out, followed by the sound of the heavy door latching.

She breathed a sigh of relief and finished securing her dressings before strolling back out into the room proper. Not wanting everyone to worry, Harper pulled back open the chat.

zealoushunter: not a baddie
zealoushunter: guild weirdo
KatieBean: pretty funny coming from a guild weirdo
zealoushunter: …
KatieBean: :3c
MyrtleStar: So what did he want?
zealoushunter: offered me a new job actually
zealoushunter: almost don't wanna say
zealoushunter: like that'll jinx it
ManicPixieDreamGirl: ♫ Secrets, Secrets are no fun ♪
KatieBean: ♪ Secrets, Secrets hurt someone ♫
zealoushunter: it was a mistake letting you two meet
zealoushunter: youre rubbing off on each other
bannedshee: THEY DO A LOT MORE THAN THAT HEYYO
KatieBean: >////>
ManicPixieDreamGirl: asdkjfkdaj

For a second, she had to physically set her phone down and take a breath. This happened constantly. A good fifty percent of their group chat was just her four friends flirting. It was cute for the first day or two, but now it was getting excessive.

MyrtleStar: Anyway
zealoushunter: anyway

zealoushunter: theyyyyy want me to live in kitesh
zealoushunter: kitezh*
zealoushunter: like some kind of superhero
zealoushunter: keeping lone vigil over the innocent denizens of the tiny hamlet
zealoushunter: lest any danger should befall them
MyrtleStar: Quis custodiet ipsos custodes?
bannedshee: please tell me ur not quoting ur god book @ us rn
XmetalXqueenX: Well, it's latin, so I guess she gets half credit
bannedshee: fuck u
XmetalXqueenX: You wish
XmetalXqueenX:;)
bannedshee: ASDKFASJDKJAS

"I could just push the little button there and leave the chat. I could just do that. What are they gonna do? Take my phone from me and force me to join again?" As soon as she said it, Harper realized that was precisely what they would do.

XmetalXqueenX: It means "who watches the watchers" or whatever
XmetalXqueenX: And I hate to be the bearer of bad news but I'm pretty sure that's you Esther
MyrtleStar: Crap. That's a big ask.
bannedshee: ESTHER YOU JUST SWEARED
MyrtleStar: Only God can judge me.
zealoushunter: so…do i go for it?
KatieBean: Wait, that means you'd be leaving the commune!! :(((
XmetalXqueenX: Like we don't already spend half our time down there anyway
KatieBean: Touche
zealoushunter: im serious
zealoushunter: its one thing to bum around for a few days and solve a mystery, or hang out there with you guys
zealoushunter: this is me becoming an official part of the community

MyrtleStar: Hon, you stopped a blood mage and saved countless lives. You're already a part of the community. Anyone who has a problem with it can answer to me.

Her face was definitely burning now. Why did Esther have to be so sweet? She was so good at saying exactly what Harper needed to hear.

nonegenderleftalchemist: Harper this is the part where you say uwu
zealoushunter: i dont know what that means
nonegenderleftalchemist: Of course you fuckin' don't
zealoushunter: well ive got time to decide
zealoushunter: for now I need to sleep
zealoushunter: which is gonna be loads of fun with these fucking hellhound bites
MyrtleStar: Harper! What did I tell you about being careful!?
zealoushunter: i was careful
zealoushunter: they didnt tear out my throat
zealoushunter: i call that a win
MyrtleStar: That's not what I meant, and you know it.
bannedshee: MOM AND MOM ARE FIGHTING
MyrtleStar: *weary sigh* Good night, Harper.

In a futile attempt to be responsible, Harper reached for the folder and cracked it open, intending to give the information a proper perusal. But the words blurred and ran together. She could let Future Harper figure out all the fiddly details. Present Harper needed to take her meds and get some goddamn sleep.

She returned to the bathroom and went to her cluster of orange prescription bottles. One by one, she cracked them open and fished out the necessary medications. She filled up the crappy disposable cup from the sink and tossed the fistful of meds into her mouth, swallowing them with the tepid, metallic water.

Once she was properly changed into her pajamas—gym shorts and a ratty hoodie—she flopped onto her bed. The poor thing let loose a worrying creak.

Harper really tried to sleep once she shut the light off. She certainly wanted to. But now, that Bridge Offer was all she could think about. It dug in deep and wasn't letting her go. She loved the commune, she loved her family, she loved her friends. And there was no shame in being a regular old Knife with steady work. But this job...

She would be trailblazing, exploring a whole new side of being a Silversmith. She would have an even more legitimate reason to be around Malcolm-Baptiste beyond spending time with Esther. And in many ways, it was the culmination of everything she wanted. She would go from being an honorary member of a supernatural community to a very real and legitimate part of their lives. All joking aside, she wasn't just being brought in to guard them from dangers. From what Fletcher told her, she was a liaison. And that meant she would have to know everyone by virtue of her position.

It wouldn't be easy. She'd built up some goodwill, but hunter was still a four-letter word to a lot of mythics. The skills she'd spent years honing would become secondary at best. Harper would need to be sociable, approachable, friendly, trustworthy— things she had thus far neglected. Her natural charisma was unreliable, and she was equally likely to make allies or enemies. Even so, she found she relished the challenge. And she wouldn't be alone.

With sleep still fighting her, Harper reached for her phone and sent a text to Esther.

think im gonna take the job.

I knew you would. <3

Her lips spread into a wide smile.

of course you did <3

Yeah, no doubt about it. That was where she was meant to be.

* * *

With a grunt, Harper dropped her duffel into Lilith's trunk. This was quite possibly the heaviest it had ever been. Rather than being packed with the essentials, it was currently full to bursting with most of her belongings.

Her parents and friends stood by, watching her with concern. Calliope cleared her throat and stepped around to peer into the car trunk. "You're just taking an air mattress and a pile of sheets and blankets?" That made it sound so depressing. She had her television and DVD player, her laptop, and her lamp too. That wasn't nothing.

"Look at Lilith. Do you think she could make it even a few miles while carting a whole bed?" She shrugged her messenger bag in next to the duffel and gave them all a confident smile. "Besides, I'm earning a proper paycheck now. Before long, I can just buy a bed." Yes, she knew all of her answers were avoiding the reality of what she was doing. She didn't want to bother anybody, or make it look like she couldn't make it on her own. Harper was a grown woman now, and she was willing to spend weeks sleeping on a crappy air mattress held together with duct tape to prove it.

"Harper," Sebastian said, voice tinged with just a hint of exhaustion and frustration. "Morgan would be more than happy to let us borrow his pickup. We can load up your bed, your dresser, and your desk too. You would have actual furniture in your apartment."

"I can't imagine Esther would be too happy about having to share an air mattress with you." God, that smirk on Nat's face. So damned smug.

And Harper wasn't doing herself any favors by instantly lighting up with a bright blush. They weren't even officially dating yet! Harper huffed, once again demonstrating how much growing she still had left. "Seriously? Must you?"

"I must."

Katie swiftly broke the tension, opening her arms wide and closing the distance between herself and Harper, wrapping around her tightly. "Group hug!" In moments, she had all four of them enfolding her, practically crushing her. "Gonna miss you, brave warrior."

She could practically hear Nat's eyes rolling. "We're absolutely going to be back down there within a week. It will be fine."

"Yeah," Calliope cooed as she finally broke off from the hug. "And your father and I will try and stop by between hunts. It's going to be fine. Besides, baby birds have to fly the nest eventually."

This was getting to be overwhelming. Already Harper was moving to climb in behind the wheel to escape this sappy nonsense. "Yes, well, anyway, goodbye! I look forward to all of you continuing to pester me for the rest of my life." She hastily fired up the engine, pulling out of the dirt lot before any of them could do something else embarrassing.

And off Harper rode, into the sunset. Or, well, into the gray midautumn day. You had to take what you could get when you were a hunter.

Bella Books, Inc.
Women. Books. Even Better Together.
P.O. Box 10543
Tallahassee, FL 32302
Phone: (800) 729-4992
www.BellaBooks.com

More Titles from Bella Books

Hunter's Revenge – Gerri Hill
978-1-64247-447-3 I 276 pgs I paperback: $18.95 I eBook: $9.99
Tori Hunter is back! Don't miss this final chapter in the acclaimed Tori Hunter series.

Integrity – E. J. Noyes
978-1-64247-465-7 I 28 pgs I paperback: $19.95 I eBook: $9.99
It was supposed to be an ordinary workday...

The Order – TJ O'Shea
978-1-64247-378-0 I 396 pgs I paperback: $19.95 I eBook: $9.99
For two women the battle between new love and old loyalty may prove more dangerous than the war they're trying to survive.

Under the Stars with You – Jaime Clevenger
978-1-64247-439-8 I 302 pgs I paperback: $19.95 I eBook: $9.99
Sometimes believing in love is the first step. And sometimes it's all about trusting the stars.

The Missing Piece – Kat Jackson
978-1-64247-445-9 I 250 pgs I paperback: $18.95 I eBook: $9.99
Renee's world collides with possibility and the past, setting off a tidal wave of changes she could have never predicted.

An Acquired Taste – Cheri Ritz
978-1-64247-462-6 I 206 pgs I paperback: $17.95 I eBook: $9.99
Can Elle and Ashley stand the heat in the *Celebrity Cook Off* kitchen?

9 781642 474732